Praise for *REMIND:*

"*REMIND* is one of a kind—the first 'utopalyptic' novel. It reads like a countdown to a catastrophic freedom the reader could never prefigure. A book written for pleasure that can be read for the best kind of fun—intelligent, surprising, and feral."

- Kirk Lynn, author of *Rules for Werewolves*

"*REMIND* is an engaging piece of dystopian science fiction, huddled and shivering in a subway tunnel, wrapped in themes of memory, privacy, identity, and class."

- Zachary Auburn, author of *How to Talk to Your Cat About Gun Safety: And Abstinence, Drugs, Satanism, and Other Dangers That Threaten Their Nine Lives* and *A Field Guide to the Aliens of Star Trek: The Next Generation*

"Like the smartest and most vital science fiction, *REMIND* gives us a world both recognizable and disorienting. It also gives us storytelling so addictive, so natural, that reading Shemkovitz's words feels like eavesdropping."

- James Tate Hill, author of *Academy Gothic*

REMIND

Greg Shemkovitz

REMIND

GREG SHEMKOVITZ

SPACEBOY BOOKS

Denver, Colorado

Published in the United States by:
Spaceboy Books LLC
1627 Vine Street
Denver, CO 80206
www.readspaceboy.com

Text copyright © 2019 Greg Shemkovitz
Artwork copyright © 2019 Spaceboy Books LLC

First printed May 2019

ISBN: 978-0-9997862-8-4

For Harper and Harvey

I know it sounds absurd
Please tell me who I am
—Supertramp

I am who I am.
Repeat after me: I am who I am.
I am that I am.
I shall be that I shall be.
Tomorrow, my dear, you will still be.

CHAPTER ONE
PEWTER PENGUIN

Back to where it began.

Eyes open. No panic. Just that morphine haze I've come to recognize over the past few days, like I'm detached from my own body. Bloodied gauze stiff against my face. A monitor clipped to my finger. Tubes and wires. It's all part of me in this hospital bed. The tightness in my joints, the subtle burning up my arms as the bed sheet drags across thin scabs where doctors removed tiny shards of glass. It's like all of me is just below the skin, but somebody else's flesh is stretched over my own like a wetsuit. At least that's what it feels like, even when I look in the mirror. Especially when I look at that girl right there. This might be the morphine talking, but I think that maybe I am somebody else.

Across the room, a large porto screen peers back at me. "Porto. News," I say, my voice weak. The screen comes to life. I just need to hear somebody, see what's happening out there. A reporter, a guy in a dapper suit, stands in front of a crumbled

1

building somewhere on the Upper East Side. Another old house has collapsed. The reporter is trying to look serious and cute at the same time. He's trying too hard. Still, I recognize his face. He's a well-known newsman. I just can't think of his name.

"Who is that?" the nurse says, as she peers cautiously into the room before entering.

I shake my head because I don't know.

"Max Neuland," she says. "That's okay. He's no good anyhow. Pam Washington is way better, if you ask me." She looks to the screen and says, "Porto. Off." The porto screen goes black. The nurse fiddles with some monitors beside me and says, "What color is my scarf?"

Her uniform is the color of toothpaste and each day she spices it up with one of those silk or rayon scarves to hide her neck. It's always pinned together with the same broach, a pewter penguin. She's a pretty lady or I bet she used to be, anyway. Working at a hospital probably wore her down a little.

"What color is my scarf?" she repeats, because I've taken too much time to answer.

I'm about to speak but my lips are chapped and sting when I move them. When I open my mouth, I can feel the stiff gauze dig into my cheek just below my eye. The nurse picks up a bottle from the bedside table and inserts its crooked straw into my mouth. When she squeezes, the lukewarm water hits the back of my throat and I gag for a second. I can feel a small ache in my stomach and chest as it goes down, like the inside of me is more alive than the outside.

"My scarf," she says again, setting the bottle aside and posing the thin fabric over her hand.

"Teal," I say, but my throat isn't clear. I cough again and repeat myself.

She holds up a corner of her scarf and looks at it thoughtfully. "It's more of a cyan," she says with a grimace. "But okay."

She raises my bed so that I'm sitting up. My hips start to ache, reminding me of the accident, how the car collapsed around me. Safety foam hadn't deployed, just spurted from their valves like whipped cream. My body jolted and crumpled as the car tumbled. I landed somewhere on a roof, I think. That sounds right.

"A roof," I mutter.

"What's that?" asks the nurse, moving the iTable closer to my bed.

"Nothing," I say.

She looks at me curiously and says, "Who am I?"

Again, I take too long to answer. She catches me studying the way her face slackens with sadness or maybe exhaustion.

"I know you know," she says.

"Nurse," I say, hesitating because I'm still unsure, even though I know it. She's said her name a dozen times. I'm just not used to having to remember. I'm trying too hard because I know I have to.

"Elaine—" she starts to say.

"Martinelli," I say, cutting her off.

"Yes," she says. "Kind of. It's Mart-In-El-Ee. Now, you say it."

"Martinelli," I say.

"Full name," she says.

"Elaine Mart-In-El-Eeeee," I say, dragging the E sound for a few seconds, until she smiles at my exaggeration.

"And who are you?" she asks.

I can sense that it's a silly question. You never hear anybody say it unless they're blind or Fried. And I guess Nurse Martinelli is asking me because I'm Fried. I can't remember anybody's name. Or maybe I can but I can't remember who belongs to those names.

"Hadley," I say.

"Hadley what?" she asks.

"Hadley Hayden," I say. It's my name in the System but I haven't gone by it for a long time. Anybody who knows me calls me Haddy. But there aren't a lot of regular people who know me. Just other Haydens.

"Say it again," Nurse Martinelli says.

I don't want to but we've been playing this game for over a week. So I repeat my name, "Haddy Hayden."

"Hadley," she stresses.

"Haddy," I fire back. I should know everybody's name. A week ago, I was like you. Just part of the System. I could recall anybody's name just by looking at their face. That's what the System is meant to do, right? Make it so we can all identify each other. No strangers. No strangers means no danger, so they say. I guess it works, if you compare now to a long time ago, before MIND formed and, well, you know the rest. Crime rate drops. People calm down. It's hard to get away with robbery or a mugging when everyone can identify you.

Of course, the System obviously doesn't work for everyone, such as the blind. What good is it to have all those faces in your head when you can't see them? Then you have the few whose chip didn't fuse like it should, which probably puts them in the third category—Fried, like me—people whose chips are damaged somewhere along the way. For me, it was the crash. I lost control of a car on the Bloomberg Skyway, went through the guardrail and landed on a roof of an apartment building, crumpled in a heap of metal.

When I first woke up from the crash, Nurse Martinelli asked me her name. First thing. "What's my name?" The hell if I knew. But think about that for a second. Think about not knowing somebody's name. You can't.

Well, I guess it's different now. But you know.

Anyway, that was back when I first woke up from the crash and I was out of it. I didn't know then what was happening. She called up a series on my porto. *Beirut Billionaire*, I think. I should have known everyone on that show. I mean, I *should* know. I still don't. I remember their names but I can't place a single one to their faces. So then she called up a portrait of George Washington. I didn't recognize him. She found another picture of him crossing the Potomac, that painting we all know. But I had to try to remember. I had to dig deep in my brain. It actually took effort. I knew who George Washington was, even though we don't have presidents now. How stupid an idea that ever was, considering how awful most of them turned out to be. But you know who he is just like you know about other long-abandoned things like golf and newspapers. So, looking at Washington, I should have recognized him but I had to apply context clues just to come around to his name.

Imagine that. I know, you can't.

That's how it works when your chip is Fried. You don't have access to the System. You aren't fed the database of faces and names that allow you to function. It's like one day you know everyone, and the next day you don't know anyone. You're a stranger. Even to yourself. At least that's how Nurse Martinelli explained it when I woke up and didn't know her name.

So, now, here I am stuck in this hospital bed. It's been over a week and I guess I'm starting to get it. I finally realize what my life will be like from now on. I'm going to have to actively remember people. It's going to take actual effort.

At this point, I almost forget about Step. Actually, I do forget Step. I remember his name. I remember his face. But the two seem somehow separate, like they don't belong to each other. And now I don't know if the sinking feeling in my stomach is because I can't make that connection or because I miss him.

Nurse Martinelli hands me my porto. It feels familiar, even with this new crack in the corner of the screen. I turn it over to find the etching of a hot air balloon that I scratched into the back. I run my thumb over the jagged scar.

"I want to play a game," she says.

"Fine," I say. When I tap the screen awake, I see that I have a message from somebody named Paul. There is no picture, which is strange because there should always be a picture.

"Let's play Scrabble," she says, calling up the game. A Scrabble board appears on the iTable between us.

Instead of reading the message, I swipe it away and put my porto to sleep. "I don't want to play that," I say. "I'm no good at it. And I'm tired."

"Humor me," she says. She gingerly taps her porto and a bunch of wooden tiles scatter across the iTable screen. My porto awakens again, and an empty tray appears. At the bottom, it reads, "Elaine Martinelli invites you to Scrabble."

She begins to tap at a few tiles, each disappearing from the iTable to reappear on a tray displayed on her porto. She's deliberating over her last choice, when she realizes that I haven't chosen any tiles. "Hadley," she says in that scolding tone.

"It's Haddy," I say.

She sighs and says, "Haddy. Please play."

I know it's not worth it to be stubborn. I'm stuck in this bed until doctors release me. I'm just being difficult out of boredom. After a moment, I say, "Random," and the tray on my porto fills with a random selection of tiles.

"Good," she says and picks her last tile. Immediately, her eyes grow wide with excitement. "Is it my turn to start?"

"It is," I say.

After a moment of thought, she taps her porto and then taps spaces on the iTable board until she has spelled the word *machete.* "Bingo!" she calls. "Look at that! 84 points on my first word."

I muster a smile because she's genuinely excited and she's a nice lady. I hate Scrabble, and she knows it. But I like her company.

On my porto, I see the tiny unread message symbol in the corner of the screen. Add to it Nurse Martinelli's cheerful humming, and I can't concentrate on the tray of letters before me. I keep staring at these little tiles, drawing a blank, like I'm not familiar with the English language. I swipe to rearrange the tiles until I see that I can make the word *fate* off of her T. When I reach for the F, my shaky finger nearly misses. I have to bring the porto close to my eyes to tap the letter with any accuracy. That's when I notice the grain in the wooden tile. A memory rushes in. A fleeting moment. The loud gaggle of a crowd. Dim lighting. I'm holding a wooden Scrabble tile, an actual wooden tile, in my fingers.

"What is it?" Nurse Martinelli asks.

"What's what?" I ask.

"You smiled. What did you find funny?" She's already flicking at her porto, probably to take notes.

"Nothing," I say. When I try to forget the memory, I can't, and a headache swells behind my eye. I press a thumb to the gauze over my temple to cancel out the pain. But now I can feel the ache throughout my body. "I just had a thought, I guess."

"Tell me it," she says.

"No," I say. "Can't I have my own thoughts?"

"Yes." She smiles. "We would like that."

"Then?"

"But it would help if you told us what you were thinking, especially if it's a memory." She grips her porto to type with her thumbs. "Tell me. Was it a memory?"

I don't want to tell her. For one, it's a good memory and I don't want to remind myself that I'm not there. It's somewhere chilly but I don't mind. Maybe it's one of those nice autumn days in System City. I must be with Step, but when I try to see his face, I can't. I keep seeing two, maybe three different faces. I recognize them because, well, they're in my head. But I can't place a name to any of them. It has to be Step. I only ever go around with him. But that doesn't matter. In this memory, I'm holding a tile. I can feel it; the edges are smooth with age and use, worn from the many fingers that caressed it in contemplation. I remember trying to trace a fingernail around the letter Q, the engraving so worn it was barely there, no different from this memory.

Wherever I was, I'm sure it was a nice place because I'm smirking again.

Nurse Martinelli's eyes grow narrow from across the iTable. I can give her just a taste, something like how I remember a wooden tile, a folded playing surface, a tattered cardboard box with a picture of a family sitting around a table, their brows furrowed in concentration, some of them smiling. I can tease her with those vivid little details.

On the iTable between us, there's an image of wooden tiles resting on a cardboard surface, all of it pristine and digital. It's a representation of what used to be a real-life, physical game. Maybe that's why I enjoy the memory or why, I guess, I like going to junk dealers and seeing all the stuff people used to have. Now, all those things that people once used—televisions, stereos, books, games—are crammed into a single device that fits in one hand. Only the basic human needs cannot be met by a porto, like food, a bed to sleep in, the toilet to eliminate, this IV tube running to a gap in the darkened gauze on my arm.

I touch a weak finger to the tube. The needle shifts under my skin, becoming one with my vein like a wire drawn into the world, and I feel all at once connected and calm.

Nurse Martinelli watches curiously. She doesn't know that the morphine tingles under my skin and makes my head go fuzzy, floating. My eyes are about to roll back into my head, tumble down my throat and roll around a hollow chest, play off my ribs like a xylophone. This sad woman sits before me, the iTable's frenetic glow dazzling the tired lines on her face, an image so serious—and why?—with those glistening scarlet lips and that cyan scarf. It all feels so poetic.

My porto chimes. It's another message from Paul.

"Hey," I say with dreamy delight in my voice. I'm a dog excited by its owner's call.

"Don't look at that, Haddy," Nurse Martinelli says.

"Why not?" I say.

"Because I want you to tell me your memory before you forget it."

"Why would I forget it?" I ask.

"You just might," she says. "We need to know if you've lost any memory in the crash."

I look at my porto screen. I don't know Paul but he has sent me two messages now. I'm about to open his new message, when Nurse Martinelli threatens, "Haddy, we can jam your porto."

"Then we wouldn't be able to play Scrabble," I say. "And you're winning."

"Tell me your memory," she says. "We need to know that your brain is still functioning correctly."

I look down again at the screen.

"What?" she asks.

"Look at that," I say. I tap the F on my porto and a triple letter square on the iTable. After finishing the word, *face*, from the C in her word, I look up with a big grin. "Triple letter."

She doesn't seem nearly as pleased as I am. "Your memory, Hadley."

"I must have forgotten it," I say.

Nurse Martinelli grimaces and then types something into her porto notes. "You must have been fed," she says. "I'll have to wait for the morphine to wear."

"I've been fed," I say, sleepy. I close my eyes for a moment, let the tingle flow to the ends of my limbs and dissolve all that pain.

Nurse Martinelli lowers my bed and adjusts the sheet over my arms before leaving. I can feel the two of me separating again, as my head floats. The gauze and burns are no longer part of me but of somebody else. I'm still thinking about that wooden tile when I open my eyes and see two unread messages on my porto screen. When I say his name, Paul, I cannot place his face, not even a faint impression like there should be. I open his first message. "We need you." It's direct and mysterious, just like the second message that reads, "You do not need the System."

I don't know what part of me wants to reply, this mangled mess just trying to crawl back from a nearly fatal crash or the curious drifter that once held a strange little wooden tile on a chilly autumn day. Maybe both parts of me, past and present, need to know more. It's not like I can't remember. I haven't forgotten a thing. But now that I'm not part of the System, I feel tremendously alone, like I've lost everyone I once knew. They've all disappeared—at least to me they have. Maybe a part of me is scared to leave the comfort of this hospital bed, the free food and familiar faces. Maybe I'm just too unsure of what's out there for somebody like me. And now the only thing I have to go on is this mysterious messenger named Paul, this faceless beacon of hope.

CHAPTER TWO
CREEPY CLOWNS

Look, my memory is fine. That's not the issue. I can recall everything back to when I was a little girl and I used to sing into my porto like a drunk idiot. That was with my first foster parents, the Beseckers. They took me in for two or three years, until I was about six. They had a son named Wayne who was about a year older than me. We got along. I asked him once what it was like to have a mom and dad. He said it was fine once you got used to calling them *Mom* and *Dad* instead of Judy and Richard. I had never thought about it that way but Wayne was tapped into the same System as me, saw people the same way.

I guess I looked up to Wayne, even while he used to steal my porto when I wasn't looking and take pictures of gross things around the house, like the cat's butt and Mr. Besecker's gnarly old feet. It was funny even if I whined about it. I probably have those pictures somewhere in the cloud. I never check.

Anyway, one day I stole Wayne's porto—at least I thought it was his—and took a picture of my fanny and left it on the screen for him to find. Too bad it was actually Mr. Besecker's porto, and Mrs. Besecker found it. Before long, I was back at Hayden House.

I did almost a year in Hayden House and then I got placed in another foster home, this time for less than a year. The Verblaauws, a French-Canadian couple who couldn't have a kid of their own, took me in because I had sandy blonde hair like them. At least that's what I heard them say in that accent, dropping the *de* from *blonde*. They didn't like me and I didn't like their diet of stinky cheeses and bitter coffee. But I relished a little in my brief brush with their upper-crust lifestyle, sharing their three-room loft in Morningside, the third room being the bathroom. I had to sleep on a small twin bed that slid under their sofa when I wasn't using it. They lived sort of a minimalist lifestyle, which I appreciated. After all, as a Hayden, so did I. Mostly, their furniture was sparse. They didn't have pictures of family or much in the way of decoration, but Mrs. Verblaauw was fond of clowns, like old-timey circus clowns and pantomime performers. So they had all these black-and-white photographs, paintings, and centuries-old cast iron statuettes peppered around the place. I called them the "creepy clowns" and Mr. Verblaauw chuckled at that. I don't think he liked them much either but he put up with it because, for as reserved as he was, he seemed to love his wife very much.

Aside from a fear of clowns, the one thing that I picked up from the Verblaauws was a love of reading. They read a lot. And because they didn't like to hear my series cartoons over their dry, upper-crusty music, I had nothing to do but read a lot, too, huddled over my porto and sitting beside the floor-to-ceiling window overlooking a building under renovation (adding floors—always adding floors), while Mr. and Mrs. Verblaauw draped themselves over the sofa and an easy chair, posing like the mannequins that used to be in storefront windows along Fifth Avenue in the old days. The Verblaauws were elegant speakers, dainty eaters, and well mannered. I was seven-going-on-eight years old and the exact opposite of them, and eventually we all sort of recognized it. Needless to say, Hayden House expected me back sooner.

Over the course of the next few years, I moved from school to school, barely getting through primary, then middle. I never finished high school. I have two more years to go. I'd graduate next spring, if I had stayed.

All the while, I stepped in and out of homes, taken in by the Moores, the Laffertys, the Del Pizzos, and once by an old lady who wasn't fit to raise her seven cats, let alone a teenager. The times in between—let's face it, most of my nights in foster "care"—I spent on the streets. This past year I jumped around sleeping pads in Queens and Harlem, scrounging for food and slumming it with other Haydens like me. There's an entire world under this city. Everyone talks about the rats, especially now that those little rodents make more appearances as the water keeps rising. But nobody talks about all the kids out there, all of us Haydens. Probably just as many of us living underground as there are rats.

Unlike the rats, I often find myself the subject of sideways glances and hushed conversations, as I dig for a half-eaten croissant in a park trashcan. On colder days, I'll be in a museum if the guard is sympathetic. If not, I'm usually hustling something. I'll make runs for this DDS carrier who calls himself Imp. He never has enough time to make his deliveries and customers don't usually care who leaves their package of designer shoes or cookware or whatever. As long as they get their package on time. Imp pays me by the delivery. I do the same for a laundry service in the East Village, not far from where I wrecked that car.

Which brings me to an all-to-clear memory.

It went something like this.

It's raining. Always raining. Especially when you just want to get some fresh air. I come out of Ziggy's, my ears ringing from Step's band, Grandpa and the Mantel Clocks, a cath-rock band like all the rest, blending elements of metal guitar and church organ. A clunky, dramatic swell of sound that lifts you up off the ground and slaps you in the face. Loud and lousy, but I like that sort of thing when it's raining. So, I'm outside on the street in Midtown, in the thick of all those tall,

tall buildings. No sky. When you look up, it's just a thin, jagged line of gray between the looming peaks of all those skyscrapers, and the rain taps your face like warm spit.

A man pulls up in a nice, fancy car. He's dressed in gray, like the sky, come to think of it, and he wears a fedora. I greet him and he greets me. We don't know each other but, you know, we know each other's names. The System and all. Of course, now I can't remember his face that well or his name, but that's the sort of problem that comes with being Fried. You can't recall what you didn't have to remember before. But back then I knew his name.

He says something like, "You look bored."

"Maybe," I say.

"You have anything going on right now?" he says. It sounds like a proposition that can go in just about any direction, most of which I'm unwilling to take.

"Maybe," I say.

"Maybe you want to make a few creds," he says.

"I'm flattered, bub," I say, thinking he might take me for a worker, as they say. "Really, I am. But that's not my scene."

"No," he says. "I need you to drive this car to New Brighten. You can drive, right?"

"Say again," I say, because I'm not used to having dapper men ask me to drive their cars. First of all, I'm a Hayden. Nobody in their right mind would trust a Hayden with their car. Second, he seems perfectly capable of driving the car himself.

"It's for a friend," he says. "But I have another appointment." He glances at his porto, probably for the time, and then looks somewhere down the street.

I'm thinking, *What kind of appointment can a stiff like this have at 3am?*

"Are you up for it?" he asks. "New Brighten. Round trip, forty-five minutes, maybe an hour. You'll be back for your friend's encore." He nods toward Ziggy's where a wave of muffled noise billows from the door.

"New Brighten, Staten Island?" I say, laughing. "I don't think I can drive across water, bub."

"New New Brighten," he says. "Brooklyn."

Of course, he's talking about that rebuild community, behind the big seawall. I've been out there before. I've seen the sign that reads, "Bigger. Better. Brighten." The old Brighten Beach is an underwater park now, if you haven't seen it. Just on the other side of that seawall, where the water keeps rising. Step and I once snuck in and swam along there, watched the old underwater town crawl beneath us. We followed those two lanes of Oriental Boulevard, the sandy foundations of old homes lining either side of the street like tombs of another generation now overgrown with brown seaweed.

"Sure," I say to the man in gray. "I can do that. If the credit's right."

"Here's the address," he says, extending his porto toward me.

I bump the rubber edge of my porto against his. My porto is pocked with paint marker and stickers. His is pristine like he just ordered a new one from MIND yesterday. An address I've never seen appears on my porto screen. Below that, I get a notification for 100 creds.

"That enough?" he asks.

"An hour roundtrip," I say. "Double it."

He sighs, swipes at his porto screen and taps it against mine. Another 100 hit my account.

"It's all funny money anyway," he says. "Am I right?" It's an old joke that nobody gets anymore, not since we haven't used printed currency in my lifetime.

Not to mention that I don't understand him. 200 creds is a lot of money for somebody like me. It could get me a few meals and maybe another pair of used boots.

But I play along and say, "Play money."

He gives a cunning little smirk and gestures for me to get in the car. I walk around the boxy black vehicle, a throwback Volvo sedan from decades ago.

"Am I going to be able to drive this?" I ask. "I'm not subscribed—"

"It's all set," he says quickly, waving his porto like it's supposed explain everything.

I wanted to ask when he did this but I suppose he could have done it from his porto any time while talking to me.

"You need a lift somewhere?" I ask.

He smirks and taps a new cartridge into his e-cigarette. He takes a drag of vapor and expels it. "No," he says. "But you drive careful now." He nods and starts down the street.

I get in and study the dashboard. It's all so foreign to me, not because it's a nice car but because I've probably only been in a car three, maybe four times in my life. I don't even have a driver's license. I can't afford to subscribe to a car, let alone ever own one. My porto should know that. It should keep me from starting the car. But it doesn't. The man in gray must have given me permission with the onboard porto, if that can be done. Don't ask me how he did it.

I tap the ignition screen and the electric motor sizzles to life. Throwback muscle cars like a Charger or a Roadrunner have a fake engine roar when you start it up. I guess they didn't bother with this one.

Because my porto isn't tapped in, I have to adjust the seats for myself. I call up a channel for more music—something old and raw like Nine Inch Nails to fit the car. I tap the address on my porto to set the GPS, and, after a moment, the car's onboard porto finds it. I'm not one to use a GPS but I don't know Brooklyn like I know Manhattan.

After a moment of adjusting mirrors and getting cozy, I'm off. Much to the GPS's chagrin, I take a few extra turns around town to get used to the car. I circle back toward Ziggy's for one more pass, hoping that Step might come out and see me. He wouldn't get my message if I pinged him. He's probably deaf from the next band.

After a few laps around Midtown, the GPS recalculating the whole way, I finally punch it up the ramp to Bloomberg Skyway, getting up high along the buildings, some of which don't reach the four-lane road above the city. Beyond those lower buildings, I can see the seawall lining the East River. Water laps just inches below, teasing an occasional splash above the graffiti-pocked wall. (Okay. I'm not sure if I'm adding that part now, but I remember spotting the sea wall from up there and thinking how it won't be long before we don't see it anymore.)

Anyway, I'm whizzing along the Skyway, my foot mashing the accelerator, even though the button on the steering wheel would do just fine. I like the feel of how cars used to drive. I wonder what it would be like to have this rush every day, whizzing around the city. I imagine careening along a country road like people used to before the migration. Open road for miles and miles.

So, I'm going, I don't know, 70 miles per hour—something crazy like that—when my porto chimes. I shouldn't even be able to get a message while driving, let alone respond to it, but that stiff in the gray fedora must have done something to the car. The message is silly. I only glance at it for a second but it's something like a question that doesn't make sense. I think it must be Step drunk-pinging me, so I reply with something equally stupid that I can't remember either. I just say, "Porto. Reply," and whatever nonsense. Well, it's not really nonsense. Just it would seem that way, I guess.

(Look, I wasn't drunk or high or anything, if that's what you're thinking.)

Anyway, I'm sort of laughing to myself when I say, "Send," and the porto chimes that the message has sent. I can't remember exactly what happens next but I must be thinking about Step, seeing him smile when he looks at his porto, his face aglow in that crowd at Ziggy's. I'm probably wishing he was with me, cruising to Brooklyn in some weirdo's car.

Then there's a muffled pop. Or a thump. Maybe it was more like a thump. Anyway, a tire blows out. I lose control of the car, jerk the wheel, hit the brake. But I've lost it. Nothing but screeching and crunching all around me.

When it's over, I'm upside-down and crushed inside the remnants of a throwback Volvo, everything around me red and foggy through the blood running over my eyes. I can't move. The motor sizzles for a moment, gives way to a dull purr before it dies. The onboard porto beeps as if sending out a distress signal. Maybe it is. My heart thuds against my chest, my breath a heavy whoosh behind my ears. Beyond that, a chorus of rain lightly taps against the twisted metal around me. Farther away, somewhere in the distance, drawing near, sirens...

CHAPTER THREE
OLD MOTORCYCLE

The day I get out of the hospital, it's been two weeks and I'm still a mess. My arm's in a sling. My ribs are bruised and I can barely take a full breath. I don't feel very well, but better. The doctor is here, swiping through my chart on the iTable with careless haste, muttering things that I don't understand. He's an older man, probably in his late fifties or sixties, tinted bifocal eyeglasses set beneath a receding hairline, and one ear pierced, which is funny to me and I'm not sure why. I should probably trust him but I don't. Maybe that's because I don't recognize him like I should. He gives me a strange, fatherly look in return before saying, "You should be fine. Just take it easy on that leg and keep rested."

"Rested," I say. "Will do."

"Push yourself to take deep breaths," he says. "It'll hurt with that rib but you don't want pneumonia." He scratches something on the chart with this finger and looks up, as if he just had a thought. "You got a place to rest, don't you?"

"I'm fine," I say.

"I can have the nurse call Hayden House," he says.

"I'm fine."

He finishes whatever he's doing on the iTable and says, "The nurse will be in to discharge you." He moves to leave and then stops short of the door. He doesn't quite look back when he says, "You're too young to—" He keeps himself from finishing his comment, and I want to see his face for some reason, maybe to know what a concerned father might look like or perhaps just to again marvel at how I don't know his name. But he leaves without turning around.

When he's gone, I slowly work my way out of the hospital bed, trying to set my feet on the floor to get dressed. Everything is shaky and I'm almost on my feet, gathering my hospital gown around me, when somebody appears in the open doorway. A man. He's tall. I can't tell from here but he might be in his late twenties, early thirties. Dark eyes accent a serious face. I'm still not used to seeing people and not knowing their names, like every face is a surprise that, like in this case, is not so pleasant. I'm suddenly concerned with details. Like his leather jacket and leather gloves, what that means. He must ride a zipbike. He fills the doorway for a moment, watching me, and I'm not quite sure if I should scream or try to run, as if there's anywhere to go. But he doesn't move, just squints at me, apparently unembarrassed by his staring.

"Yeah?" I say. "You mind?" I gesture for him to leave or look the other way.

"Hadley Hayden," he finally says without following either of my commands. His voice is deep, almost hushed or sore.

"Yeah," I say, backing toward the bench where my jeans are folded beside my boots.

"Do you know who I am?" he asks.

"Should I?" I say, trying to keep an eye on him but now feeling a strange shame for not being able to call up his name.

"You don't know who I am," he says, taking a step into the room. "And that's why I'm here."

He comes a bit closer, unbuttoning his jacket. I've seen this posture before, the stiff squaring of mass to seem more imposing, looming. It's usually from GCs—good citizens, if you know what I'm talking about, the folks who always want to confront you. Can't let you live. The ones that the System relies on to rat you out, because the whole thing wouldn't do much good without a snitch to name names. They try to make an example of us Haydens, usually with fists. It happens a lot especially when three or more of us gather somewhere. Then we're suddenly a "gang," and soon we have a posse of GCs on us.

People take the law into their own hands. They think they know us or they own us, just because our names are all the same. You probably don't care about any of this if you're not a Hayden. But to us it matters a whole lot. It becomes an issue of life and death when you got half a dozen GCs coming at you. They're always juiced-up young guys looking for a fight, acting like they're just trying to clean up their neighborhood, even when they're a long way from home. Maybe that's why they come after us, because they're scared.

Then you got GCs looking for a good time. They prey on Haydens because most of us are girls. And some GCs are just drunk or had a bad day and try to take it out on us one way or another. Sometimes it gets ugly, especially when you have enough male Haydens around. I'm talking about big boys, seventeen, eighteen, or nineteen, as big as football players, just as hopped up on adrenaline as any GC. Everyone's ready to stand their ground. Hayden boys usually don't care what happens. Less at stake. GCs are usually too stupid to see that. Keep coming at us.

So, here I have a GC in my room and I'm just one half-naked girl, unsteady on her feet and barely able to gather up her jeans.

"Beat it, creep," I tell the man.

He steps closer, now reaching into his jacket, and all I can think is that he has a gun or a knife. Sometimes GCs come armed. I look to the open door, hoping that the nurse will show up. The man follows my eyes to the door. A doctor scampers by. Then a nurse slowly shuffles past, pushing a boy in a wheelchair. Regular hospital traffic.

The man works his hand around under his jacket. I'm scrambling to get my jeans on, grab a boot as a weapon, when he pulls out his porto. He removes a glove with his teeth, tucks it under his arm, and scrolls through some notes.

"Hadley Hayden," he says. "Seventeen. Runaway. In and out of Hayden House. Juvi records indicate three counts of theft. Minor larceny. Possession of tobacco, one count."

"Who are you?" I ask, but he keeps reading aloud.

"Got a lot of short-term addresses on you. Fosters, I suppose." He grimaces and continues, "Recently involved in an accident on the Bloomberg Skyway. Uninsured. Unlicensed. Pulled from an unregistered vehicle. Not reported stolen."

"You almost finished?" I say. "I think I know how this story turns out."

"According to the System," he says, raising his voice above mine and still looking at his porto. "Hadley Hayden was deceased."

I'm not going to lie. As alive as I am at this point, it takes me a second to register what I'm hearing.

"You were dead," he says.

"Well," I say, presenting myself alive and trying to be casual about it. "Not anymore."

"But for twenty-four hours you were," he says. He tucks his porto away and puts his glove back on. "Why is that?"

"You tell me." I grab my clothes and say, "You mind?"

He looks away toward the wall. I quickly clip my bra and pull on my shirt and hoodie. When I have everything on, I notice the giant rip running up the side of my jeans. My hoodie has small holes in it, and there's blood streaked up the sleeves.

"The thing is, Hadley, the responding officer found you alive in that car," he says, still looking at the wall. "When I got the call, I looked you up. You were in the System, only you were dead."

"System's wrong," I say. "Do we need the doc to confirm it?"

The man peeks around to make sure I'm done dressing. Then he comes closer, until he's on the other side of the bed from me. "Has anyone contacted you lately? Somebody you might not know?"

I laugh. "Besides you?"

"Special Agent Stevenson. Off System Unit." He pulls his coat open to flash a badge. "Besides me."

"I'm off the System," I say.

"You are," he says. "Mostly."

"Mostly," I say, and force another laugh. I sit on the bench and lace up my boots, the whole time wondering where the hell the nurse is.

"You're a Hayden," he says.

"Does that make you care less?"

"The opposite," he says. "Has anyone contacted you?"

"No," I say, because I still don't know what he wants from me. "Should they?"

He seems curious but not upset. "May I see your porto?" he asks.

The porto sits on the bedside table closest to him. He gestures toward it and I come around the bed, one boot still unlaced. "I don't think so," I say. "Not without a warrant."

"I don't need a warrant to check your porto," he says.

It takes all the energy I have but I quickly step between him and the bedside table, grabbing my porto before he can. "I'm not sure that's true," I say.

"Maybe," he says, with a smirk. "Besides, responding officers say your porto was wiped clean."

I turn it over in my hand. I don't keep much on my porto, but I suddenly remember the 200 creds I was given for delivering the Volvo. I flick to my account. It's wiped clean, zero balance.

Agent Stevenson looks at his porto and says, "Officers report that you were mumbling something about a man who sent you."

"Look," I say. "I was out of it then and I don't have anything to say now." I move toward the door and he steps in my way. I can smell the leather treatment on his jacket. I can also smell tobacco on his breath.

"The man who sent you," he says. "What did he send you to do?"

"I don't know of any man," I say.

"Listen," he says. "My job is to figure out what happened, what led to you becoming..." He nods to indicate my Fried noggin.

"Becoming Fried," I say, planting a finger on a bruise covering my temple.

His eyes flicker with a mix of compassion and suspicion.

"We know you weren't intoxicated," he says. "But the car's onboard was wiped clean too."

"Sounds like a dead end," I say.

"I suppose," he says. He buttons up his jacket again. "But tell me, then, where'd you get the car?"

I'm not sure I even want to answer that. It was a legal transaction. The man in the fedora gave me creds to drive a car. Innocent enough. No reason to tell this officer. But his eyes are locked on me and he isn't moving out of my way. I'm about to say something when a nurse walks in. She stops suddenly and sizes up Agent Stevenson before presenting a hospital-issued porto to me.

"Miss Hayden," she says, still glancing at Agent Stevenson. I don't remember this nurse but I've seen her so many times in the past two weeks. "I have your invoice and prescription. Where should I have the medication sent?"

Agent Stevenson is watching, listening. He still hasn't moved out of my way.

"I'll pick it up myself," I say. I hold out my porto to hers. The prescription and invoice appear on my screen. I catch the list of charges totaling 53,988 creds. Balance due: 0. Not that I could have or would have paid it. But I wonder why I don't owe anything. Agent Stevenson must read the shock on my face, and he peers at my screen before I turn it off.

"Is there somebody to pick you up?" the nurse asks.

"Yes," Agent Stevenson says.

"No," I say.

He flashes his badge to the nurse and says, "I'll take her from here."

The nurse gives him a cautious glance again. "Fine with me," she says. Then she steps into the hallway and returns with a wheelchair. "It's a rule," she says.

Agent Stevenson waits behind the wheelchair and nods for me to sit. I tuck my porto in my pocket and reluctantly ease myself into the wheelchair. Agent Stevenson waits patiently, a content look on his face. He doesn't have anything on me but I've come to learn that truth doesn't always matter in the battle between Haydens and the law.

"Is Hadley under arrest, Agent Stevenson?" asks the nurse.

"She's in good hands," Agent Stevenson says.

The nurse glances my way, concern washing over accusation. "Rest up," she says.

Agent Stevenson wheels me out of the room and into the busy hall. He says nothing as we move toward the elevator, passing rooms where nurses, doctors, and family members lean over patients—more faces I cannot name. A hollow pit of dread forms in my stomach. The more faces I see passing in the hall— young and old, tired and alert—the larger the pit in my stomach grows. I'm not sure what to expect when I get outside with all those people. Not knowing. And this man, Agent Stevenson, steadily moving us along the corridor. I wish the nurse had

25

confirmed his identity.

We reach the elevator and wait. People keep coming and going, up and down the hall. Sideburns, glasses, a yellow ribbon in dark brown hair. She's fat. He's short. A gap in his teeth. Who are they?

On the elevator, Agent Stevenson doesn't press a button, satisfied that his floor has been pressed by one of the three people already on the elevator. I wonder if it's the ground floor, where I'm headed, or one of the parking deck levels that are also lit up. I'm the only one sitting and when I glance up to see the other passengers, I can't bring myself to ask any of them who this man is pushing my wheelchair. I can't bring myself to admit to them that I don't know.

We stop at a few more floors along the thirty-four floors we must descend. More strange faces get on. Big nostrils. Five o'clock shadow. Agent Stevenson stands beside me, quiet and reserved, like a statue. We stop at another floor. Two doctors exit. Two get on, chatting about something technical. High-pitched voice. Mole on left cheek. Thin eyebrows. I don't recognize a single face and I suddenly feel like I've entered a new world where I don't belong. Each time the doors open, I'm compelled to leap from the chair and run as fast as I can away from Agent Stevenson. I don't know what will happen or what he'll do once I get to the ground floor, if that's where we're headed. Each floor that ticks by makes my stomach heavier. Am I ready for what's down there, what's outside this building? And what if Agent Stevenson takes me into the dark, secluded parking decks?

I lean forward and tap the already lit ground floor button, asserting my destination. Agent Stevenson doesn't flinch.

When we reach the ground floor and the doors open, a few passengers exit but Agent Stevenson doesn't move.

"Our stop," I say.

"You don't need a lift?"

"I don't." I try to stand but he pushes the wheelchair forward into the backs of my knees and I sit back down. I kick my foot forward to stop the elevator door from closing. Finally, he rolls me out of the elevator.

The hospital lobby bustles with people carrying balloons and flowers, others hang their heads in sorrow and worry—all these strange faces. Doctors and nurses work their way with mechanical determination through the confluence of people. Other hospital staff gab and nibble pastries by a cart like it's just another day. And I suppose it is. I want to feel comforted by all these people, feel safe that we're in a public place. And I have to keep telling myself that just because I don't know them doesn't mean they don't know me. I'm safe. As long as they know who I am and who Agent Stevenson is, he can't do anything.

We get to the doors and I can smell the exhaust from outside, a familiar stench that oddly settles me for a moment. This hospital is air so clean, too clean. We stop short of the door and Agent Stevenson waits, holding the chair steady. I slowly stand up, my hips still sore. My knuckles are raw and my head is heavy. When I get to my feet, I turn to give him a mock reassuring look, but my head only drops in a pathetic nod.

"Somebody did you a solid," he says. I know he's referring to my paid hospital bill but I don't reply. So he says, "Maybe a guardian angel."

"Maybe," I say.

"Does that angel have a name?" he asks.

"I guess I'm not very good with names," I say.

He shows a sad smirk and says, "Is it the same person who gave you that car?"

"I guess I don't remember," I say, faking amnesia. I know he doesn't buy it but what's he going to do? I start to leave and he sets the chair aside to follow me out.

"Hadley," he says, putting a hand on my arm. "It's not

the same out there."

"I've only been in here a couple of weeks," I say.

"That's not what I'm talking about," he says.

He means that I'm going to have to navigate without the System. Maybe I'm naïve at this point. But I can't imagine it will be that hard to get around without knowing everyone around me. People did it for hundreds of years before us.

After a moment, he says, "You're tough. I get that. But be careful."

"Sure," I say, hoping that I'm as tough as he thinks.

"Here." He pulls out his porto. The screen wakes to an image of an old motorcycle, and he catches me looking before he swipes to his ping app. "Harley Davidson," he says, without looking at me. "It's just an old motorcycle, like a zipbike. Forget it." He quickly shoots me a message, and my porto chimes in my pocket. "Now you know how to contact me if you remember anything."

"I'm fine," I say.

He nods and I turn to see where I'm headed. Anywhere but here, I think. Of course, in between here and wherever I'm going are all those unfamiliar faces. A baseball cap. Sunglasses. A beard. An upturned lapel. I don't know these people. I'm Fried, I tell myself, maybe even out loud. I see is a cane, worn shoes, a red metallic coffee cup. From now on, everybody I meet will be for the first time, like Agent Stevenson.

I look back to see his face again, to remember it. He's watching me. Leather jacket. Gloves. His eyes narrow against the sun. He's clean shaven. Creases run from his nose down around his mouth to meet his square chin. His hair is dark and short. Real short. No grays. He buttons his jacket cuffs. Clenches his jaw. He's very serious as he studies me in return. Sunglasses in hand. I don't know if he's a threat but he's my only familiar face for now. Bloodshot eyes. A scar near his left eye. I have to remember it all.

CHAPTER FOUR
CRESCENT MOON

There are things I wish I could forget. Like almost everything having to do with my birth parents. You wouldn't think I actually knew them. Why should I? I'm a Hayden, an outcast, a byproduct of this country's lousy history. Take a massive economic crash and a government trying to recoup by selling off any non-urbanized land to American Indian tribes. Cram everyone into a dozen or so select cities, like this crummy place, leaving behind skeletal suburban remains where tribal colonies now grow amidst an otherwise abandoned and barren rural landscape. The result of that great migration is overpopulated cities with a half-assed unwritten one-child rule stoked by certain meager government incentives. You get abandoned babies—dead or alive—left at fire stations and churches. Usually girls because, you know, it's more important to pass on the family name than to spare a life. You get thousands of unwanted children roaming the streets. You get the Haydens. You get me.

So, let's look at how one becomes a Hayden. Maybe you don't know.

Take my situation.

I was found wrapped in burlap, down near Wall Street. Never mind, just yet, how I know. I'll get to that just like I'll get to my parents. But first, somebody found me, little baby me, lying there on Wall Street. This was back before the water reached that far downtown. I was probably crying—at least that's how I imagine it, for dramatic effect.

So, this somebody, this *hero*, let's say, called up Hayden House, who took me in. There, a woman named Miss Ula Mae brought me up. She brought up lots of kids. To this day, Hayden House has raised tens of thousands of children, each of us put in the System once we're discovered, and each of us given the last name Hayden. Our chips were implanted upon entry to Hayden House, mostly because there needed to be some way of identifying us. Of course, you have so many kids with the same last name, you start to run out of first names, which is the reason why so many of us have funny names like Pin or Mace or one of Miss Ula's pride-and-joy Haydens named Iggy. Though, he died not long ago, so I guess they can reuse that one. That is if Miss Ula wants to give another baby that sweater she knit for Iggy, the one with a big crescent moon on the front of it. He loved the moon. I bet he died howling at it.

With so many Haydens and so little room in Hayden House, this also means you'll come across a lot of us underground or on the street. Not all the homeless are Haydens though. Of course, you know that already if you even pay attention to who's all out there. That beggar outside Central Park Zoo, the guy with one eye? He has a face. He has a name. And it isn't Hayden. I don't know what it is now. But, you know.

Then there are the few—very few—Haydens who make it somewhere. This is the woman in line for coffee that seems a little weathered, a little knowing, and when she turns around in her suit and fancy updo, she takes your breath away because there's no way she's a Hayden. But she is. Or the receptionist sitting behind a big modern front desk at that tech firm. She's got those smart glasses and that take-no-crap smirk. You might not bother to look her in the eyes but she's one of Miss Ula's. And, sure, I wonder sometimes if that'll ever be me. There's a chance, I guess. After all, they came up just like I did, on the street.

So then you have to ask: if so many of us are without a place to live, why don't any of us get out of the city? Like we're pioneers or something. It's a perfectly legit GC-type question. Never mind that nobody else would dare explore that terrain. But we're dirty Haydens. Practically scavengers. Well, you took the same history classes I did. You know who's out there and where we get our tribal tobacco. You've probably never ventured out, but you have a pretty good idea that you don't want to. I'm not saying it's lawless out there. I mean, I don't know. It's just uncharted. Or it's re-charted, just not for a city girl like me.

I should know. I've been out there. Step once took me up the Hudson. Craziest thing we ever did. He got hold of somebody's zipbike. Never said where he got it. It had a full charge and the day was just starting, so we went on up to that place they used to call Poughkeepsie. They say the Delaware and Mohican tribes have taken it back. Not that it was obvious. It just looked like an abandoned town. Old distribution warehouses rose from weeds and overgrowth, their weathered signs mucked with rust. Trees and vines and shrubs grew everywhere. Not exactly what you'd find on one of those old postcard things people used to send to each other. But it was lovely. For one thing, no exhaust or steam rose in the air, just smoke from chimneys or cooking fires. Tribes kept few street lights on. I heard once that closer territories like this were still on a power grid that tethered away from the city, but they had to put up with constant throttling. Made electricity unreliable. I heard from somebody that their power might go black for days at a time. I can't imagine.

All this is to say, it felt like the earth was swallowing up this small industrial town and that somehow made it a cleaner place. Like it was becoming one with the natural world, just like the way they talk about the tribes. They're one with nature or something.

Anyway, I was thinking all this as we crossed that rusty, rickety bridge from Highland, our tires humming above the Hudson. In town, Step drove slow and cautious past storefronts that looked old and unattractive. But I could see inside where shelves were stocked with goods. Meats hung from ceiling joists. I don't remember a lot of color. In fact, there was something dull about everything. I'm not saying things were antiquated out there. I think they had portos, or something like them, and cars and all the same stuff you find in the city. Just, it wasn't branded, I guess. Some things were. But not a lot. You see tribal folks in the city. I'm sure they take things back to their reservations. I don't know. Anyway, we drove real slow to take it all in. Anybody who saw us either waved or seemed indifferent. Nobody made a fuss. Not like you'd think.

We drove north as far as old Rhinebeck, with its beautiful hills and dilapidated mansions. Step wanted to take me camping, something he had heard about people doing back in the day when it was safer. He was always talking about how people used to just take their cars out for a drive, that if you looked at old maps, you'd see roads running like veins all over the country and it was all free to explore. "Imagine," he'd say, looking off somewhere in his mind, like he'd seen it himself. "Just imagine."

In old Rhinebeck, we ended up lounging in a meadow, taking in the sun. Step went on about sleeping under the stars, building fires, cooking meals over coals, and hiking trails through the wilderness—stuff I'm sure he would never do. It all sounded like tribal life to me. At least that's how I imagined tribal life until we saw it for ourselves.

But if you knew Step, you would know that he's not camping material. He knows his way around the city. He can charm you with his goofy smile, his soft voice. But that's his strength, knowing people, meeting people, navigating the social order. Put him in the wilderness and he'd try to dazzle the squirrels into building him a fire. I doubt he's ever seen a cigarette lighter. But I listened to him confess his dreams all afternoon. We napped and talked, with my head on his lap as the sun moved across the sky. After a while, we were resting in the shade of tall trees on the edge of the meadow.

I can't begin to explain the serenity of it all. Wildflowers peeked from tall grass in the distance, peppering the green—so unbelievably green—landscape with pinks, purples, and yellows. Step plucked a dandelion from the millions of white little globes that surrounded us. He blew the seeds and those tiny tufts floated away and across my nose.

I want to tell you that you've never smelled such clean air in all your life, never felt such a soft and forgiving world. It would knock you out.

The sun was about to set, and we watched the sky grow orange and then pink behind the trees.

"Look," he said. "I read about this somewhere." He pulled a flint from one pocket, his tiny bar of steel from another. "I've always wanted to do this." He drew the steel toward the flint, holding them above a plush part of the field where dandelions clung like a vale above the dry earth beneath. He struck the steel bar against the stone.

"What are you doing?" I asked.

"Watch," he said, and struck it again, this time sending a spark from the stone and into the field of dandelions. Suddenly, a ring of tiny flames grew from that point and just as quickly spread outward.

We leapt to our feet and ran a short distance away. I'll admit I was scared. I couldn't believe what he had done, and I was sure somebody would come out from the nearby houses—as abandoned as they appeared—and chase after us.

"It's okay," Step said, taking my hand. We watched the ring of fire grow, consuming dandelions in all directions. As it came toward us, he gave my hand a gentle squeeze and said, "Just step over it."

"What?" I was terrified. Look, you've never seen flames move like this. Things like this don't happen in the city. Nature doesn't act like this in the shadow of high-rises. The Earth—its trees, and plants—it's all so alive. Its fire too. And I was petrified by what it might do to me.

"Step over it," Step said, a strange and knowing tone to his voice. "It's okay. There's nothing on the other side."

"It's hot," I said.

"It's not," he said. "The flame is barely there."

I grabbed his wrist with my other hand and pulled myself closer to him.

"I've seen videos online," he said. "Kids used to do this all the time way back in the day."

This only confirmed my notion that kids back then were savages.

Step chuckled at my fear and said, "They did this with dandelions and leaves. Man, you should see the smoke." He was getting excited now. "One kid poured gasoline all over his lawn, threw a match and it went up—woosh—real quick, like a flash. The ring of fire spread and was gone in an instant."

He was squeezing my hand tighter as he spoke, and still the ring grew closer. Neither of us had ever seen fire move like this. You don't see it much in the city. It's usually just smoke from high up in an old building. Sprinklers take care of it too quickly. When it was just about to reach our toes, I was sure I'd get burned. My legs were paralyzed with fear. Then Step shouted, "Now!" and we both hopped over the quiet flame and landed safely on the other side. The ring kept on burning until there were no more dandelions to consume.

Looking back, it was really nothing. But it also was so exhilarating.

Later, as we approached the city, the wall of skyscrapers

jutting upward like rows of decrepit headstones, I thought about that meadow and Step's silly little fire, the excitement and embarrassment that I felt as we stood in that ring, bald dandelion stems tickling our ankles. Nature can so easily retaliate against us city kids. Its power is so enormous as it calmly whispers for us to retreat to our loud streets, our drowning lights, or, she says, next time might not be so pleasant. That day, Mother Nature told me to leave what I don't understand. Stay put, girl, she said. Stay put where you belong.

CHAPTER FIVE
HERON

Falling back into life on the street is hard enough, to say nothing of having a hospital bed and three meals for most of that time. In fact, I may have found this to be the most difficult part of moving in and out of foster homes, from comfort to concrete. The readjustment period seemed to get longer and longer each time. But there I am, weaving through a current of people outside the hospital. I find myself staring at faces, so many unfamiliar faces. And I wonder how I would have acted before the crash. Should I even look at them? Do I keep my head down like everyone else, consumed by my porto or tracing the cracks in the sidewalk?

While it's comforting to find that nobody is looking at me, as I study each face I see nothing but mystery. I have no connection to these people. I may not have known them before but I would have known who they were. And I suddenly feel a strange sense of anonymity, like I don't exist if they don't look at me. Of course, you know, anonymity isn't real, not anymore anyway, like some long-ago eradicated disease.

For a moment, I remain a stone in a river of people, when a delivery guy nearly plows me over. He stops and mutters, "Hadley," as he skirts around me. I quickly say, "Hey," stifled by a tinge of regret, or maybe guilt for not knowing his name. Then I keep moving with my head down.

From the hospital, I work my way through the East

Village and over to SoHo. There, I figure I can gather myself, maybe drop in on a Hayden who works at a boutique on Spring Street. But when I try to think of her name, it doesn't quickly come to mind, especially when I picture her face, or try to anyway. She has a unibrow. I'm sure of that. Like that Mexican painter. What's her name? Frida? Just like her. But now I'm thinking of Frida, not my friend, and I can't come up with a name. I try to think of what I might have said in the past. "I'm headed down to Pitchfork and Co. to see..." but I can't think of her name. When I reach the shop, I peer through the storefront window, and I don't recognize a single person. She might be that girl leaning over the counter. If she looked up, maybe I'd recognize her. But probably not, and I can't bring myself to find out.

I keep walking west, and the farther I go, the more my hips and back ache. Still, I need to keep moving until I see somebody I know. With all the Haydens roaming about, I'm bound to know somebody. I head to the High Line where a bunch of them are usually pushing tribal tobacco. It's been awhile since I walked up there and I immediately remember how much I love the view. I wish I could have seen it in its heyday, before the city lifted height restrictions on development around Chelsea. They say it used to be like walking through a floating forest, what with all the vegetation. But now these tall buildings block the sun, and what little foliage that could survive is now sparse and gnarly like it's always wintertime. It makes me wonder if anything can really ever *live* in the city.

At the overlook above 10th Avenue, two kids I'm sure must be Haydens are, just as I thought, not-so-discreetly selling tobacco to passersby. The girl wears a thermal under two t-shirts, fingerless knit gloves, and faded gray jeans with the knees torn open. There's a general uncleanliness about her that surpasses the normal punk look that she's going for. With her, a boy, maybe fourteen years old, is dressed in a dirt-darkened canvas jacket, a knit cap and brown overalls. He's digging through a hemp shoulder bag for sacks of tobacco that they've parsed themselves, probably from a bulk crate that somebody brought in from the outside territories. Of course, nobody knows who brought it in. That's part of the business. Everybody knows where to get it, just not where it came from. These kids are working the lunch crowd, letting people smell the tobacco. If it's been a slow day, they'll let people roll and light a cigarette, even though it's illegal.

I don't want to approach either of them for fear that I don't actually know them. I'm about to sit on a nearby bench and wait to be noticed, when the girl waves to me. She trots over and I give a halfhearted wave back, still unsure if I know her. The closer she gets, the more I think I might recognize her, but I still have this worried feeling because I can't place her name, not even if I try. Messy bob hair. Too much eye shadow.

"Haddy," she says, without the H, like *Addy*. She holds out her fist and I tap it with mine, like I'm knocking on her knuckles. This is a good sign. And she knows that I go by Haddy. "What's it like?" she asks.

"Just seeing what's what," I say, trying to keep it cool, despite my unease.

Her tired eyes lock on the scratches that cross my face, the scabs on my forehead, the bruises that seem to be spreading around my ear and along my hairline. She looks me up and down, almost repulsed by the blood and scabs. Then her eyes widen in realization. "That's right. You were in a wreck weren't you? Nuts, chicky."

I tuck my bruised and scabbed hand back into my pocket and say, "I'm fine."

"You look like hell," she says, gesturing to my ripped clothing.

I haven't gotten back to the Junction to see if I have

anything in my stash.

"Step's looking for you," she says. "He said you disappeared that night."

She walks over to a bench and I follow. I'm reluctant because I can't remember her name but I know her. This is a girl who used to wet her cot until she was about six years old. I remember that because it was usually boys who had that problem at Hayden House. Not a lot of boy Haydens though, which is probably why so many weren't potty trained so well. I guess it's a different process or maybe Miss Ula's staff didn't know what they were getting into. It's kind of a girls' club over there, and when one goes so long still wetting the bed, you tend to remember it. Just, I can't place her name and it's making me really anxious.

"Seriously, you alright?" she asks.

"Yeah," I say. "I don't know what happened." Of course, I remember enough to know how I got so banged up. I just don't know how I lost control of the car in the first place.

We sit down and she rolls a cigarette. She pushes up her sleeves and says, "It's getting kinda warm today, you know?"

She has a small tattoo on her wrist that I recognize. It's a primitive black outline of a bird, its beak absurdly long and almost reaching her palm. I suddenly realize that she's not the bed wetter. I can't remember who that girl is but I know I didn't meet this particular girl until I was older and living in the Junction. That makes me feel a bit better. The Junction is about the safest place to meet somebody, because if they know how to get down there, they must be a Hayden.

You probably already know this but there's an old junction north of 57th that flooded a long time ago like all the rest. But this one is a few levels below the old A line. When they built the seawall and pumped all the water out, some original Haydens found that the vents led all the way up to Central Park, perfect for quick access and for smoke to escape when we build fires to keep warm. Now we call it the Junction, a place for Manhattan Haydens to meet and lie low. You probably know it as some mythical place to avoid. Maybe you should keep it that way.

Of course, if you ever find yourself down there—but I don't know why you would unless you're a Hayden—you'll know it's the Junction by all the graffiti. Over the years, each of us has come to mark our place down there, usually with something that we thought best symbolized ourselves. Drawings and paintings climb the semi-arched ceiling and creep down each way of the four tunnels leading from the Junction. I met this girl—whatever her name is with the bird tattoo—when she was sketching that same bird along the wrist of a tall column. She used one of those fat paint markers. I remember watching her and thinking that I couldn't make out what she was drawing but it reminded me of the birds I once saw out near Jamaica Bay.

"An egret," I said to her.

"No," she shot back. "This is a heron." Only, she said it like *yeerrrr-on*, cutting off the H.

I would have explained that an egret is a heron but I didn't want to ruin the moment. There's something special about leaving your mark in the Junction, like you've staked your claim on the Hayden family tree. I remember doing it myself, finding an unassuming bare patch beside an old circuit box tucked near the floor. As if channeling something deep within me, I closed my eyes and took a snapshot of the first thing that came to mind—a hot air balloon. That's what I drew. How stupid, I know. But it's been sort of a thing with me. I can't explain it. I don't have much of a desire to ever fly in one. In fact, I'm not even sure they're still around. I just like the shape, I guess.

The lunch crowd picks up on the High Line, and I watch as the heron girl finishes rolling her cigarette. She balls up another square of rolling paper, removes a flint she wears

40

around her neck, and strikes it twice against the steel brace of the bench, until a spark leaps against the balled paper in her other hand, creating fire. She brings the fire to her cigarette and takes a long drag before offering it to me. I pass and try to ignore people looking at us as they walk by.

"So, where'd you see Step?" I ask.

She exhales with a big plume of thick, sweet-smelling smoke and says, "Not sure. Midtown, I guess. He was running umbrellas."

That's one of Step's tricks. He steals umbrellas from lobbies all over the city. They're easy to grab by the door and get away quick. He then sells them from a backpack up and down old Times Square.

"You think he's still up that way?" I ask.

"Not today," another girl says, coming up behind us. She's older, like in her mid-thirties. Bleached blonde hair, but tasteful. Good posture. I can't tell if I know her. Deep laugh lines cut through her weathered face.

"Hey, Cam," heron girl says, offering her cigarette. "What's it like?"

Cam. Or Cammy. That's her name. It's short for Camera or some old car part. And just knowing that much fills me with a strange sense of ease. She's dressed nicely but her face shows the wear of being a Hayden. In fact, she's an original, one of the first to take our last name.

Cammy takes the cigarette, watchful of the people passing by, in case a GC wants to say something about the tobacco. "He's probably bumming scraps at the market," Cammy says through exhaled smoke. "We're cooking tonight for Repats."

She's talking about Repatriation Day, when the new-old territories were officially ratified. I'm sure you don't bother celebrating it. I mean, it's the sort of holiday that people celebrate only to accept the current state of things. If anything, it's in celebration of the law that put us in this overpopulated mess in the first place, and what had led to us Haydens being where we are today. Of course, Haydens celebrate it because we rarely miss an opportunity to party.

"Just ping him," the girl says to me.

"I thought about that," I say. "But my porto's been wiped."

"Really?" the girl says.

"From the crash, huh," Cammy says, casually. I shoot her a look because I don't know how she would know that. Then she says, "You look like hell."

"What are you going to do?" the other girl says. She seems deeply concerned. "I mean, don't they back up portos or something? They have to, don't they? I mean, think of what you'd lose. Dex once lost his porto, and MIND just—."

"They tried," I say, cutting her off. "Even the hospital couldn't retrieve my data."

"That's crazy," the girl says. Her eyes beam wide, as if a tragedy just unfolded before her. "It's like you might as well be dead."

"Leana," Cammy says, balefully. And suddenly I know this heron girl. Only, I'm not much more at ease from her. I must not know her that well, I guess. "Your porto isn't your life," Cammy says.

"Well, I mean," Leana says. "I guess not. I don't know." I look at her face again to see if I can place her name to her face. I can't but she seems a little more familiar. I'll have to remember her hazel eyes, that one crooked tooth, and the dropped H.

"Believe me," Cammy says to me. "It's not that big a deal. Don't worry."

"I know," I say. "I'm fine."

"They'll make you believe it," Cammy says. "Don't get me wrong. You don't want to lose this thing." She takes a long drag from Leana's cigarette.

"You know," Leana says, pulling out her porto and turning it over in her hands. "I got a feeling they track us with these things."

"No kidding," Cammy says, half-joking because it's obvious that we're tracked. Anyone who thinks otherwise is a fool.

"Not that we're worth watching anyway," Leana says.

She tucks her porto back into the waste of her pants.

"Tell me about it," Cammy says. She looks at me and says, "Step will be there tonight. We'll start the pit at 7."

"I'll be there," I say.

"Me too," Leana says eagerly.

Cammy hands Leana her cigarette. Leana looks at it disappointed because it's nearly smoked down to the nub.

"Leana," Cammy says quickly. She nods toward a cop coming down the High Line.

Before I can even say, "See you," Cammy has made her escape, swiftly walking in the opposite direction.

Leana whistles to her partner across the way to cut his business short. She flicks the cigarette butt into the shrubs, and I'm pretty sure the cop sees her do it. Leana gets to her feet.

"Come on," she says. I can tell that she's looking to me for an escape route. I'm sort of known for that. Our portos have a GPS but I got the city mapped down to the tiniest nook. Leana wants me to lead us to safety somewhere.

I think to run but I haven't done anything wrong and it would hurt too much, anyway. So I quickly say, "Take the stairs above 12th. This cop will radio for whoever's walking the beat down below. Don't worry about them."

The boy scrambles with his tobacco and hemp shoulder bag, and the cop quickens his step.

"Hey," he says, calling above the crowd.

"When you're down there," I say to Leana, "run back the other way until you hit 13th. Then cross over to the substation.

Behind it, there's a ladder. You know the substation, right?"

"Sure," Leana says, but she doesn't sound confident.

"You can't miss it," I say. "I'll hold him. Just get to the substation. Take the ladder to the top and climb up into the rafters just underneath the High Line. You probably won't even need to go that far."

"But what about you?" she says. The boy arrives and takes her arm. He's smart and keeps his head tilted down and away from the approaching cop so he won't be recognized.

"Go," I say. "When you're safe, ping anybody nearby for a distraction."

Leana smiles thankfully and they run off just as the cop arrives. I stay put on the bench.

"Hey," the cop says. "You."

I'm looking away like I'm too busy with something else. It's intentional.

"Look at me," he barks. When we're facing each other, he says, "Okay, Hadley...Hayden." He sighs because he knows that us Haydens won't make it easy. "Where did your friends run off to?"

"Who?" I say.

"You know who," he says. That's when I know he hasn't seen their faces. Otherwise, he would have their names.

"I'm not sure to whom you're referring," I say.

"Cut the crap, kid," he says. He puts out his hand for my porto. I slap it into his palm and he starts thumbing through it. Of course, he's not going to find anything.

"There ain't nothing on here?" he says. "What the hell?"

"I keep it clean," I say, taking it back. "Can I go now?"

The cop talks into his watch. "Got anything down there, Five?"

The watch squawks back something I can't understand.

"Looks like you'll have to do," he says, taking my arm.

"Come on," I say. "You don't have anything on me."

"You're a Hayden," he says. "There's something on you. There's always something on you Haydens. Besides, you look like you've been hit by a train."

He gestures for me to stand and come with him, like he's going to take me to the station. Only, I know he's not going to, and I stay where I am. He sighs and sits down beside me.

"If I search you and find—" he starts to say.

"And find nothing," I say. "Because if you touch me, I'll scream."

"Don't be like that, kid."

Neither of us moves. He knows that I can make this harder for him and I know that he can get fed up enough that he will take me down to the police station, where, even though he'll have nothing on me, he can at least make me sweat until somebody from Hayden House takes me in for mandatory lockdown.

"Just tell me their names," he says. "They're Haydens, right?"

"Probably," I say.

"Probably?"

I want to act like I'm kidding, but I'm not. After all, I don't know their names for sure like I used to. Maybe he sees this on my face because he says, "What's the matter?" He sounds genuinely concerned when he adds, "That train that hit you take your tongue?" He nods to my bruised and scratched up face. I suddenly don't get the sense that he's a GC-turned-cop like I expected.

"I'm—" I start to say, but I can't. I don't know what he'll think if I tell him I'm Fried.

"Look," he says with a strange tone of compassion. "I'm just doing my job."

After a moment, I say, "I—I don't know who they were. Okay?"

His eyes narrow on me, as if he's looking at something he

45

has never seen before. When it seems to register, he quickly shifts in his seat like I'm some sort of fragile thing. It feels like several minutes but he really only studies me for a second or so.

"Wait," he says. "Look at me." He reaches to turn my head toward him and I slap his hand away. We both know that my doing so is enough to take me in for assault on an officer. And I freeze with caution.

"Look at me," he says, his voice with a slight edge to it.

When I look, he removes his sunglasses to reveal a pale impression of those frames stretched from ear to ear. Creased skin drags away from his eyes as he squints. They're brown eyes. Bloodshot.

"What's my name?" he asks.

I don't say. His glasses have also left an impression on the bridge of his nose just below where his brow folds over as he squints against the sun.

"You're Fried," he says. It's like he's trying to find the reason in my eyes. "What happened?"

When I don't answer, he pulls out his porto and swipes at the screen. He says my name into it. My record appears. He's about to dig through my history—a few minor brushes with the law, a lot of what I already told you—but then his watch squawks again.

The other Haydens are on the move. Like I hoped, Leana called for some Haydens to run the cops for a bit. There's enough of us around that if you simply send out a ping that you're stuck somewhere, there's at least half a dozen bored Haydens who will throw on their masks and make the cops chase them in every direction.

The cop gets to his feet just as a leather-clad Hayden in a nylon skull mask dashes through the startled lunchtime crowd. The cop shouts something, looks back at me like I'm still at fault, and then takes off after the kid. Running cops is easy and it nearly never fails, as long as you're relatively quick on your feet and you know your way around. Some Haydens make a game of it.

I waste no time in leaving, work my way into the crowd as another cop comes striding by in pursuit of the masked Hayden. Somewhere in the distance, I can hear another Hayden laughing and taunting another cop.

The thing about being a Hayden is that you might be homeless but you're not alone. You have people around who will help you out of jam. You have a lot of the same problems as the average drifter, like where you might sleep tonight or where your next meal will come from, but you know there are a hundred or so people within a five-minute walk who can help you for at least one night.

That, of course, requires knowing people, which I do but I don't...not anymore.

I've been walking for half an hour now and still I recognize no one. My hips are killing me. My feet are tired. I used to be able to walk for hours. That's an important skill to have as Hayden. You can't sneak onto trains. Porto scanners will catch you and you'll be fined straight from your cloud account, if you have any credit. So, I walk. But now I'm mad at myself for being so tired. Only, I'm really just mentally tired. Actively trying to read people, trying to make sense of my new life as a Fried person. It's exhausting.

I need to sit down but when I look up, I'm on Broadway and 23rd and there's nothing but sidewalk and scaffolding. I've climbed scaffolding for a quiet perch many times but I'm not about to now. There's no way I'd make it even one story.

I shuffle over to Madison Square Park and take a seat on a park bench beside a smelly, old homeless man. He's not a Hayden. Too old. But you do a lot of this as a Hayden, find yourself killing time in public places. Sometimes the hustle gets old. You don't have the energy to keep going, just have to sit down and collect yourself. Otherwise you'll get nowhere.

Of course, you sometimes just need a place to sleep for the night. We all have our places. I'll go to a hospital emergency room and fake like I had a spill or that I ate something bad. They make you wait forever to be seen, plenty of time to sleep in a warm place. A lot of Haydens do this sort of thing, especially on rainy days, find cover in a cellar stairwell or under a loading dock or on a sheltered park bench like this one.

I hear that it's a lot like this in the other cities. I don't know what they call their Haydens or if they even have as big a problem as us. I know each city runs things differently at this point. The only thing we share is the System, so I assume, but even that would be more or less useless if nobody's traveling anymore from one city to another. Still, if there are a few thousand homeless kids in Los Angeles, Houston, or even San Francisco, they're probably running similar hustles, searching similar dumpsters, and killing an afternoon on similar park benches.

I just wonder how many of those kids are beat up and tired, even scared, like me. How many are unsure if they can navigate like they used to now that they're Fried? I lean forward, elbows on my knees, head in my hands, and I think about why this has happened to me.

When I lift my head again, I follow the cement path before me and remember a boy. His name is Tommy. I can see his face. My heart grows heavy with regret.

"Hungry?" the homeless man asks. He picks through an oil-stained canvas bag and withdraws the crust from an eaten slice of pizza. "Go ahead," he says. His raspy voice forces its way through a mouthful of chewed pizza crust. "I don't mind."

It's not raining today and the sun beats on the man until he's practically sizzling with stink. He says, "Go ahead," again before taking another bite. He turns a little more my way and gestures to my belly. "Might be important."

I don't realize it at first but my porto chimed in my

hoodie pocket. When I pull it out, I see there's a message. It's another one from Paul. It says, "Do you feel alone?"

I suddenly get the sense that I'm being watched. Maybe it's just somebody messing with me. Or it could be spam. Either way, I want to write back and say, "Who are you?" or "Leave me alone!" Try to stop this Paul from bothering me. But that would just bring more pings, I'm sure. Before I can talk myself out of it, I fire back, "No." Because I don't feel alone. I'm sharing a park bench with a perfectly fine, albeit stinky, homeless man.

Then I wait. And the more I wait, the more I start to feel like my response was rude. Of course, I don't know why I care or why I want this Paul person to write back.

The smelly man turns and says something.

"What's that?" I ask.

He presents the stained canvas bag again, opened before me to reveal an assortment of pizza crusts like they're potato chips. "Take one."

"I'm fine," I say. I'm actually really hungry. Being off the IV, I feel a little weak.

He glances at my porto and smiles, flashing the few teeth he still has.

"Stupid things," I say, and I turn my porto over on my lap.

"Makes a handy flashlight," the man says, and takes another bite of crust, tearing at it with mostly gums. He chortles to himself.

A breeze rustles the browning leaves in the trees above, and for a moment, the man's stench is replaced with crisp clean air. Above the murmuring leaves, there's a faint and hollow creaking of metal in the distance. With each gust, it gives a dull whine somewhere above us. The man locks in on it and smirks.

"Listen, Haddy," the man says, leaning in close and whispering. "Can you hear—?"

Haddy? I look to the man and say, "Do I know you?"

"Of course," he says and goes back to listening to the breeze.

I wait for him to explain how we know each other but it's clear that he's distracted by the metal sound.

"I'm going to find it," the man says. He gets to his feet and shuffles down the path toward what I suppose is a distant wind chime.

In my lap, my porto sits lifeless. No new message. So, I type another reply to Paul, this time saying, "Sometimes." I reluctantly send it.

The breeze lulls and then gusts again, and I close my eyes to enjoy the way it brushes across my face. That mournful metal groan cries nearby. I open my eyes again to the concrete path beneath my feet. Again, I can see that boy. Tommy. What else could I do?

My porto chimes. I look down at it in my lap. The screen comes alive with a new message from Paul. It reads, "I know."

CHAPTER SIX
CANDLESTICK

I think, for most Haydens, loneliness isn't an issue. We're basically a family and we're all over the city, practically crawling on top of each other. We also know our place in society. So, we don't yearn for much. But because I know my past, and I know who and where my family is, this stupid longing nags me.

Like I said, I was wrapped in burlap. Somebody found little baby me on Wall Street. Yes, before it was under water.

I don't remember those early years, obviously. And I certainly can't recall lying there on the cobbled street, crying into a burlap sack. But I remember my parents because I met them years later.

When I was eleven, my mother tracked me down through Hayden House, and they confirmed my story. Hayden House keeps impeccable records, probably for the sole purpose of reuniting parents and children. It's one of the things I don't like about that place, if you really want to know. It feels like they keep tabs on us. But worse, they make it so that unloving parents can track down their kids, and usually when those kids are old enough to bring extra income to a household. At least Hayden House has the decency to keep hardcopies, actual physical paper, of those records rather than keeping them in the cloud. Who knows what would happen if people suddenly had access to every Hayden's past with one little hack.

Anyway, all of this is sort of moot. The name-changing process is so difficult and in the few instances where it ever gets that far, most of the kids end up running away before their birth parents regain custody. For Haydens, it's hard to give up what little life we already know.

In my Hayden House record, I had been found on a Sunday. A maintenance man almost threw me into a dumpster, when he heard me screaming. I was cold and hungry, so he called Miss Ula to come down and pick me up. It was morning when people from Hayden House got there, and the maintenance man was gone. Apparently his shift had ended and he didn't care enough to stick around and make sure I was okay.

Time passed and I was eleven years old and living with a family in the Bronx—the Moores, if I remember—when I got a ping from Miss Ula about how my birth mother was waiting to see me. Miss Ula, forever the saint, had told my mother the whole story and, apparently, my mother nearly wept. For all the horrible things that led us Haydens to her doorstep, Miss Ula felt like there was still more good than evil in the world. And she didn't see any harm in reuniting a child with her neglectful parents.

My mother was still crying when she saw me. I was nearly crying, too, and I don't know why. I can't imagine I was happy to see her. But, I had to admit, it was like I was looking into a mirror at an older version of me, like those silly apps that will age your picture to show you what you'll look like when you grow old. And because I saw her, I knew her name. It was like I already knew her, when, really, I didn't. I almost said her name, too, though I really didn't want to. After all, her last name—Karp—was my real last name. And if my last name was Karp, then the System was wrong. I don't think an eleven-year-old kid can handle something like that. The one constant, the System, being wrong. Even worse, if I accepted that last name, I would no longer be a Hayden, which was the only thing important to me, even if I didn't realize it until that moment. All I knew, everything that defined me, came with my name.

Mrs. Karp, as I try to remember her, reached out to hold me but I kept one hand on Miss Ula's leg, maybe because I was afraid of leaving.

Miss Ula said, "Go ahead, Haddy. That's your mommy." She was tearing up, too.

I remember asking, "Where's my father?"

"He couldn't make it," Mrs. Karp said. "He doesn't know I'm—" She choked on her sobs and turned to Miss Ula. "What if we made a mistake?" she said. "Can we take her back?"

"That depends on her foster parents," Miss Ula said.

I knew the Moores wouldn't care. I was already sneaking out with other Haydens, smoking old tribal tobacco and lifting food from the market. They wanted to get rid of me. It was only a matter of time.

"Can you find out?" Mrs. Karp asked. She looked to me. "Would you like to come home?"

Home. What a stupid word, I thought. It made no sense to me. How can I consider her place home if I'd never seen it before? It's sad, now that I think about it. An eleven-year-old girl having that sort of thought.

I gave a reluctant smile because Miss Ula seemed eager to see this work out.

"I'll come back next week," Mrs. Karp said. "You make sure it's okay and I'll be here to come get you. Okay?"

Miss Ula rubbed my back and I nodded that it was okay. But it wasn't okay. I was scared. I didn't want to move again. I didn't know where they lived, and I didn't want to find out. That is, until Miss Ula asked, "Will Mr. Karp join you? I'd really like to meet him."

"Oh, sure," said Mrs. Karp. "I didn't tell him I was coming here. He'll be thrilled that I found you though." She reached to cup my face in her hands and I leaned away. This seemed to upset her but she quickly let it pass. Then she said, "Your father's a custodian over by the Stock Exchange. Isn't that neat? He works nights, usually."

It took me a minute to put together the Stock Exchange, Wall Street, and a janitor who "discovered" me.

I didn't let on that I knew something was fishy but I'm sure I was trembling with fear or rage or shock.

"I'll make sure he comes next week," she said.

I shrunk back behind Miss Ula, who could tell something was wrong with me. I didn't say anything more. The next day Miss Ula went ahead and asked the Moores if they were planning to adopt me, because otherwise I ought to go home with my birth parents. Sure enough, they didn't even have to leave the room to contemplated it. So, once again, I found myself back at Hayden House, this time awaiting my birth parents.

I'm not proud of what I did next but I did it, and I have to live with it.

A few nights later, I snuck out of Hayden House to go down to the Stock Exchange. As far as I've ever known, the Exchange has been a façade, sort of a relic or a historic site. Nothing actually happens there anymore. It's all done in the cloud.

Anyway, by this time, I think the water had already filled the Brooklyn-Battery Tunnel, and it was still a few blocks away, certainly not like it is now. I huddled in the shadows and waited for Mr. Karp to come out with the trash like he apparently had when he first discovered me. I must have waited three or four hours before he came out with a hose and pressure washer to spray down the front steps. He was a stout man, not like I would have imagined him. He had a beard and thick-rimmed glasses and a floppy hat. He wore coveralls that made him look dumpy. I hated him right away.

I crouched back and watched him hook up the hose and

crank the washer's motor. He methodically sprayed the steps, walking the length of them, starting with the top step, taking great care. I wasn't this perceptive then, but now that I think about it, I would have loved to see him stand where he left me, to see if it weighed on him in some way, what he did. You know, just see his shoulders drop in a fleeting moment of regret.

When he was done, he disappeared to do whatever else. I waited where I was for his shift to end. By then it was morning and commuters were starting to crowd the area, perfect for me to hide among as I followed him to the subway. He didn't see me, and I wondered if he would even know who I was if he had. Had his wife mentioned meeting me? Did she tell him my name? I watched him from the other end of the train car as it emptied the further we got from Manhattan. We were headed to Queens. I followed him off the car and down to the street. Another ten-minute walk and I was standing outside his house, a small row home toward the end of the block. For some reason, I decided to sit on a stoop down the way and watch their house. It was morning and people were coming and going. Traffic had picked up again. Before long, he emerged from his house with a young boy. I thought maybe the boy saw me, so I kept my head down. He was no older than eight, carrying a backpack too big for him. The two of them walked to the boy's school, and I followed. The whole time, I could feel something stir in me, a hollow sense of jealousy. But why? I hated this man. I did. That's what I told Miss Ula when she made me leave the Moores. "I hate them," I said. "I hate the Karps."

"No, you don't," Miss Ula said. She hugged me and I let her because part of me knew she was right.

Once at the boy's school, Mr. Karp hugged him and sent him off. Before shuffling up the steps, the boy looked back and I saw his face. His name was Thomas. Thomas Karp. But Mr. Karp called him something I didn't quite hear, maybe Tom or Tommy or even Tom Tom, like one of the Haydens I know.

All I could think, standing there outside his school, was how he stole my parents. They gave me up so they could have him. For that reason, I became fixed on him.

Over the next few days, I sat across from the boy's school. I could smell their lunches from the exhaust fan outside the cafeteria kitchen. My stomach growled and ached, but I stayed put until the boy came out. And then I followed him home. I didn't have a plan. I just wanted to see him.

I did this for three days, sometimes snapping photos with my porto, as if I were some private detective. I watched the boy arrive with his father and walk home on his own after school. But on the third day, the boy stopped at the curb across the street from me. I thought he was going to tie his shoe or maybe he forgot something and was about to turn around. But he just stood there, his head sort of bowed, and he looked at me. I should have walked away or told him to buzz off but I didn't. I sat still, watching him look at me. Then he crossed the street toward me.

"You're Hadley Hayden," he said. I knew a lot of boys his age but they didn't have his innocence. I had never heard that quiver, the subtle upward inflection of genuine curiosity common of boys—innocent, youthful boys—his age.

"You're Thomas Karp," I said.

"Tommy," he said.

"Tommy."

He shifted under the weight of his big school bag. After a moment, he took it off, dropped it beside his feet. I could see little paint markings on the front pocket, the sort of doodles a bored kid might make. Only, these were an odd shape like railing banisters or candlesticks.

"Looks heavy," I said.

"It's not," he said. "I don't like carrying it though."

"What's all in there?"

"Just stuff," he said. "My lunch box. Gym clothes. My

mom makes me bring an extra bottle of water. She says the school water is bad." He nudged the bag with his toe. "Is the water bad at your school?"

"Yeah," I said.

I stood up and smoothed my shirt. I remember it was an old dress shirt that an older prep school boy might wear. It was too big and a little dirty. I think Thomas noticed this.

He looked down again and said, "My mom said your name the other day."

"Are you sure?"

"Yes," he said. "I remember. She told my dad your name, and then she said you were their daughter."

I didn't say anything. I wanted to be angry. Why was his mother complicating things? How could she be so reckless? After all, this boy could not possibly understand what was going on.

"Does that make you my sister?" he asked.

I don't know if I was about to cry or if I was just disgusted with the whole situation. But I looked away and didn't say anything.

"Where do you live?" he said.

He didn't know about Haydens. He was an innocent boy whose mother probably wanted to give him the world, and then probably did all this against her husband's wishes to stop meddling. I wanted to march over to their house and kick her in the shins. Here was this helpless, sheltered kid. But he had everything. He was the reason I was on the streets. He couldn't possibly handle knowing what happened to me. It would shatter his world. And that, I thought, would break his mother's heart.

Precisely what I wanted to do.

"Would you like to see where I live?" I said.

"I don't know," he said.

"Sure you do," I said. I took a step toward him. He didn't move. I put a hand on his arm. "Your mom—*our* mommy asked me to show you."

He looked me over. Those sad, innocent eyes. So naïve. I think he might have fancied me in that awkward boy way. "Maybe I should ping my mom," he said.

"No need," I said, taking his hand. I felt much older than him, and I probably exuded that maturity. The streets will do that to you. "I already told her."

"Oh," he said, and he reluctantly tucked his porto back in his school bag.

We walked for a few blocks toward the train. It felt wrong to do this. Believe me. I'm not proud. But I wanted to hurt this family. I didn't want to do anything serious, just scare them and make their perfect little happy lives feel a little less comfortable.

He suddenly stopped, let go of my hand, and said "I can't."

"No?"

"I'm sorry," he said.

"It's okay," I said. "I just thought you wanted to see where I live."

"I do," he said.

"Well?"

I waited while he pondered it some more. He was scared and rightly so. And that vengeful little version of me was relishing each moment. I started to step away and said, "Look, Tommy. I have to go. It's okay. I just thought you were grown up enough to hang out with me."

"I am," he said.

"Don't worry," I said. "Maybe I'll see you again some time." I started to walk away.

"Wait," he said. I knew I had him then.

I stopped and looked back. "It's okay," I said. "You're not ready."

He didn't say anything, just licked his lips and then

dropped his head. I started toward the train again, listening for his footsteps behind me. I didn't want to turn around to see if he was following me. I thought he might but I couldn't hear him behind me. When I reached the stairs to the train stop, I looked over and saw that he had followed me but was now standing across the street and looking up as I ascended to the platform. He saw me look, so I gave a fleeting wave good-bye, that final touch.

The train came soon after and I got on. Before the doors closed, I saw Thomas board the car at the other end. He didn't come over to see me. He acted like he wasn't following me. So I acted like I didn't know he was there.

The whole way back to Manhattan, his eyes were peeled in the underground darkness as lights streaked past the window. I watched him and thought how sad it was that he was so excited by the city. Or maybe it was sad that I didn't care. Still, I had no idea what I intended to do with him. Not that I should care. *He* followed *me*.

We reached my stop and I let him follow me to the street. When he emerged from the subway steps his face lifted toward the tall buildings, eyes first, then chin, until he nearly fell over with awe.

"Oh, Thomas," I said. "I didn't see you there. Are you following me?"

Startled, he looked down and said, "No. I mean—" His eyes drew upward again, before he looked at me. There were maybe two years between us but he seemed so young, so innocent. Or maybe I was just too grown up. Either way, he was little. And when I looked at him, I just wanted to take his hand. My little brother's hand.

"I've been here before, you know," he said.

"Cool," I said.

"Truly," he said. "My parents took me to a science museum. Where is that?"

His parents. As if they weren't my parents too. I didn't know why I was so angry. I didn't want them. I didn't care about Thomas and especially not his mother or father.

"Not very far," I said, but it was over fifty blocks away. I was having trouble thinking. This naïve little boy. How much I pitied him. And, yet, as I look back, I must have envied him too.

"Oh," he said, almost sad.

"Anyway," I said. "I should get going. It's good to see you again." I was done with him. I just wanted to go back to Hayden House, serve my time and get on with my life.

But, of course, he followed me again, keeping half a block between us. I took a few turns, tried, maybe in vain, to shake him. Finally, when he got caught up at a traffic light, I waited, acting like I needed to tie my shoe. I led him to Madison Square Park because I had no other plan in mind and, with its reputation for being a Hayden hangout, I guess I wanted to see what he would think. After all, the Haydens were basically my family.

But when I got there, I could tell that there was something unusual going on. There were a bunch of people over by that big elm tree. You know the one. And I'm talking about the nasty riot that happened a few years ago, if you remember. A whole bunch of GCs. A mess of boys from that prep school. Just as many Haydens. Everyone barking threats. More GCs poured in from the university, all of them surrounding these Haydens.

When I turned to stop Thomas from entering the park, he was already there, already too close to run when the brawl broke out. A Hayden started swinging a pipe and everyone went berserk with chains and bricks, people leaping at each other. I just remember the howling and screaming. The cries for help. Thomas stood there frozen. This sheltered little boy a witness to mayhem, a confirmation of everything he'd probably been told about the city. I went to grab him but a GC started for us with a wooden paddle, bloodlust in his eyes. I reacted the only way I knew how. I ran. I took off as fast I could. I knew where to escape and I kept running.

But Thomas, when I looked back, was nowhere to be found. I called for him over the screams. I even doubled back a little, hoping he might be hiding in the shrubs. All I saw was his book bag on the path. I cried his name. But there was no answer. I watched that flurry of violence spill from the park and into the adjacent streets. Somewhere in that melee was a scared little boy that I led to the slaughter.

CHAPTER SEVEN
BOXING GLOVES

Thick smoke lingers at the ceiling of the Junction, lazily waiting to escape through two small vents. As the current shifts from one tunnel to the next, smoke snakes between them, crawling along the tunnel ceiling and luring more Haydens to the pit of smoked meat and potatoes at the center of the Junction floor. I can smell it from my stash a few hundred feet down the south tunnel, and it's driving me crazy. I haven't eaten all day, and before that, I was mostly fed through an IV bag in the hospital.

I grab a pair of baggy men's corduroy pants from my stash, cinch them with a belt, and throw a jacket over my hoodie before joining everyone else under the dome. Firelight flickers against a collage of tags and graffiti that covers the Junction walls. The highest of that graffiti—a bunch of animal shapes, a pickup truck, a baseball bat, a weird boat-like vessel that appears to be carrying apples—is darkened by smoke, making those figures seem like prehistoric hieroglyphs. They tell a story of this place's inhabitants, past and present.

The fire stretches along fifteen feet of the tracks. Embers and freshly placed wood are contained between the rails, over which different meats—whatever Haydens could muster—smoke and sizzle and smell like heaven. People pick pieces of pork and chicken from the fire, use splintered pieces of wood or bent scrap medal for plates. They pass drinks. Somebody got hold of a few massive jugs of clean drinking water, which is always in short supply down here. A dozen or so bottles of vodka make the rounds. Cans of beer chill in a puddle where the floor dips away from the old tracks.

Parties down here are always interesting, like a hundred different moments are going on under the same roof. It's one unorganized mob where there might be people hooting and hollering in one corner and another group lounging, usually doped to near unconsciousness, on the other side of the room. People fill in around the tracks, tiny factions of Haydens bickering or laughing. Somebody screams but barely raises concern. Another person laughs manically in the corner, a haunting, inhuman cry of intoxication. Whatever they're passing around over there, I don't want it. But at least they're having fun. And it's good to be back among friends. At least that's what I'm trying to tell myself. I have so many names in my head. Cal, Mindy, Stump, Law, Prilly. They're here, somewhere among these faintly familiar faces. But I can't place them. This is my family. I'm a Hayden. And I'm trying so hard to feel like it.

You're part of them. That's what I have to tell myself. *They're your family, Haddy. You know these faces. Look around.* Piercings, ratty clothing, tattoos. Tangled hair. Sweat and dirt. That girl with the cane. That guy in a suit coat and a Mohawk. *You know these people.*

I'm supposed to belong here. I just don't feel it.

An arm comes across my shoulder. I look and see a guy in his late teens, maybe early twenties, just like so many other people here. But when I look in his eyes, I feel a calm come over me. *This is Step, Haddy.* Of course. He smiles and pulls me toward him for a hug. He holds me tight, squeezes his arms around me. He has to be Step. I want to cry. I recognize him. At least I think I do. But the fact that I second-guess myself, the idea that I wouldn't know Step, of all people, just kills me. He leans back and looks at me. He smiles and, for a second, I start to notice things—the thick, dark curls around his ears or the way his eyebrows slope away like he's always sad or doubting you. He reminds me of a basset hound, in a way that he seems trustworthy, if that makes sense. Well, it does to me. Maybe that's all that matters, what I feel when I'm with him. Because that's not something you get from the System. Moments of face-to-face contact aren't the same as sterile screenshots frozen in time and shown to you through some chip in your head. You know the expression: *You'll know it when you see it?* It's not, *You'll know it when it's presented to you.* I think you have to be active. (I don't know. I'm just riffing.)

"Damn it's good to see you," Step says, grimacing as his eyes scan my bruises.

He squeezes my arms and smiles. I wanted to give him a big hug but he says, "We're jamming now. Let's catch up in a bit."

He folds into the crowd to make his way over to his band who are huddled around their gear beside the only power source to the Junction from a mainline box near the west tunnel. Just above their instruments is Step's tag, a scribbled clock, and above that the words, "Mantel Clock rocks!" I don't know if he wrote this before or after his band formed but he claims he's always had the name floating around his head, just waiting for the right sound.

The band does no sound check, probably because they don't have a sound guy like they would in a normal venue. Without an introduction, Grandpa and the Mantel Clocks jumps right into it, instruments barely meshing until the third measure, a throng of sound that cuts through the crowd's murmur and rises with smoke and ash to the domed ceiling. It's a mess of noise that comes at you, makes you feel something with each crash of a cymbal, each pounce on the electric organ. Step seems at home among his bandmates.

The rest of us watch or listen as we feast and mingle.

Somebody hands me a strip of charred beef on a stick. I don't know who she is but she puts her arm around me and says something into my ear that I can't hear over the fuzz. I just thank her and she moves on. The beef is warm and smells perfect. I savor it as I watch Step sway before an enthusiastic audience, his bass guitar hung high on his chest.

My jaw hurts as I chew the tough meat, and I wonder how long it will take to recover from the accident. It occurs to me before long that the last time I heard Step's band was the night of the crash, when I was still like everyone else here. I was just another Hayden. The thought makes me feel very alone and invisible, even among these people I call my friends.

I feel in my pocket for my porto and think about Paul's last message, those two simple words: "I know." For some reason, this makes me feel better.

***

After a couple of weeks on the street, I start to settle back into my Hayden routine, not just physically but mentally. I try to forget about the crash or Agent Stevenson. I'm a Hayden. I have other things to worry about, like surviving. The rest of my energy goes toward making do. Nobody knows yet that I'm Fried and I'd like to keep it that way. I just wonder how I'll ever break it to Step, if I can.

Today, he and I are working the Upper East Side. I told him that I'd like to keep whatever we do legit for a while. I'm not in the best shape to run from the cops or whatever trouble we might find ourselves in. So Step sets us up with some window washing equipment—telescoping squeegees, rags, and buckets of soapy water. We go knocking on brownstones to see if anyone will hire us to wash their windows.

I'm not the prettiest girl in the city but I'm not afraid to admit that I look a whole lot better than most Haydens, which is why I'm often the front girl for hustles. I can be persuasive, so I've been told. The trouble is I don't look so good right now with faint bruises still lingering around my face. So, when this middle-aged man answers the door I'm knocking on, he grimaces a little.

"Y'all mind if we wash your windows?" I employ a southern drawl that probably hasn't existed in decades but has a sweet sentimentality kept strong by movies.

The man knows I'm a Hayden but I bat my eyelashes and flash a sympathetic grin. I can usually lay on the charm. Step waits down by the curb with our equipment so as to not pose a threat, especially if a GC answers the door. And if a potential customer doubts my abilities, they see Step is with me and expect that he's the labor, I'm the dealmaker. Even if I still pull my own squeegee. We make all the right moves.

I sweep back a tuft of hair for effect, but this action must also reveal a still-swollen scar on my hairline. The man narrows his eyes in disgust, lurches his head back.

"Just get off my stoop," he says, and shuts the door.

We spend a good chunk of the morning trying to get somebody to bite. Finally, an old lady lets us wash her front windows and *only* the front windows. We haven't had much luck to this point, so we take our time with this lady's house and carefully wipe down trim with rags.

To reach the second floor, Step climbs a tree in front of the house. He thinks this will give him a better angle on third-floor windows, as well. But he catches a glimpse of the elderly woman inside. She's not doing anything intimate but she screams when she sees Step. She curses him, calling him a peeping tom. Unfortunately, Step, being how he is when I'm not watching, flips her the middle finger. And like that we're stuck without getting paid. Step has a few choice words for the lady but she doesn't bother to respond. All we hear in return is the front door lock.

"I'm done," Step says, working his way down the tree. "Stupid lady." He shakes off his squeegee. I tell him to take it easy but he doesn't seem to hear me. Instead, he considers the bucket of soapy water in his hand. Then he tosses the water all over the lady's first-floor windows, negating the work we did. Inside, the lady shakes a fist and curses us to leave.

"I'm hungry," Step says, ignore the raging woman, as if none of that even happened.

"Okay. You pick," I say, knowing that when Step gets worked up, he's difficult to bring back down. But he turns my simple accommodation into a weapon.

"You don't mean that."

"I really do, Step."

"Don't do that," he says, and starts to walk. "Don't make me out to be the picky one."

We've had this conversation enough times for me to know that Step is the pickiest eater I've ever known. Where we eat has never been my choice, mainly because I'll eat just about anything and anywhere, like most desperate Haydens. Whereas, Step has adopted some fake paleo-vegetarian-type diet because of all his allergies and peculiarities to texture—crispy but not so much, never too slimy, and always easy enough to cut with just a fork. He refuses to use a knife.

"I'm not going to argue with you," he says, after I don't dignify his confrontational tone with a response. "Let's just hit up Reggie's."

Of course, I could have guessed we would end up at Reggie's Veggies the moment he suggested we wash windows on the Upper East Side.

I don't know how this place stays open. There aren't a lot of vegetarians anymore and it's difficult to come by good produce in the city. Most of it is tasteless hydroponic junk that places like Reggie's Veggies end up steaming until they're the consistency of baby food held in the shape of broccoli or asparagus or carrots. I suspect this is why Step likes it. But he's also so allergic to everything good that he often doesn't like complicated meals. He has places that he trusts, like Reggie's Veggies, where he can order steamed veggies with nothing on them. He'll add the salt (not too iodized), his own pepper (course ground), and maybe butter, only if it's organic, which is rare to find. The way he eats isn't extravagant but it's finicky, especially for a Hayden. I know he's a lot like me, in that we bumped around from foster home to foster home. But in his case, I imagine foster parents couldn't put up with his dietary needs. Heck, I find it annoying. That's why I order things like seasoned grilled veggies tossed in oil with a flight of exotic mustards. When the waiter asks if I'd like to know what's in the mustards, I say no. The mystery alone makes Step squirm.

And yet, for its mediocre menu, the place is surprisingly busy. More than half the tables are full. As usual, most people entertain themselves with their portos, instead of interacting with their dining companions. It's a narrow, brightly lit dining room with tables lining each wall from front to back. Above the tables are pictures of boxers in the ring, mostly people I've never heard of. A lot of the photographs are black and white.

We sit at a table by the window, so we can watch our equipment that sits on the sidewalk outside. Step is anxious as usual, his leg gyrating at its regular rabbit-like cadence. I have to separate the salt and pepper shakers from clanking together. I don't say anything because I think he might still be fuming about the old lady. But it turns out to be something else entirely. He cranes his neck to see something down the street.

"What?" I ask.

"Are we being followed?" he asks. He ducks his head and then peeks again in the same direction. I turn to look and he says, "No. Don't look."

It's worth noting that Step has terrible eyesight. With all

the carrots he eats, you would think his vision would be better but he probably needs some strong glasses that he can't afford.

"Who is that?" he says.

"I can't see if you don't let me look." I say. I realize, of course, that if I look I'll have to know who the person is. But, of course, I won't because I'm Fried. I haven't told Step and I just don't know how he'll take it. It's not like being Fried is looked upon like a disease. It's just rare. It's a handicap, and maybe I don't want to be pitied or seen as weak. Most of all, I can't help but feel alone like I can't connect. If I let on that I'm Fried, he might treat me differently or act uncomfortable. And, frankly, I'm not prepared to deal with it getting around, having to explain myself or put up with somebody who might want to mess with me because I'm vulnerable. Haydens need to keep their weaknesses hidden.

Still, I feel like I should look, in case we're in danger. It might be a GC. I turn slightly and Step puts out his hand to stop me.

"He might see you," Step says. He covers his mouth with his hand. "I saw him earlier when I was up in that tree. He was sitting in that same car but parked down the street." Step squints. "I think he's vaping. Is he vaping?"

"Let me look," I say.

"No," he says, his hand still curled around his mouth like he's about to cough.

"Why are you covering your mouth?"

"So he can't read my lips," he says.

"Is he that close?"

"He's right across the street," Step says, and acts like he's taking a drink of water. "He's just hanging out, watching us."

"What's he wearing?"

"I don't know. Shades." He squints again for a better look. "Maybe a suit."

It doesn't take me long to guess who might be following us. I can think of only one man dressed like that and smoking an e-cigarette. The same man who sent me to Brooklyn in a stranger's car.

"Does he have a hat on?" I ask.

"What?" Step chuckles.

"A hat. Is he wearing like a fedora?"

"No. What does that matter?"

"I'm going to have to look," I say. I have no idea why he would be looking for me, maybe to follow up on the accident, for insurance purposes. Or maybe it has more to do with why that Agent Stevenson guy came to see me.

"Okay," Step says, leaning in close like we're conspiring. "Act like you're going to reach for the Sriracha on the table behind you and then take a look."

"That's stupid," I say. "What about this bottle right here?"

Step quickly slaps the bottle from our table and it skids under another table across the narrow restaurant.

"What bottle?" Step says. "Now you'll have to reach over and—"

"What the hell?" Somebody at another table says, "What the hell, Hayden?"

When we turn to look, we find, of course, a pack of young guys who look none too pleased with a projectile bottle of Sriracha coming at them. And like that, the table of fellow patrons has become a young, angry group of GCs. And us two Haydens have just disrespected them. That's how it happens.

Two of the GCs slide back in their chairs to stand up. The other two watch like whatever is about to happen will be entertaining. These guys are big. It would take only one of them to easily dispatch the two of us.

Step looks down at the table in front him as if he's ashamed of what he's done. He says, almost too lightheartedly,

"Here we go."

The one who yelled over to us starts toward our table. He has on a sweater and work pants. But I'm more concerned about his boots, which I imagine will soon be used to press Step's face into the linoleum floor. The other guy is taller and has a more intimidating build, but he seems to be following his partner's lead.

"Why don't you two go beg somewhere else?" the booted man says. "You're stinkin' up the place." He keeps a comfortable distance, not getting too close to us "dirty and unpredictable" Haydens. Stories go around about Haydens pulling knives or wielding other strange weapons. These legends make us sound like hooligans, when the reality is that most confrontations are provoked by GCs. Anything a Hayden produces during a fight is usually out of self-defense.

"We're sorry, guys. Seriously," I say, because I'm not in the mood to run. There's really nothing else we can do. "It was an accident. Look at my friend here. He's sorry. He feels *really* bad about it." We all look at Step, who doesn't seem the least bit remorseful.

"We're just trying to have a nice meal over here," the booted man says. "Minding our own business. And then you two go ahead and throw a bottle at us."

"I know," I say. "And I'm sorry. Please accept our apology." It's difficult to be cordial when it's clear that this guy will find joy in pounding us to a pulp.

"That's not the point," he says.

"You don't have a point, Todd," Step finally says, emphasizing the guy's name. "A guy like you can't muster a string of thought long enough to even qualify as a point."

"Hadley," the taller guy says. "You better shut your boyfriend's lip."

It didn't even dawn on me that I should know this guy's name but now I feel very isolated again, like the confrontation between them is among another species.

"Listen to you, Stephon," Todd says, and he drags out the *ffff* sound. "Such a pretty name."

Step snickers to himself and looks down. I can see him gritting his teeth. He hates his name. He shakes his head and says, "Todd, Todd, Toddy, Todd." Then Step looks at me and says, "This guy isn't listening." He casually leans back in his seat to address Todd. "He doesn't have the capacity for understanding language." Step points a finger to his own head. "Not a lot going on upstairs, if you catch my drift."

Todd is standing no more than four feet away and Step is talking about this massive gorilla of a man as if he isn't even there, like he's somebody on a porto screen who can't hear him, no threat at all.

Todd takes a step forward and Step raises his hand in the air like he's waving for a waiter to bring us the check. Only, he doesn't want the check.

Step says, "Reggie will take care of this."

Like I said before, Step knows everyone. He's usually a smooth talker, makes a lot of friends when he wants to. He could probably smooth things over with Todd and his cronies. But he doesn't have to because he's already friends with Reggie. Now, I've never met Reggie but the place is decorated in boxing paraphernalia. The Reggie's Veggies logo is a set of boxing gloves, which never really made sense to me. So, I'm suddenly relieved to think that Step can simply call his friend, the restaurant owner and boxer, to come out and take care of these guys.

By this point, the other two GCs have risen from their seats and take post behind their booted friend. Todd reaches out to grab Step by the collar, when the kitchen door swings open. Everyone stops and turns to look.

There's Reggie, a short, elderly Asian woman who looks barely strong enough to hold open the door. And suddenly I'm not certain we'll walk away from this one alive. Reggie stalks out to the dining area. She takes her time, sizing up the group and nodding to other diners. She walks up to the group of us— Step and I versus the four buffoons. She looks at Step and points a thumb back toward the other four.

"Yeah," Step says, a strange quiver of intimidation or respect in his voice.

Reggie pivots on a heel, her entire being no larger than one of Todd's legs. She looks up at him and says, "Go now."

"Listen, lady," Todd says.

"Oh no," Step says, playfully. "You don't want to talk back to—"

Reggie shushes Step with a stern point of the finger. She looks back at the four GCs with scorn in her eyes. "You all go."

Todd looks to his cohort and laughs. He turns back to Reggie and says, "You a fighter?" He waves a finger toward some of the boxing photos on the wall. "You knock me out?"

It occurs to me that Step knows people everywhere probably because he's bound to find himself in this sort of predicament. Only, I'm not certain Reggie is the right person for the job.

Reggie points to the door and says, "That's the door."

Todd considers the situation and a smile crawls across his face. But just as he sucks in to let out an obnoxious laugh, Reggie flicks open a butterfly knife, a swift glint of metal that flickers before she has the blade held confidently close to Todd's crotch. Stunned, he freezes, standing gingerly on his toes as Reggie draws the shiny blade deeper against his groin.

"Go now?" Reggie says.

He nods feverishly in agreement. The four of them politely push in their chairs and file out. Whether or not they paid, Reggie doesn't make a fuss about it.

With another quick flick, Reggie folds the knife and it disappears into her chef's coat. She turns and walks up close to

Step. He looks up to her like a child to his mother, and she wipes something from his shoulder. Then she slaps his arm and says, "Don't be stupid."

"Sorry, Reggie," he says, sort of laughing. "Why do you even let idiots like that in here?"

She raises her hand to slap him and he flinches. She points a scolding finger in his face and shakes her head. She says, "No more," and storms back to the kitchen, where the cook who had been watching scurries back to work.

Step chuckles and looks outside where the four men gather themselves and glare at us through the window. Step offers a condescending wave and Todd gestures a threat. Then he leans over, picks up my telescoping squeegee and bends the aluminum pole over his knee with ease.

"Come on," I say, and flip him the middle finger.

"Damn," Step says. He smiles at me like nothing serious just happened. "I totally didn't see that coming."

The four GCs walk off, and that's when I see the black car and the man inside it. It's the man from the other night. The man who gave me his Volvo. He's watching the GCs move down the street.

"Geez, Haddy," Step says, probably noticing my grimace. "Relax. I'm sorry about all that. But we're fine now."

Our food arrives before I can say anything, and Step digs in. I glance back to the black car, then pull out my porto in some reactionary gesture of defense. Though, the only thing I can think to do with it is ping Agent Stevenson. Not that I can trust him. I just think he's somehow involved with whatever has this guy camped outside the restaurant.

"Put that thing away," Step says. "Don't be lame."

"Shut up, stupid," I say, not in the mood to hear his voice right now. We're able to talk this way because we're like brother and sister. At least he annoys me like I imagine a brother might. "Almost get us killed and you're eating like nothing happened."

He shoves a massive forkful of bland steamed broccoli into his mouth and smirks with chubby cheeks.

The man in the black car is looking down, and I can see a faint glow against his face from what must be his porto screen. Something tells me he'll keep turning up and I'd rather find out why before that *why* happens. On my porto, I call up Agent Stevenson's contact to ping him. I type, "We need to talk."

When I look up from my porto, Step is scolding me with is gaze. He has no idea, and I don't know where to begin. I realize that if I'm going to meet with Agent Stevenson, I'll have to do it alone. No Step or his quiet saviors like Reggie.

I flip Step the middle finger and finishing typing my message, "Somewhere public," and hit send.

Step's face is one of ecstasy, his cheeks full with bland veggies. My porto screen is blank. No reply. So, I tuck it away in my pocket. When I reluctantly look out the window again, the man and his black car are gone.

CHAPTER EIGHT
UNICORNS

I'm supposed to meet Agent Stevenson in less than an hour but it feels like I might not make it. I'm absolutely dying of boredom. As I look around the classroom at all these tired and apathetic faces, it's clear that the rest of my GED classmates would also rather expire than to suffer one more minute of this.

It's my sixth night here over the last two weeks and I don't think I've learned anything I didn't already know from the first three times I was sent to this place. Not that it matters. This is part of the Hayden House package. Every time a Hayden makes the news or Hayden House gets word that one of us is in trouble, they try to intervene. Hayden House's approach is subtle and mostly unproductive. They offer counseling or other programs when a Hayden is arrested or fired from a job or, in my case, has a near-death accident. In most cases, they do the bare minimum to establish a routine for the Hayden in need. The thinking is that by reinforcing a foundation in my day-to-day life, I'll be able to better recover from whatever trouble got me here. They make themselves out to be lifelong guidance counselors. But the real trouble is that they have only a few options for us. They might find us volunteer work or sign us up for a community exercise program. Sometimes a psychiatrist will offer free hours in a clinic so we can lie about having abandonment issues and feed whatever lame textbook cases the psychiatrist thinks we resemble.

I keep getting dumped with GED classes, always at the same place and always with the same tired instructor, Mr. Kilroy McNabb, whose peculiar affinity for unicorns—an assortment of unicorn pins on his bag and jackets, a unicorn tattoo on his forearm, unicorns on his socks peeking from his short pants—creates the strange sense that his class is for children and not for adults. I just wish other Haydens were here. We'd own the place. Instead, we get sent to sites all over the city. They know better than to lump a bunch of us together.

And now there's a new layer of misery to the equation. I'm Fried. This, I've come to learn since the crash, has made everything—I mean every last thing in my life—a much larger chore than it needs to be. Take my first night back in GED class. We were reading from a history text app and Mr. McNabb walked us through review questions at the end. Beside the first image of some old historic US figure, there was a made-up question, written as if the pudgy old man in the picture was addressing us directly. It read, "I'm a polymath—author, political theorist, inventor, printer, musician, scientist, among other things. Who am I?"

"Can anyone answer number one?" Mr. McNabb asked the class.

There was the usual creaking of wooden chairs as we shifted in our seats. Most of us have much more important lives during the day, so nobody has energy. Out of the dozen of us, there's probably only one or two who actually want to be here.

"Sounds like a fella needs to get laid," said Vince, a jokester who sits in the back and has been coming here for nearly a year.

"Thank you, Vince," Mr. McNabb said, trying to calm our laughter. "Now, seriously." He looked around the room and his eyes landed on me because I'm too stupid to look away. "Miss Hayden."

"That's right, Hayden," Charles growled. Charles stokes

fires and apparently doesn't like Haydens.

"Miss Hayden," Mr. McNabb said. "Can you answer the question?"

The kicker to this question was that the answer was right there in the guy's face. Anyone on the System would know his name without even really knowing his name. They just have it right there in their brain. No effort. That's our education system for you, asking you questions you already have the answer to.

So, it wasn't that the class was stumped by the question so much as they just didn't care to participate. Answering this question would just lead to the next question, which would lead to another. The longer we could prolong this first question, the more time we could burn, which, in turn, meant we could avoid the next lesson. After all, this is the lightest form of punishment for most of us. Actually, they don't call it punishment. Most parole officers and counselors call this *rehab* or *life-long learning*. Whatever they call it, most of us want to stay here as long as we can because it beats more labor-intensive options.

Fortunately for us, Mr. McNabb has even less drive to move through the material any faster. He's stuck in this room, whether we move on or not. If it isn't us, it'll be another crop of dropouts.

"Miss Hayden," said Mr. McNabb again, with a little more prying.

I looked at the picture again. The man was balding but had a mullet. His lips were pursed with a strange arrogance. He had the sleepy eyes of a man who didn't need to worry about where his next meal would come from. And judging by his chin, he could afford to miss a meal or two.

I searched for details, then searched every corner of my mind for the answer but the more I dug, the more I realized I was just rolling through all the names I'd ever heard and had somehow retained without a face. The names reeled through like one of those old Rolodex things, cards flipping over themselves, blurring into one faded flicker of text.

I couldn't do it.

"I'm sorry," I said.

"Miss Hayden," Mr. McNabb said, sleepily. "Please just say a name." He'd been working from this same text app for so long and he'd asked these same questions so many times, he wasn't about to lose his patience over my inability to answer. "We're all waiting."

"I really don't know," I said, exhausted with the charade. Hiding my condition had gotten me nowhere. I didn't know anyone here. There was nothing to be ashamed of. Why didn't I just come out with it?

"Of course you know," he said.

"Shoot," Vince said. "We all know the dang answer, kid. He used to roll on a hundred-dollar bill."

"Go ahead and say it," Charles said.

"Yeah, girly," an elderly woman named Muriel said. "Don't be so stubborn."

"Kids," Vince said.

"Haydens," Charles said, sneering.

"I can't," I said, frustrated. "I can't do it. I don't know." I threw down my head and knocked it with my knuckles. "I'm—" I looked up again and said, "I just can't."

A wave of realization swept over the class. Everyone seemed to know what was wrong at the same exact time and the room went still. It was awkwardly quiet. Nobody wanted to speak. They just knew.

After that night, the class dubbed me "the Fried girl from uptown" because nobody really knew where I was from. But Vince caught me hustling tobacco uptown last week, and now I'm from uptown. That's how the class works. You either call the shots or you don't. Vince calls the shots. Charles takes shots. Mr. McNabb doesn't bother to care what happens. He gets paid no matter what happens with us.

Every class since that day has been just as annoying as the last. If the question asks for a name, a classmate will say, "Uptown's got it," or "Call on the Hayden." Mr. McNabb now speaks to me much more slowly and loudly, as if I can't hear. Last class we were put into groups to present on the great wars. I was grouped with two classmates who introduced themselves as Martin Luther King and Mickey Mouse because that's apparently funny.

It has gotten so bad that each class I slink deeper into daydreams, trying to tune out the insults and sideways glances. Mr. McNabb will blather on about something, and I'll start dreaming about what I can do after class, maybe head off to Ziggy's for a show or see if some Haydens are throwing a party. I've even started to mess around on my porto like the other students. After all, the teacher doesn't jam our portos like they did in primary school. I'll download a bunch of game apps or look at stupid pictures of people's food. And sometimes I'll go back and read those short messages from that mysterious sender named Paul.

When I look up, Mr. McNabb is diagramming the last century's redistribution of territory, and I'm among a class of wandering minds. I have my porto on my lap, as if I need to be so discreet. I flip my porto to the last message from Paul and decide to write to him for once.

"History is killing me," I write.

I imagine Paul is somebody about my age and sitting in a very similar night class across town, bored to death. My ping will brighten his evening. Then again, he's probably much cooler than that. I bet he's out with friends, having a nice dinner somewhere in the Village. He probably has access to all the finest places in town, the ones I don't even know about and can't imagine what they look like on the inside.

Of course, if that were the case, then why would he

bother talking to me?

Mr. McNabb is just about halfway through the Second-Phase Migration, where he talks about the time middle-class citizens could finally move to the cities. This, he explains, was met with great resistance from the top 10% who were given prime pickings in each city. But they were the constituents who fought for—rather, funded—redistribution in the first place. So, at the risk of sounding like a crusty, I get why they got dibs. Mr. McNabb seems slightly emotional about this, as he explains the financial turmoil that came with a shift in housing options for the middle 40%, which was nothing compared to what the last 50%—those well below the poverty line—would face once they had a chance to migrate.

Despite the ridiculous unicorn patch on his sweater, I have to give Mr. McNabb some credit. He seems to care about the course material. I almost feel bad that I haven't been paying attention, but then my porto vibrates on my lap. I quickly check it. It's Paul.

"History might kill us all one day," he says.

I wish I could hear his voice to know if he's as compassionate as I imagine. Or is he being snarky. All I hear is Mr. McNabb's nasally tone and I can't get it out of my head.

"What do we do about it?" I reply to Paul. I suddenly feel connected with somebody. It doesn't matter that we've never seen each other or that I can't picture his face just from his name, even though I'm sure he can picture mine.

Mr. McNabb starts talking about the people who live outside the cities, mostly Native American tribes but also plenty of outcasts.

My porto vibrates again. It reads, "We write the future."

It's like the perfect slogan. I can feel it in my spine.

I read Paul's ping again, "We write the future." It's great.

"When?" I reply, trying to keep his attention.

"Now," he replies almost immediately.

I don't even know what this means but it fills me with hope. We don't know each other but it feels like he understands what I'm going through. Miss Ula used to tell us Haydens that we ought to write our own history (kind of what I'm doing now, I guess) since we didn't have families that could pass down our histories to us. I always thought of it as a way to take control, write it from the loser's perspective for once. I guess I never took Miss Ula's advice seriously until I started this. I hope you find it helpful.

Before I can ping him back, Paul writes, "Come see me."

I don't know what to say. I can't reply. I suddenly imagine what would happen if I met him in person. I try to picture his face and where we would meet. It doesn't matter. I can't possibly meet him. I'm an outcast. A Hayden. Fried. He knows this already.

My porto vibrates again. "You'll like it here," he says.

I take a deep breath and write back, "Where's here?"

"Nowhere nearby," he replies.

I can feel the hair on the back of my neck stand up. I look around the room. Nothing but bored faces.

"Where?" I write. "How do I get there?"

He doesn't reply as quickly, and I think that I might have scared him somehow. I want to write him again, but I'm afraid he won't reply.

Mr. McNabb keeps lecturing about the typical life in the territories. "We're talking about a true downgrade of life," he says. "Not at all like what you know of life here in the city."

I already know this having been out there, even though it was just that one time. It's pretty obvious the moment you leave the city, cross that river, and see how desolate and dark it can get. I look around and wonder if any of these people have been outside of the city, if they even dared.

"It's no place for us," Mr. McNabb says. "I admire them. Those people fend and fight. They're practically hunter-gatherers. Who can tell me what a hunter-gatherer is?" After nobody flinches to answer, he says, "Anyway, those people out there, they are off the grid, off the System." Mr. McNabb looks at me now and says, "Maybe even Fried."

My porto vibrates but I don't look down at it. Mr. McNabb keeps staring at me and I'm too afraid to look away. The pause in his lecture prompts others in the room to look my way, including Vince, who says, "That's you, girl. You Fried."

***

After class, I check my porto. Paul's message reads, "I'll send somebody for you."

I'm down on the street now and I half-expect a car to pull up with his *somebody* behind the wheel. Maybe the magic of the moment has worn off but I don't want to reply. He's probably just messing with me anyway, like my classmates do. Maybe this is what it's like to be openly Fried—constant ridicule. As if I didn't get enough of that for being a Hayden. Now I'm a Fried Hayden, the perfect combination of need and vulnerability.

Agent Stevenson was supposed to meet me outside my GED class but I don't see him anywhere. It's late enough that not a lot of people are around, fewer than I wanted but this was the only time he and I could meet.

I stroll down to the corner to see if he's standing by another entrance. That's when he steps from a dark doorway that I just passed and says, "Hadley."

"What the hell, man!" I say. I want to punch him for being such a creep.

"Lean against the wall," he says. "Don't look at me." He stays in the shadow but I want a better look at him.

"Why?" I ask.

83

"Just do it," he says. "You're being followed."

I look away from him and cautiously lean against the wall, trying to appear like I'm waiting for a bus or a taxi. "That's why I contacted you," I say.

"I checked the onboard porto on that car you were driving," he says. "It was recoded."

"So," I say, not sure what to make of this news. "Are you blaming me for that?"

"I want to know more about this man who gave you the car," he says. That's when it occurs to me that Agent Stevenson, aside from the biker getup, acts an awful lot like the man who paid me to drive the throwback Volvo. He's mysterious and cold.

"Why should I trust you?" I say, and I turn to look at him. His black leather jacket, gloves, and dark hair fold him into the shadows a bit too well. I can see from his posture that he's frustrated, and I suddenly feel the emptiness of the street around us. Any lights that are on in the buildings across the way are behind thick, faraway windows.

"You know who he is," I say, accusing but cautious. "Don't you?"

He nods for me to keep leaning against the wall. I comply.

"Stop playing around," he says. "You do, too. He's on you all day."

"And how would you know that?" I ask.

"You say he paid you but there was no credit on your account," he says.

"Do you think I would drive a car to Brooklyn for some jerk if I didn't get paid?" I muster a laugh and say, "You're a sharp one, Stevenson."

"Okay," he says. "Fine. Did you know I found your birth parents?"

"Whatever," I say, deflecting his attack.

"I thought maybe you were going to see them that night," he says. "Maybe go see your little brother."

"Screw you." I start to walk away because nothing feels right about this situation, and now he's just pissing me off. But he grabs my arm and turns me around.

"Your brother lives in the city now," he says. "Did you know that?" When I don't say anything, he shakes my arm and leans in close. "I have the notes right here on my porto. You want to know how Thomas is doing?"

I glare at his hand like I might bite it and he removes it from my arm. I'm sure my fear is evident but I try my best to keep composed.

"Look," he says, "I need to know everything that happened that night. Anything you can tell me. Was he tall? What color hair did he have? Or was he bald?"

"First, you tell me what you know." A couple walks past but pays us little attention, probably because I'm a Hayden. I wish that Charles or Vince or even Mr. McNabb would walk by, but I think they've all gone home.

Agent Stevenson watches the couple until they're a good distance away. "All I know is that he was the last person to see you before you were supposed to die."

"*Supposed* to die?" I say. "Was that your hope? Was it all your doing?"

"Look, kid," he says. "I'm not fond of you. And you being a Hayden doesn't make matters any better."

"Go to hell, man," I say. "I don't know why I pinged you in the first place."

Agent Stevenson takes a deep breath and pulls his hands away from me. I can tell he's angry, like I know something he needs and as soon as he gets it, he'll go ahead and strangle me where we stand. He could do it right now. His hands linger in his jacket pockets, and I imagine one is cradling a knife, waiting for the perfect moment to thrust it into my gut.

"You have any friends go missing lately," he asks through his teeth. "Any of your dirty little buddies?"

I don't want to entertain his attack but I start to think of a few Haydens who I haven't seen in a while. There have been a few, like that girl—Sierra, I think was her name—who fell on the subway tracks just before an oncoming train. Apparently she was so preoccupied with her porto, she didn't realize how close she was standing. Some Haydens say she was pushed but I think that's just people trying to make controversy with some GCs. It's just as plausible that she was distracted. Then there's that other girl who lost her porto. A Hayden found it somewhere in one of the tunnels leading from the Junction. She ended up vanishing, and I think her porto is still around somewhere, probably out of commission. Then, of course, there's Iggy, whatever happened to him. I just remember seeing a picture of him at Hayden House not long ago. The System told me he was dead.

"Streets aren't good to you Haydens, are they?" Agent Stevenson says, with a snide grimace.

I don't like the vibe I'm getting from him. Before I can tell him to get lost, a cab comes down the street and I wave for it with my porto.

"Where are you going?" Agent Stevenson says.

"Leave me alone," I say. I step into the street and start toward the cab.

"Hadley, wait," he says. Just as I get into the cab, he grabs the door and says, "Others are going to die." I can't get the door from his grip. "You understand? Your friends will die."

"Just," I say, pulling on the door. He let's go when I say, "Just leave me alone."

He steps away as I shut the cab door. I tell the cab driver to take me to Central Park South. We pull away and I watch Agent Stevenson get smaller through the rear window, one hand still in his pocket, the other in a gloved fist at his side.

CHAPTER NINE
SOCCER BALL

All the way back to the Junction, I expect to get a ping from Agent Stevenson or to look out the rear window of the cab and see him tailing us on his zipbike. Instead, the trip is short and uneventful, and I'm back under that great big domed ceiling where I'm supposed to feel safe and secure among my friends. But I don't. I feel better but not comfortable.

A bunch of Haydens are lounging around, killing the evening as usual, like a family might sit around a porto projector in their living room and watch whatever series people watch these days. Only, these people are watching a small fire crackle on the tracks where a couple of Haydens have foil-wrapped potatoes cooking in white hot ash. After the night I've had, this is exactly what I need, to be among friends. I have to learn to trust these folks, even if I can't recall who they are. I'm learning though. I'm taking in their faces, trying to associate names. Roman sits across the room, huddled under his long hair, reading a book draped over his blanketed lap. He collects old books, the paper kind people used to read when everything wasn't digital. Yancey lies in the dirt beside Roman, his bulky tattooed arms bent back, big hands laced behind his head like a pillow. He dozes off and comes to. He asks Roman to read him a story and Roman tells him to screw off. Yancey goes back to sleep. Step, with his dopey basset hound face, listens to music on his porto through some ear nodes. He drums a song against his thighs, letting the patter echo off the domed ceiling of a quiet Junction. He looks at me without taking out the ear nodes and nods. I nod. He smirks and goes back to drumming on his legs.

Cammy, still in her business attire, sips from a beer, her tired eyes and crow's feet adding to her weathered appearance. She's drinking with two older Haydens, one I don't know and the other is Nona, a Greek woman with a thick nose, dark hair, and even darker eyes. The three of them carry on like I've seen them do.

"Feels like college," Nona says. Her voice is rough and deep.

"Like you'd know a damn thing about college," says the other girl, with a deep laugh. She wears dirty cargo pants and a Metro uniform shirt. She's a bus driver. "Besides, I don't think college kids sleep in subway tunnels."

"You see enough of them bumming around Union Square," Cammy says. "They try too hard."

"I like the art students," the other girl says. "The other day this one dude got on the bus with all his block prints. He must have had two suitcases full. All of it of the same image of really cool-looking octopuses. Is it octopi? Whatever the hell." She takes a drink from her beer. "This dude didn't have the fare so I says to him he can ride free all day if he gives me one of them prints. So he pulls out this crazy one of like ten different colored octopi-puses-whatever. Kind of trippy. And he rode with me uptown and back down. Made good company."

"Where's the print?" Nona asks.

"Oh," the girl says. "I don't know. I think I chucked it."

They laugh and look around at the rest of us younger Haydens.

Nona sits a little away from the fire and says to me, "Thought we lost you, kiddo." She taps the overturned bucket next to her and says, "Come on up. It's warmer."

I get up and join them.

"Lost another one yesterday," Cammy says. "Took a bullet, I hear."

"What was her name?" the other girl asks.

"Don't know," Cammy says. She looks up at the domed ceiling, scans the chaos of paint and chalk. "There," she says, pointing. "She did the soccer ball."

Everyone listening looks up at the graffiti hovering overhead like spirits. When I glance back at the three women, I notice Cammy looking at me.

"Haddy over here," Cammy says "She's living on borrowed time."

"You that girl who nearly died?" the other girl says. She grins a mouthful of twisted, rotten teeth. "That you?"

"I'm still here," I say.

"Oh damn," the other girl says. "Kid's got a mouth."

She finishes her beer and tries to crush the can against the ground. Unsuccessful, she tosses it aside and grabs another one.

"Better be careful," Nona says.

"Damn right," says the other girl.

"They don't know nothing about nothing," Nona says.

"Not like it used to be," Cammy says.

"You'll get killed out there soon enough," the other girl says. "System won't do jack to stop it neither."

"Never stops the crap that counts," Cammy says. "Mass shootings every other month. How many are done by somebody who doesn't want to be known for it? System plays right into their hands."

"Didn't stop OGC," the other girl says.

"Son of a bitch OGC," Cammy says. "That's a different story altogether."

The other two jeer and shake their heads. I glance at Nona beside me for clarification, but she just seems sad. When I look back at Cammy, she says, "The original. The worst of 'em."

"What a no-good slime ball," the other girl says. "Probably the worst there ever was. Should have never let him near this place."

"Wait," Step says. He comes over and sits on the rail to stir the fire and throw on another piece of rotted timber. "You mean, this guy, this GC, came down here? To the Junction?"

"No," Cammy says. "He knew we were down here but he didn't know how to get here."

That's when I notice that Nona has gone silent. She looks sick, almost disgusted. She balls her fists and starts to breathe heavily through her nose.

"He was some big shot up top," Cammy says. "Got word of us from his shoeshine girl, a dumb kid who used to come over here from Broadway Junction over in Brooklyn. Anyway, I guess this GC—"

"OGC," the other girl corrects Cammy.

"Yeah," Cammy says. "The OGC got curious about the other end of the social order. He must have heard we knew how to party, if you know what I mean."

The other girl makes a gesture like she's smoking a joint and says, "Dude would lurk around up top and wait for a young Hayden to come out. Hit her up for some scag or a good time."

"So, you saw his face," Step says. "You know his name."

Cammy and the other girl look to Nona, who's been rocking with her arms around her knees.

"What was it, Nona?" Step asks.

"Step," Cammy interjects.

"What?" he says. "In case I run into him." He punches a fist into his other hand.

Nona looks across the group of us, her eyes dim. In a timid voice, she says, "Reuben Mayfield."

"Dude had credit," the other girl says. "What are you going to do, pass up a great meal, a night on the town? What did we know back then?"

Cammy shakes her head disapprovingly. She puts up her hand for the other girl to stop talking.

"What?" the other girl says. "I mean I'm not going to live like it didn't happen. We didn't know any better."

"Just shut up," Cammy says. Her eyes go to Nona, who stares at the ground with a blank face. "Okay? We're chill."

"What?" I finally ask, because I have to know. I can't imagine what would haunt Nona like this. She's a grown woman, a tough Hayden. She's seen and been through more than most women her age.

"The things he did," the other girl says. "Nobody knew until one girl couldn't take it and killed herself." She peered over toward the wall and pointed to a typewriter. "She was super young. Real innocent. Finally, somebody spoke up. Then another girl came forward. Then another and another."

"He must have preyed on ten different girls in a span of a summer," Cammy says.

"But like," Step says, leaning in. "What did he do?"

"Look, Step," Cammy says. "This didn't happen last week or last year or even in the last decade. We were barely teenagers."

Step's face slackens with horror. Nona starts readjusting herself in her seat, not quite ready to walk away but clearly not comfortable with this conversation. I'm not either, and I can't imagine what these girls went through.

"What did you do?" I ask. I have to know. I keep imagining rabbits popping up from the ground and getting snatched up by some nasty rabid fox.

"We didn't do anything," Cammy says. "We vowed to castrate him if he ever came around again but he just disappeared."

"I'll murder him," Nona suddenly mutters to herself.

"Is he still out there?" I ask.

"Definitely," Cammy says. "He's around. Because we haven't had a chance to kick in his balls. The System would never stop somebody like him. Men with power. That's a much bigger, much more corrupt system. Can't touch a man in power, not if you're a woman, and especially not if you're a Hayden."

"Reuben Mayfield," Nona says. "Never forget it. Never forget his face." She looks at me and says, "Don't you forget that name."

Nona sits with her legs tucked close, her chin resting on her knees. I understand right away when I see the hurt in her eyes. It's haunting. I can't imagine what she endured, and all I can do is say, "I'm sorry."

"Never again," Cammy says to her.

"I'll kill him," the other girl says. "I swear."

Nona's face trembles in a flicker of fire light. She says, "Never forget."

***

Neither of us can sleep, so Step and I take a stroll. We head down toward the theater district, where the lights are brighter. The street is wet with drizzle, bringing up that faint smell that Step likes to call *concrete sweat*, like the streets have their own body odor. We walk lazily like we have no place to go, just trying to wind down some.

"Imagine what it must have been like back in the day," Step says, looking up at the glimmering marquee lights. "Did you ever see pics from when this was like a place to be?"

"Strange times," I say, recalling a booth at the Hell's Kitchen antique market. "Remember those old black-and-whites? The lady said they were from tourists. What a funny thing. Go visit a city and take pictures. How weird."

"Yeah," he says, and snickers to himself.

"They talked about it in my GED class," I say. Mr. McNabb would ramble on about how people used to travel around the country like it was no big deal, like there was something worth seeing out there. He called it *road tripping.* "Weekend getaways," I add.

"Travel," Step says. "Vacations. What a strange concept."

"Who would want to come here?" I say.

"Here," Step says. "I get that. But elsewhere..."

"So," I say. "You've never had the desire to check out one of the other cities?"

"I don't know," he says. "Not really."

"Remember when we got out, just drove north?" I hook an around his. "Don't you just want to get out of here? Go somewhere else?"

He gives me a strange look, but then he smiles and says, "That was a good time." He puts an arm around my shoulders like I'm going to help him walk, like he's a wounded soldier. We keep walking like this, a little awkwardly. "But, I mean, people were crazy back then. Things were different. We couldn't go much farther than we did. Not like they used to back in the day." He stops walking. "Besides, look at this place. Look at this beautiful city."

All I see are drowning lights, cracked concrete, and litter everywhere. I haven't seen the stars or the moon in days. Everything is washed out and dirty. Don't get me started on the people. What's worse is that I probably never noticed this before the crash. But now that I'm forced to take in the details, to observe and interpret everything, I can't help but feel out of place, like I was meant to be elsewhere. They renamed it System City for a reason. And now that I'm off that System, I just don't identify.

I'm sure this realization shows on my face because Step looks at me like I'm crazy. I take my arm back and let him stand on his own.

"What's up?" he says.

"What?" I say.

"Haddy, come on."

"What?" I say again, defensively.

"I don't know," he says. "You've been acting different lately."

Looking for an excuse, I say, "Maybe it's that Reuben Mayfield creep." When I think about it more, that might be part of it. I just feel vulnerable and disoriented. I don't recognize people and it scares me. Most of all, I don't feel like I belong, least not with the Haydens, my closest family. I don't know any of them anymore.

"No," he says, shrugging that off. "That was forever ago. Don't listen to them. And if you see that sicko, walk the other way. Simple as that. It's not like he was snatching girls off the street in a cargo van."

I don't bother to point out to Step how insensitive he's being. I get it. Mayfield wasn't a kidnapper, so much as a manipulator. But that doesn't make him any less a threat.

"I don't mean that Mayfield guy exactly," I say, trying to pivot the conversation. "Look, I just mean the idea that somebody like that can be out there preying on people."

"Gees, Haddy. You're smarter than them."

"Than who?" I say. "Than Cammy? Than Nola? What the hell, Step?"

"It's not that," he says. Then his eyes train on mine like he's trying to see through me. I don't know if he's angry or just upset. "It's something else." He looks down like he's collecting his thoughts. "I mean, you're here but, you know...like you're happy to see us but not really. Like you're all reserved and cold." He stops and shakes his head, steps away. He runs his hands through his hair.

"Yeah?" I say, a bit on the offense. "Go on. What else you

got?"

"No," he says. "You." He nods for me to talk.

"I don't know what you want me to say."

"I want you to tell me why you're so distant lately."

Here's the thing. Even now, still after all this, I don't think I see in Step what I used to, back when I didn't have to and we were just best friends for whatever unexplainable reason. I think you might understand now what it's like to be Fried or confused or, at the very least, unsure of who you're talking to. You sort of have to read a person. And you give up whatever comforts you once had with them.

With Step, I'm still trying. I want him to be the brother he used to be, the man in my life that I could always depend on no matter what. But I can't because I'm always trying to be sure it's him. And the only way to know is to tell myself it is him. So, do I trust myself the way I trusted the System?

"I came to see you at the hospital," he says. He looks down and wipes his mouth. "I got this feeling that you were dead and tried to contact you." He laughs to himself like it sounds ridiculous now. "I mean, your porto was offline. I couldn't reach you." He looks genuinely sad like he's back there now. "They had you all drugged up and bandaged. I barely recognized you. I couldn't stand to see you like that." I think he might cry. "And now—"

He puts a hand on my shoulder. I don't know what I want him to do. I just stand there. Watching him, waiting.

"Tell me," he says.

"Tell you what?"

"You know," he says. "It's not obvious but—"

"But what?"

"Say it," he says. "Tell me what's going on."

"Nothing," I say. I start walking again but he doesn't move. When I look back, he's still standing there. "Come on, Step," I say. "Let's go."

"Why don't you just tell me?" he says. "It's me, Haddy. Come on."

I don't want to talk about this. He doesn't know. He's just playing me, trying to get me to admit something, the persuasive prick.

"It's pretty crappy that you can't talk to me," he says.

I stop and laugh at his comment, acting like it didn't sting. I look back and say, "Stop being so dramatic, Step."

"You're being a coward," he says with an edge of anger. "You know that? I'm here for you. I've always been here for you."

"What the hell does that mean? You want to fix me? You want to make everything better? Fix the broken Fried girl?!"

He's stunned. His eyes go wide and he doesn't move. All he can muster is a timid "Really?" He looks almost disgusted with me.

"Yeah," I say. "I'm Fried."

"That's—" He takes a deep breath, pauses. "That's okay. That's fine. I mean, I've known people who are Fried."

"Great," I say, passively.

"No," he says, stepping closer. "It's okay."

"Yeah, Step. It's okay. I don't recognize anyone. I'm in a world of strangers and I can't tell who's who. That's it. No big deal. Just a glacier of loneliness is all. It's okay that I don't know anybody."

He doesn't say anything, so I add, "Shoot, I don't even know you."

"Oh, come on," he says. "Don't say that. I'm sorry. I'm just—you know." He puts a hand on my arm. "I'm here for you. I'm here to—"

"Fix me," I slap his hand away. "I get it. And I don't need to be fixed. I'm not broken." I know if I keep going, I'll be crying before long.

He shakes his head, his eyes still trained on me. "You can

trust me," he says. I can see tears forming. My heart sinks. "You'll be—"

"Don't," I say.

I can't tell if that's sadness in his eyes or pity. It's like I'm somehow a different person than who he remembers. And that's the thing. Maybe I am. Maybe he doesn't remember me. He doesn't even know me. He only knows the version of me that the System feeds him. I'm nothing but a photo and a name. I mean, why do we have to be what the System makes us?

"You know you can always talk to me," he says. "I mean—" He reaches for me but I step back. "Come on, Haddy. It's me. It's Step."

"Are you?" I say, after a moment. "How can I trust you?" Still trying to fight back the tears. "I don't even recognize you."

For a moment I hope it breaks his heart because it sure breaks mine. He says nothing. What is there to say that isn't already on his face? Those sad eyes. That furrowed brow. I still have to say his name to myself. I have to gather details from what I see, how he acts, what he says. I have to *remember* him.

And what does he see when he looks at me? Who knows? At the moment, I suspect he sees a person he might no longer know, somebody he may have never really known at all. And when he digs deep to find what he really sees in me, maybe he'll find nothing but pieces, tiny little shards of what we were. I don't know or care or wait around to find out.

CHAPTER TEN
SKULL

I get as far as Madison Square Park, find my bench and plop myself down. The night breeze is cool against my tear-streaked cheeks but I'm done crying. I'm through with trying to find my place, with acting like I belong.

My hip hurts from all this walking, and by favoring this pain I'm starting to feel a sharp tinge in my other ankle. I just need to sit and gather myself. I have nowhere to go. Step will be waiting for me back at the Junction, and I don't want to see him now. I don't want to see any of them. I just want to leave, find somewhere new. I know too much of this city. I'm tired of it and it's bored with me. I just need something new. Someone different. Somebody like me.

I turn my porto over and over in my hands, wondering if maybe Paul is available to chat. I call up his last message saying he'll send somebody to get me. Strange, sure. But maybe he's a high roller like I suspected. Maybe if I say yes, I'll be whisked away in a big old limousine with Chardonnay and fresh fruits. I'm stupid for dreaming like that, of course, but whatever. He's new. He's different. Like me.

I write, "Why should I come see you?" I set my porto beside me on the bench and watch the shadows in the park. Skeletal shrubs line these walkways. A rat scurries to a nearby trashcan and disappears inside. On the path, I think I see something in the shadows. A bag. A book bag. But I know nothing is there.

My porto chimes.

"Because you're one of us," Paul replies. "You're off the System."

I want to believe him. With those words—*you're one of us*—comes a lightness in my head. He understands me. I don't know how he found me but it makes sense now why he has contacted me. I'm just like him.

"Where are you?" I ask.

A moment later, he writes, "Outside the city."

Can he really be? I want to believe him. Just talking to him, this faraway friend, makes all my pain fade. He's not part of this mess of a city. He's somewhere clean and green and probably very quiet. I bet there are no GCs or Haydens or bad memories where he is. It sounds perfect.

"Please come see me," he writes.

I have nothing here, I tell myself. I am nobody, and I can't bear to think how tomorrow will be no different. I'll wake. I'll hustle. I'll worry for my next meal. And for what? For nothing. I have to leave.

"Madison Square Park," I write. "Send somebody."

"Done," comes the reply. It feels so final. So sure.

I wonder how long it will take. Even if this person doesn't come until daylight, it's worth the wait. I'm leaving town. I'm finally getting out. I can practically feel that cool, clean air, just as it had crept along the green meadows in old Rhinebeck. I want to be surrounded by those fields, under those trees. I close my eyes, lie back on the bench, and I dream about where I'm headed. For once I feel like I have a future, even if it's completely unclear. At least it's somewhere else...

I must have dozed off but I don't know for how long. When I wake, I look around to find the same darkness, the same dirty park, and I start to feel like an idiot for thinking that anything would be different. I'm smarter than to hope that some stranger will come and save me.

Over the murmur of distant traffic, somewhere among the rustle of tree branches and that tired creaking in the distance, I hear footsteps. More than one set. People talking. Young people. Young men.

I don't move because they might not see me. They might be on the other side of the park and just walk right by.

"What's that?" one guy says, his voice is not quite deep, just scratchy.

"Bro," another one says. "This place is crawling. I've never been down here at night."

"Shut up, already," a third guy says. His voice is clearer but not as deep as the first. "Who knows why the hell he sent us."

"Sent *you*," the scratchy voiced one says.

Their feet shuffle along like they're considering whether or not to keep walking. They're apprehensive, which means they don't know this place. I do. If I run and can get away, they won't find me. I know every nook and cranny of this town. But my legs ache, and I probably don't have much of a lead. There's nothing I can do now but sit up and be ready. When I'm seated, back against the bench, my legs planted on the path, I can see three guys, no older than fifteen or sixteen. They're standing against the glow of a street light near the same entrance I took. I can't see their faces, not that it would matter. They see me though. One even points. Another pulls his friend's arm back down, slaps him in the shoulder with the back of his hand. Their silhouettes are each unique. One is tall and scrawny with a big head like a lollipop. Another is short and stocky, no neck and his arms hang away from his body like he has too much bulk in the midsection. The third is fit, proportioned, and stands confidently beside his awkward friends.

"Dude," the tall one says. He looks down toward the fit one. "That's a Hayden."

I wonder if I can act crazy, maybe lunge at them like a rabid animal. I bet they'll run in fear back to their prep school a few blocks away. They're not the first boys I've seen around here at night. They get out sometimes, tease themselves into thinking they're part of the big city. It's cute, if you think about it. But these are the first to acknowledge me, and I'm not sure what to make of them.

"How can you tell it's a Hayden," the stocky one says. *It.*

"It's her," the fit one says, a confident tone.

The fit one creeps closer like he's going to sneak up on me. He's cautious but assured in the way he steps toward me. Nobody addresses me. The stout kid says, "No way, man. What are you doing?" But he follows the fit one as they approach.

"Tommy," the tall one says. "What are you doing? I...I'm..."

They keep coming. I lean forward, make sure I can take off if I have to. The fit kid doesn't let up. He's almost at me before I see his face, his eyes, like they found what they've been looking for.

"Hadley," he says. He stops. His friend remains behind and to the side of him. The tall kid is still near the entrance, scanning the street for anyone who might get them in trouble. "Hadley Hayden," he says again. His hair is neat, parted down the middle. His chin and cheeks are soft but the rest of him is defined beneath his button-down shirt. When the light catches his face, I can see his eyes. Those eyes. I don't need the System to tell me whose eyes those are. I know. I have them burned in my brain, judging me, screaming for help. They're the eyes of a boy who lost himself in this very park, the last time I saw him.

I ran away. That's what I do. I run. But he didn't. Thomas stayed and watched the fight unfold, frozen by fear. He braced himself when that GC came for him. I came back to find him. After the riot—what turned out to be a mutually planned brawl—a lot of Haydens were rounded up and sent back to

Hayden House. The GCs, at least the college kids, probably had a pep rally as punishment. There was no clear winner in the fight. But I remember now that several Haydens returned the next day to ceremoniously unlock a bike that one of the GCs left behind. They hoisted the bike up into the massive elm that stands above all the cherry blossoms. For days, I'd return to the park, looking for any sign of the boy. I found his book bag near the shrubs, its contents gone. Nothing but candlestick drawings left to tell me whose it was. A week later, back at Hayden House, Miss Ula took me aside. She said that Mrs. Karp had called to say that she had made a mistake in tracking me down. Miss Ula paused before saying this next part, probably unsure if she should tell me. But she believed in honesty and openness. She told me that Mrs. Karp, the woman who was supposed to be my mother, never wanted to see me, that I was never to go near her family again. I was angry and sad and regretful. When I look back, I think I wanted Mrs. Karp to want me back, even if I resented her.

I felt this way partly because I wasn't certain if Thomas ever made it home. I watched the news for days, hoping there was never a story about a missing boy or a body found. I was too afraid to go see for myself, to make sure he made it home.

I never knew until now.

"It's actually you," he says. He stands so close now I have no room to stand up. He's practically on top of me.

I'm too shocked, even afraid, to make sense of what he says.

The tall friend comes closer and now he and the stocky one stand behind Thomas. The tall kid is awkward and pimply. The stocky kid wears the same blue button down as the other two, only his is unbuttoned, letting his belly spill out beneath a tight black t-shirt with a skull printed on the front.

"Time hasn't been very good to you," Thomas says.

I'm a wreck. I'm an outcast. And I'm frozen in my seat,

unsure of what to do. Thomas looks healthy and sure. He's come a long way.

"You know her?" the tall one says.

"We met a long time ago," Thomas says, his eyes fixed on me. We have the same nose, the same cheekbone structure. I wonder if he remembers, standing before me now, that we're siblings. "This Hayden," he says, nearly hissing it. "She tried to teach me a lesson."

"Haydens are scum," the stout one says.

"Yes," Thomas says. "Yes, they are."

I'm paralyzed. I can't move. I just want to apologize. That's all I ever wanted, to let him know that I didn't mean for any of that to happen. He leans over slowly, his face close to mine. He gently picks up my porto from the bench beside me.

"You know," he says. "If I hadn't had my porto that day, I don't know what I would have done."

"Thomas," I say. "I'm sorry."

"What's a Hayden need a porto for anyway?" asks the tall friend.

"I don't know," Thomas says. He regards the porto in his hand for a second and then he winds up and throws it hard against the stone walkway. The porto breaks into a few pieces and skids away into the shadows. Its screen blips one last time and goes dark. I'm suddenly defenseless. Three against one, and I have no way of calling for help. Not that I can even think or move. Thomas stands before me, acting out whatever revenge fantasy he's long been concocting. And I know I deserve it.

He turns back from watching the porto die. His smirk dissolves into disgust as he looks at me again. "Where the hell do you animals live anyway?"

"Look," I say. "I never meant to hurt you. I—"

"You didn't hurt me." He raises his voice. "A pathetic Hayden like you? What can you possibly do to a guy like me?" He laughs and turns to his friends for recognition.

I want to remind him that we were young. I was stupid. I want to say that I didn't know how to handle finding my parents, and I did what I did because I was scared, like I am now. I want him to see that we're related, and that he doesn't need to hurt me any more than I already do.

I'm certain he can already see it in my eyes. If he can't, his friends must be making the connection. But when I look to them, their dim faces show nothing but blind anticipation. The more Thomas speaks, the more excited they appear to become.

"Look at me," I say. "Thomas, look at my face. My nose. Look at my eyes."

"Don't," he says. "Don't bother." He takes a step back.

I stand up so now we're face to face. He's a few inches taller, but there's no mistaking it. We're brother and sister.

The stout kid's eyes dart back and forth between us, then suddenly grow wide. He says, "Dude. She's—"

"Shut up," Thomas says. He looks at me. "Don't pull your Hayden crap on me." He reaches to grab hold of my arm and I kick him in the knee. He bends in pain while I leap over the bench, over the wrought iron fence behind it, and dart through the dead flower beds to get away.

"Get her!" Thomas shouts.

I can hear them grunt as they come after me. They're not far behind but I'm certain that if I can get to the other side of the park, I can lose them. Dirt and mulch slip under my feet. I try to keep an even stride as my hips scream with every kick. I can barely keep my breath. But I run like they're right on my heels.

I don't make it as far as the fountain, when the tall one takes me down. He has me by the waist and he starts to climb on top of me. I punch and throw my elbows, trying to get myself loose. He has me pinned, sitting on my legs and his hands hold my arms down. I scream as loud as I can.

"Shut up," he demands, almost whispering. "Shut the

hell up. Stop screaming."

I keep screaming and he tries to shake me to stop.

He locks his legs over mine in some sort of wrestling maneuver and he leans his weight against my arms, driving me against the stone path. My head hurts where I hit the ground and my elbow stings where I landed. I try to wriggle free but he keeps a tight grip, growling, "Hold still."

We struggle for a moment when it occurs to each of us that the other two boys, Thomas and the stout kid, are nowhere in sight. They can't be that slow. He looks up quickly, eyes searching around us.

"Guys?" he calls, his breath short and shallow. "Hey, Tommy, you there? Luke?"

It occurs to me then that he has no idea what he's supposed to do with me. He has me secured mostly by his weight. Otherwise, he's trembling, not from adrenaline but from fear.

"What are you going to do?" I say in a hushed but firm voice.

"Shut up," he says. To the park around us he calls, "Tommy! Hey, Tommy! Come on. I got her."

"You don't know what to do with me, do you?" I say.

"Shut the hell up," he says through his teeth.

"They're gone, buddy," I say. "They've ditched you."

Just then, somewhere in the park, there's a cry. "No!"

We both freeze. The tall kid's breath quickens. I can see panic in his eyes. He almost loosens his grip.

That's when we hear somebody running and then Thomas leaps over the wrought iron fence from the flowerbed and hits the pathway running past us. "Run!"

The tall kid watches him flee. We both look back to where Thomas has come from and find a man walking steadily toward us. He's tall, probably taller than this kid, and much older. He has a pea coat and a beanie. One hand twists and a telescoping club extends with a *snap*.

The tall boy climbs off me, whimpering in panic. He steps on my arm, trying to make his getaway, when the tall man takes out one of the kid's knees with the club. The kid screams and the man throws him effortlessly across the path. The kid skids against the fence, gets to his feet, and scampers off. I struggle to get on my feet but there's no way I'll get away. He's already standing over me. He looks down at me and for a second I just want him to hit me, to end this madness.

He scans the park from where he stands, probably for any other attackers. I contemplate kicking him in the groin, when he looks back at me and extends a hand. I don't take it. I don't move. I'm just lying there on the cold stone path, looking up at this man, when I start to cry. Maybe it's because of Step or Thomas or a combination of everything, but I can't stop. The man stands up straight again, looks away, and sighs.

I try to gather myself again. I wipe the tears from my eyes and when I look up, I see something odd. Above the man's head, high up in the elm that looms over both of us, a rusty bicycle dangles from a branch, its rear wheel bucking in the breeze, its pedals squealing and whining half rotations—this unlikely wind chime. The man follows my gaze and looks up too. The bike's rusty chain creaks with a somber groan.

The man extends his hand to me again and says, "Paul sent me." His voice is gruff, but the S sound give a tiny whistle. He says, "I'm Weston."

I reach up and he grabs my wrist. He effortlessly lifts me to my feet.

"Thanks," I say.

"Not a problem," he says. He looks at my elbow, touches the tear in my hoodie. He looks a little concerned as he examines my head where it hit the ground.

"I'm fine, man," I say.

"Weston," he says.

"Yeah, Weston." I touch my head and it stings. When I look at my hand, there's blood on my fingertips.

He takes a deep breath, bobbing his head to affirm that everything is okay. I think he does this more for himself than for me. He seems relieved that the commotion is over.

"I saw your porto back here," he says.

We walk around the landscaping, following the path. As we pass a shoe on the path, Weston points and says, "Chubby kid's," as if taking inventory.

We come around a bend in the path to find my porto is in pieces, clearly no longer functional. Weston picks up the pieces anyway.

"Don't bother," I say.

"We will fix it," he says.

He rounds up all the pieces and cradles them in his hands. I offer to take them in my hoodie pocket but he refuses. He removes his beanie, revealing his shiny shaven head. He places the pieces in the beanie and holds it like a sack. "This way," he says, and we start toward the way I had come into the park earlier.

"Are you sure you are okay?" he asks. "Should we get you to a hospital?"

"No," I say. "Of course not." I'll live. I'm shaken up, for sure. But since the accident, I can say I've lived through worse.

When we're out of the park, a thought hits me. I stop and say, "How did you get here so fast?"

Weston sighs to himself. "Ask Paul that when you see him," he says, and leaves it at that.

CHAPTER ELEVEN
CELLO

If you've never left the city, you're missing something. Imagine all the noise and the lights and the looming buildings, all of it.

Now, think about how you move through that unforgiving world. Feel how it surrounds you like murky, tepid water devouring each of your senses until you're practically drowning. Not just the stabbing LEDs or the roaring trains. The aggression. The violence. The judgment. How it holds you down, leans into you with the weight of all those people, the good and bad, until you can no longer breathe. Not that you want any more of that exhaust and stink in your lungs.

Now, picture this: beneath it all, there's a tunnel. A way out. And you descend, slowly at first, that light and noise fading behind you, trying desperately to chase you like an echo, until it's gone, leaving only the hum of your tires. You punch it faster, those tiny lighted markers zipping past your window, one, then another, and another, faster and faster and they become a tiny flicker pulling you deeper until there's only two bright, thin lines drawing you forward. The dull dot of an opening appears in the distant darkness, grows, pulls you out into a new world. A world of machines and industry. Lifeless. Pounding. Grinding. It's where, when you looked across the river as a child, all those towers of exhaust and smoke rose into the air like the land was on fire.

The road carries you right through all that, reminding

you of how the city's light and noise came to be, where all that hard concrete was mixed, where that steel was forged. This burning industrial land goes on and on. And just when you think that it will go on forever, getting louder and brighter until it's screaming, you come upon a ridge, around a curve of jagged outcroppings, and before you can blink, it's gone.

You have your heartbeat, your breath. Music swells from the onboard porto, a mesh of stringed instruments, a flute racing through it. The landscape becomes a living watercolor of browns and greens, gracefully rolling by your window, stretching into the dark horizon, with only the moon floating in that enormous star-filled sky to cast a pale blanket of light over this sleeping world.

Out here I can forget everything, lose myself. As a Hayden, I've become accustomed to finding comfort in the least welcoming arrangements—beneath an overpass, wrapped in musty blankets beside a dumpster, huddled under a scrap piece of corrugated metal to hide from the rain. This is where a Hayden finds respite. Perhaps that is why I can relax in a car driven by a stranger to a place I've never been, far away from everything I've ever known. Warm air pours from the dashboard vents, and I can't help but think about all those places I once found safe and secure. It makes me think how comfort is relative and that, as I gaze out my window at this beautiful landscape, the idea had to come from somewhere.

Weston catches me yawn.

"Is it the music?" he asks.

A dreamy melody mingles about the car, a line of basses marching beneath a taut chorus of clarinets. I take in the smell of the car's leather interior, sink into the plump seat.

"It's fine," I say, not looking away from my window. "I haven't slept."

"I can turn it down," he says.

"No," I say, and put my hand up to stop him. Though, he

doesn't try. "Leave it."

He hums a measure with the music, a soundtrack to the serene world beyond our headlights. I can hear Weston take a deep breath. Maybe he's tired. More likely, he's just as relaxed as I am. Who wouldn't be?

"Can you hear the cello?" he asks. "I always listen for the cello."

I close my eyes and try to focus on a single instrument, pluck one voice among the orchestra. But I can't make out a cello from the rest. I open my eyes again to see meadows on the edge of the road skidder past. Hills crawl by in the distance. I say, "It's very nice."

CHAPTER TWELVE
MUSHROOM

We reach a small town in the very early hours of the morning, and almost immediately I can smell a trace of sulfur through the heat vents.

"Is that something to worry about?" I ask.

"You'll get used to it," he says. "It's not so bad in the colony."

Off the highway now, the scenery passes slowly by my window. Like a lot of places outside the city where tribes haven't taken over or recolonized, this town is mostly abandoned. Homes are in disrepair, unsalvageable, and smothered in dead vegetation. Larger buildings are boarded up or crumbling. At some point—judging by the overgrowth, probably long ago during the first or second migration—somebody tagged the buildings with spray paint. They must have had free reign, leaving their symbol—a plump mushroom—on surfaces all the way down the main street through town. It's the last sign of life having been here.

What sets this apart from other towns is that the ground appears to be cracked in many places. I think I see smoke billowing from an empty parking lot where the concrete has split. We drive over rough terrain and the car jolts and jostles.

"What is that?" I ask.

"Just a speed bump," he says.

I look back and see a jagged fissure in the road, not like

the smooth speed bumps I'm used to. When I look ahead again, I see a glow in the distance, like we're coming upon a stadium or giant parking lot just beyond the hills.

"Is that another city?" I ask.

"No," Weston says. "That's the colony."

Before long we round a curve and clear the hills to find what looks like a modest, simple community of small, single-story, concrete buildings. The lights are not as extreme up close as their impression against the darkness from afar. Rather, because there is no other light for miles, the combined glow of low-strung lights along each walkway between buildings is enough to create this otherworldly luminescence.

We pull up to a building and Weston helps me out of the car. I can feel my hip, elbow, and head still hurt as I stand up. The air outside smells faintly of sulfur and it burns my nose.

"You'll get looked at," he says. "We have an onsite nurse. For now, let's eat."

He takes me to another building that looks like all the rest—concrete, tinted windows if any, and gray, steel doors. Inside, there are three long tables with chairs. It's a cafeteria.

"I'll fix us something," he says. "I'm hungry too."

I follow him into a cramped semi-industrial kitchen where he tells me to sit at the steel-topped island. Everything looks new and clean, and I wonder what I've done to deserve being here. I'd feel better seeing who else is around. I have to tell myself that if I was actually in danger, I'd probably already know it.

Weston doesn't speak as he prepares what smells to me like one of the best meals I will ever have. I watch as he tosses cubes of tofu, sliced fresh pepper and onion, with spices and oil, in a deep pan. He heats some rice that he pulls from a large container in the refrigerator. All the while, my stomach is screaming.

He plates up the food and slides one over to me with a

fork and a glass of water.

Before I can take a sip of water, he says, "You'll get used to it."

I don't know what he means until I bring the glass to my nose and it reeks of sulfur just like the air. I wince at the odor.

"It's okay," he says. "It's well water but it's safe."

"What is it?" I ask. "I could smell this for miles."

Weston snickers to himself. "You'll see tomorrow," he says. He takes a bite and chews it thoughtfully. "So, you're a Hayden. We've never had a Hayden."

I find this startling. He doesn't seem disgusted or judging. But of course he knows I'm a Hayden. I wish I could know his last name. I'm just too afraid to ask.

"Is it obvious?" I say, joking.

"Not really," he says, and finishes chewing a bite. "We're all Fried here."

He lets a fleeting, warm smile draw across his face and I find this to be tremendously comforting. I've found a new place for myself, where people understand what I'm going through.

"A nugget of advice?" he asks.

"Sure," I say.

"Remember—they don't know more than you. The System tells them what they appear to know."

I'm not sure how to take this. I suppose I get it but it doesn't immediately make me feel any better. He takes another bite and watches me, almost studying me. Maybe he thinks I'll figure it out soon enough. Or maybe I just hope I will.

We eat quietly for a moment until we hear somebody coming into the cafeteria. Weston quickly shovels three huge forkfuls into his mouth, wipes his lips, and stands before the kitchen door opens to reveal a middle-age man. The man doesn't look at Weston, just at me, and he smiles.

"Miss Hadley," the man says, stepping toward me and offering his hand. "I am Paul."

He is not who I expected. I don't know what I expected. Somebody younger, maybe. Instead, Paul is a man of medium height, medium build, brown hair with some gray on the sides, a little male-pattern baldness, glasses, and what appears to be a cotton-blend tracksuit. Aside from his smirk, there's nothing remarkable about him. He is, by all means, average, almost so unremarkable that he stands out for it.

I get to my feet and shake his cold, somewhat soft hand.

"Please, Miss Hadley," he says. "Have a seat. I see that Mr. Weston has provided food." His eyes scan our plates before locking on Weston.

"Yes," Weston says. "I thought it would be better to stay up and wait for you than to—"

"Yes," Paul says.

"And, well, Miss Hadley was hungry—"

"Of course," Paul says.

"Do we have a place for her—?"

"Miss Hadley," Paul says.

"Miss Hadley, yes, sorry." Weston steps around the island and gathers our plates, even though I haven't finished. "Do we have a place for Miss Hadley to sleep?"

"Of course, of course," Paul says. "Mr. Owen will be leaving today. Miss Hadley can have his quarters."

"Okay," Weston says. More to himself, he says, "Mr. Owen."

Suddenly, the dark and mysterious Weston has become a yes man to Paul. I'd find this comical if I wasn't suddenly ill at ease.

"Have you any bags?" Paul asks.

"We—" Weston starts to say, but then stops himself. Instead, he quietly cleans our plates and puts them away.

"I have nothing," I say, a little more embarrassed than I probably should be. For some reason, I feel compelled to explain. "I'm...between places."

Paul's eyes widen as if tickled by what I've said. A thin smile creeps across his face. "Between places," he says. "It is for that exact reason why you belong here." He holds that erect posture, his smile fixed in place, perhaps waiting for my response. But I have nothing to say, so I smile awkwardly in return. After a moment, Paul looks to Weston and says, "Mr. Owen?"

Weston nods, quickly finishes drying the dishes, and scurries out the door. Paul walks toward me, his hands folded behind his back. We're alone now and I can feel myself becoming unsettled again. He comes close, only the corner of the island between us. He rocks like a bored child teetering on the balls of his feet.

"You will like it here," he says.

"I hope so," I say, trying to mask my apprehension.

He smiles, an almost mechanical response. I have to assume that a man in his position—whatever that is—can see right through me.

"No worries," he says. He leans in again, his belly pressing against the metal island top. His eyes fix on my face. "Have you had more trouble?"

"What do you mean?" I ask. *More* trouble? What is he implying?

He points to my head and then my arm. "Your bruises," he says. "I see blood. Are you okay?"

"I'm fine," I say.

"You are not fine," he says, his voice shifting suddenly, like it had with Weston, a direct monotone. "There is no such human condition," he says, but quickly replaces his serious tone with a forced giggle. "Yes, yes," he says, taking a deep breath. "You will be okay."

"No worries," I say.

"Indeed," he says, almost delighted. "Indeed, no worries." He looks at his watch. It can't be later than 3:30 or

4am.

"Oh, and my porto," I say.

"Ah, yes," he says. "Again, no worries." He draws in a sudden breath, raising his chin like he expects me to say something and he'll hold his breath until I do.

"Weston said you can fix it?"

"Yes," he says, with a large exhale. "Of course. Of course."

As a Hayden, it's an instinct to try to read people, find out their weakness to exploit them for survival. Now that I'm Fried, it feels more like a necessity for simply remembering people, like Agent Stevenson's restrained hatred for me and all Haydens, or Weston's reserved demeanor crumbling under Paul's mere presence. With Paul, I see now that he's the sort of person who tries to sound like he's on top of things. He wants to appear in control. I'll have to remember that. He doesn't question what's wrong with my porto or how it might have broken. It's evident that he compensates for his unimposing appearance by exuding confidence. It works.

"Is there anything else?" Paul asks. Before I can answer, he says, "Forgive me. You most certainly have questions. Let us save your queries until after you are rested, at which time I will give you the full tour."

"That sounds good," I say.

He gestures for us to leave the kitchen. We walk through the dark cafeteria and out the front door. Outside, I still cannot see much but small buildings and lights glistening off the damp gravel walkway. A few buildings down, Weston's car shines in the same light. It's a nice black sedan. Seeing it in the distance like this makes me think of the man in the gray fedora, and I feel a chill.

Two people come from a building and move toward the car, Weston's long silhouette followed by another man slouched under the weight of a large duffel bag. The second person, I assume to be Mr. Owen, scampers to keep up with Weston.

Beside me, Paul watches the same shadows across the colony. He brings his wrist to his mouth and says, "Porto. Ping. ES. Linens. Cabin 4B. Now. Send." He flashes a smile and says, "Just another moment." He looks away from Weston and Mr. Owen, as if bored, and directs his attention to smoothing a patch of gravel under his feet.

I watch Weston take Mr. Owen's bag and throw it in the backseat of his car. He points his finger and says something to Mr. Owen. Mr. Owen's hands make frantic gestures as he speaks. Weston points to the passenger side of the car and, after one last gestured plea, Mr. Owen bows his head and climbs in.

"We have the stars," Paul says.

"Yes," I say, distracted. We both look up at the sky but I glance over at Weston's car with just my eyes. "They're amazing," I say.

I wish I could hear what Weston and Mr. Owen are talking about, but the car doors close and soon they drive away.

"Have you seen the Aurora Borealis?" Paul asks, his eyes still fixed on the stars.

"No," I say. "What's that?"

"The Northern Lights," he says. "Sometimes they are visible as far south as this, and they are utterly breathtaking."

Not a moment after Weston's car disappears in the surrounding hills, another shadow scampers toward the building with a pile of what I assume are the linens Paul demanded. Paul gestures for me to walk with him, and we slowly stroll toward the building.

"Maybe you will see them," Paul says.

Before we reach the building, whoever brought the linens emerges again, wipes his brow and scratches his head. Then he looks our way and quickly scurries off again.

"I trust you would find them to be lovely," Paul says, walking close beside me.

"What's that?" I ask.

He stops and looks at me, accusing. "The Northern Lights," he says. I almost expect him to say, *duh,* but his face maintains a compassionate smirk.

"That would be lovely," I say, matching his elegant tone.

"Yes," he says, patting my back. "Yes."

We reach the concrete building—or cabin, as he calls it—that looks just like the rest, and he lets me into a dim hallway with roughly ten other doors. The first door on our left has a letter B on it. It has been left ajar. Paul stops here.

"This is your room. It is your space," he says. "You should have everything you need for the night, including towels and a toothbrush. There are two bathrooms halfway down the hall."

I reluctantly reach for the door handle to my room.

"Please," he says. "It is your space. Only you can enter."

I step across him and slowly open the door to a small room. In fact, it's a tiny room, slightly larger than the bathroom I had in the hospital. A newly-made bed with a folded towel and a toothbrush on the pillow takes up most of the room from end to end. There's a bedside table with two drawers and beside that a metal chair. There's barely enough room to swing the door open completely.

I look back to Paul. He says, "Will this do?"

"Yes," I say.

"We will get you new clothes," he says, trying a comforting smile as his eyes scan my outfit. "Tomorrow."

I smile in appreciation, even though I'm still quite unsure what to think. I give a slight wave and a nod as I close the door between us. That's when I notice the door has no lock.

I'm tired but also too wired to sleep. So, I sit on the bed and watch the door. Paul's shadow lingers for a moment before moving on, and then I hear the entrance to the building open and close. It feels like I'm alone in this building but there were many doors along the hallway. There must be others sleeping in similar rooms next to mine and across from me. I remain seated on the edge of the bed, staring at the door handle for as long as I can stay awake.

CHAPTER THIRTEEN
ACORN

A lack of a clock, porto, or window in my room makes it difficult to know how long I've been asleep. My head is heavy when I lift it. My mind is foggy. I need water. It's dry in this tiny room, the concrete walls almost chalky. People shuffle by in the hallway, whispering. When I roll out of bed, I feel where my head hit the ground last night in the park. That was last night. It feels so long ago, so far away. I guess it is.

I'm afraid to put my bare feet to the cold concrete floor. But when I do, I find that it's surprisingly warm, almost too warm, like a stone left out in the sun. I'm not sure what I should do now, if I even want to step out into the hall. So, I stay in bed a little longer, taking in the tiny room, the towel and toothbrush. I try the first drawer in the bedside table, open it a few inches to find it empty. When I go to close it, I hear something I missed roll around inside. I open it again to find an acorn and nothing else.

Two people are talking in the hall. Their shadows come together at my door. It doesn't take long before I realize that they're talking about this room.

"He never sleeps this late," one says.

"Heard a little fussin' late last night," says the other voice. They're both men's voices. "Sounded like he was having words with Weston."

"What a tool," the first one says.

Then comes the knock. "Owen, man. You in there?"

I hurry with my boots, trying to make as little noise as possible. They knock again. The knob turns and I get to my feet as the door clicks open. I can either try to stop them from opening the door or just face whoever it is. Instead of stopping them, I grab the knob and quickly pull the door open. Before the two men can trap me in there, I slip between them and into the hall. Neither looks threatening, especially as they freeze with surprise. The pale one lets a startled whine seep from his dumbstruck face.

"Bathroom," I say, and point. "This way?"

"Uh," says the other man. "Is Owen in there?"

"The bathroom," I say again.

"Yeah," says the pale man. "Blue doors."

As I walk to the bathroom, they peer into my room and wonder out loud where the heck Owen is and just who the heck is this girl.

There are two single-person restrooms. I glance in the first one to find a bunch of shaving cream cans, razors, toothbrushes, and assorted colognes. It must be the men's room. But when I step into the second and lock the door—thank goodness there's a lock—it, too, is cluttered with men's toiletries, including an electronic thing that I can only assume is a nose hair trimmer. Then there's the hair everywhere. I mean everywhere. Tiny bits of stubble, along with other suspicious tangles and tufts that even a Hayden like me finds disgusting.

I wash my face and hands, try to tame my hair as much as I can, feverishly scrambling to get out of this filthy bathroom. By the time I open the door, a small crowd has assembled in the hall. Their faces span a spectrum from stunned to mildly curious. It's a peculiar welcoming party. For a moment we stand in silence. None of them says a word. So I say, "Morning. When's breakfast?"

A few of them look at each other, maybe as if to say, *Did*

she just speak?

I excuse myself and they open a path so I may pass. On my way back to my room, I hear, "Darlin'." I look back to see an old man with a drooping face. He holds up a finger and, in a vaguely southern drawl that may actually be the real thing, says, "Sorry to say, we're about to set down for supper."

***

The cafeteria is smaller than I remember from the night before probably because it's filled to near capacity with unfamiliar faces. Its size also makes for a difficult nonchalant entrance. I take one step inside and conversations taper almost immediately, silverware settles, and heads turn. It's a fairly diverse group for the few dozen people sitting about. While there are more men than women, there seems to be no other majority in the room, not by age or ethnicity. If I didn't know that this place was meant to help the Fried, I would have no idea what brought this group together.

Paul rises from his seat across the room. "Friends," he declares, and lets the room settle a bit more. "Please welcome our new resident, Miss Hadley Hayden."

A momentary murmur sweeps across the room, something about me being a Hayden, and yet it doesn't seem disquieting. I can hear somebody say I'm not the first. Clearly annoyed by their reluctant welcome, Paul begins to clap, and soon the room erupts into a generous, yet somewhat eerily mechanical applause. People get to their feet to greet me. Some shake my hand as I move through the room. Others wave. A few still don't seem so enthusiastic but I suppose I wouldn't either.

"When you get a chance," Paul says to the group, cutting through the fanfare, "make sure to introduce yourselves."

Clapping subsides almost as awkwardly as it began and

people go back to eating and chatting. Paul gently puts a hand on my arm and leads me to the kitchen.

"That was nice," I say, trying to be polite.

He smiles and helps me fill a plate from the serving line. "I think you will like it here," he says.

After I gather my plate and drink, Paul guides me back to his table, where the two men from outside my door are sitting among others. Everyone at the table seems cordial, if not overly well spirited, and they make room for me to sit.

"TJ," says a Hispanic man, waving from a few seats away. His smile is wide and bright.

"Renee," says a black woman, sitting across from TJ. "Not that you'll remember." She wears thick glasses with loudly colored frames.

I wave back to them and to the others.

One of the two men from the hallway stands up and says, "Trevor," and extends his hand. We shake hands. "Sorry about earlier," he says. "We're—"

"Idiots," Renee says.

"Eager," Trevor says back. "Misunderstood."

"Pete," says the other man, the pale one. "She's right. I'm an idiot."

"We were just talking about what happened to Owen," Trevor says, as if I knew Owen simply because I slept in his former room last night.

"Some folks are just ready to go back, I guess," says Pete.

"He seemed to like it here just fine," TJ says. "He was just saying the other day—"

"Mr. Owen will certainly be missed," Paul says, cutting off TJ. Before anyone else can speak, he raises his glass of water to the table. Others follow with their waters, teas, and juices.

"To Owen," Paul says. "Good man."

"An okay man," Pete says.

"Just fine," Trevor says. "But a hell of a scrabble player."

Others nod in agreement. Paul smirks.

They drink.

"Yeah," Renee says. "But Hadley—it's Hadley right?"

"Yes."

"You're alright, Hadley," she says. "I can tell."

"Oh, can you?" Pete says.

"Sure thing," Renee says. "Got to be tough to end up here."

I'm not sure how to take that.

"Did I hear correctly," Trevor asks. "Your last name is Hayden?"

I don't respond other than nodding. Instead, I take a forkful of lasagna and hope I don't have to speak for my last name. Back in the city, such a remark would be followed with a threat.

"I'm pretty sure it was something else," Pete says. "She wouldn't be—"

"You deaf, Pete?" Renee says.

"Yeah," I finally say. "I'm a Hayden." I present my beat-up hoodie, sniff my armpit, and say, "Is it obvious?"

They all laugh. Then TJ says, "Listen, kid. I came to the colony in the same clothes I wore to the hospital after falling from four stories of scaffolding. You bet I looked like hell too."

"Oh," Trevor says. "So, you're saying Hadley looks like hell?"

TJ blushes and everyone laughs. We finish dinner and there is no other mention of my being a Hayden. As far as they're concerned, I'm just another one of them—Fried. It's unusual, for sure. I almost don't believe any place could be so accepting. Renee flashes a warm smile and I want to think I'll be okay here. But the survivor in me says, don't drop your guard just yet, girl.

***

After dinner, Renee, TJ, Trevor, and Pete show me around the colony. It's really not all that big. The buildings are almost exactly the same in look and size. Beyond the cafeteria are the three cabins. Two more buildings are for memory, as Renee puts it, and one is a recreation space. There's a basketball court and a small pond for swimming, though it reeks of sulfur. We walk past a giant fire pit with logs around it for benches. That's when I remember the smoke I saw the night before. I look around to see where it might have been. We're surrounded by hills but in the distance I can see a little bit of smoke trailing in the air.

"What's that smoke?" I ask.

The four of them look in the same direction, toward thin tufts dispersing as they rise into the dimming gray sky. "Those are the underground mines," Trevor says. "They've been burning for well over a century."

"Longer," Pete says.

"Isn't it crazy?" Trevor adds.

"Before Paul started the colony, nobody lived around here," Pete says. "Not even before the first migration. All those buildings you saw coming in? Those are from forever ago, back when this was a little mining town. Somehow fires started underground and everybody just left."

"Couldn't stand the smoke," TJ says.

"No," Renee says. "They left because it smells like somebody passed gas."

I laugh and she smiles.

"It does," she says. "I know you're not used to it yet. We all know how you feel. We've been there. I bet you want to barf right now."

I don't want to throw up but this sulfuric stench is intolerable. "So," I say. "Then why build here? Why put a colony

125

right on top of—"

"Farts?" Renee adds. "The colony is built on ground farts. You can say it."

"If you think about it," Pete says. "It's the perfect geothermal setup. Tons of energy at the ready. Free heat. If you can channel it like a mill, you can turn it into electricity."

"Which is how we can be off the grid," TJ says.

I'm not sure why this would matter, but when I think about it, it's comforting. Somehow it ties into the whole idea of us being off the System. We're not tethered to the city in any way. I'm suddenly overcome with ease, like nobody is watching me, no Agent Stevenson or mysterious man at every turn, no Hayden House to come calling when I do something wrong. I've found myself in a completely opposite world, where trees instead of buildings stand proudly. And there's no possible way that thousands of children could be living below us with the rats and cockroaches because there's nothing beneath us but earth and fire.

For some reason, I'm compelled to say just that, "Nothing beneath us but earth and fire."

"That's the absolute truth," Trevor says.

"You said it," TJ adds.

The sun has set and we're all watching the faint wisps of smoke dance above the dark hills. It's so calm and quiet that I can barely believe I'm here. I stare deep into the shadows and see only the sway of trees, maybe the movement of an animal like a trick of the eye. It all seems so serene and natural. The landscape is as alive and welcoming as anyone here.

"Take it in," Pete says. He inhales a hardy lungful of air.

I draw in a deep breath and nearly gag on the sulfuric fumes.

"Farts," Renee says, waving a hand before her nose. "Don't forget the farts. Nasty."

CHAPTER FOURTEEN
BEAR

The following morning, we file into two vans to go take a hike. I grab a seat next to TJ.

"Got rid of the hobo look, I see," he says.

I found a few sets of clothes outside my door this morning—two pairs of pants, some shirts, a sweater, and this coat. There was also a winter cap, which I have stuffed in my pocket. Everything fits pretty well, which makes me wonder how they knew my size. I tend to wear my pants looser but these fit better. The shirt is nice too, but the collar comes too close to my neck.

Weston drives our van. Trevor drives the other van. Passing through town just outside of the colony, I get to see the cracks in the ground as the vans hobble over them. Smoke sweeps from meadows and parking lots, tangles in the breeze and disappears. The smell of sulfur finally fades as we leave the area and enter more wooded terrain. We drive for a while, skirting a ravine, and it's almost too much nature to believe. Low-hanging branches encroach our way, reaching in from massive trees that line the road. Roots push up through the pavement along our path. The forest goes forever into darkness in both directions from the road. So many trees.

"It's really amazing, isn't it?" TJ says.

"You see pictures," I say. "But this is overwhelming."

TJ takes a picture of the trees with his porto as we pass

them. He shows me the picture—a slightly cock-eyed shot of a bunch of spruce trunks, most of them blurred in motion. He looks at the picture and smiles.

After a short while, we come upon an old gravel lot that's partially wooded with weeds and small trees. Paul exits the other van and scouts the premises, which seems roughly overgrown but subdued by the autumn frost.

"We've never been here," TJ says. He snaps a picture of the gravel lot with his porto. I find it odd that he does this but then I see a few other people doing much the same with their portos. They point their portos at trees, a shrub, paw prints in the mud.

"No worries," Paul says to me. "Your porto will be ready soon." He turns to Weston. "Right, Weston?"

"Absolutely," Weston says.

"Your clothes are suitable?" Paul asks.

"They're good," I say, and tug at the collar of my shirt. It feels a bit taut against my throat, like it's trying to choke me.

"You are not your clothes," he says, offering a small dose of philosophy. "You are you."

Paul walks over to a trailhead. I watch Weston rustle through some supplies in a compartment toward the back of the van. He opens a backpack and inspects a water bottle, a small knife, and a compass, before slinging the pack over his shoulder. Next, he pulls a rifle and ammunition from the van. He inspects it and then looks at me and the horror that must be on my face. He casually says, "For the bears."

"There are bears?" I ask.

"It's their land," he says, as he props the gun against his shoulder and joins the group by the trailhead.

I'm nervously gripping my pant leg when a middle-aged lady who introduces herself as Penny, says, "Bears are my spirit animal." She's a small lady, not the sort of person you would think of as a bear. "Do you have a spirit animal?" she asks.

I snicker and say, "A rat?"

She cringes, as if I'm being serious, and says, "Are you afraid of the outdoors, or just bears?"

"Neither," I say, immediately realizing that this isn't true. "Maybe bears."

She smiles and says, "For good reason. I was scared too. But I'd love to see a bear." She flashes another smile and squeezes my arm before joining the others who have gathered around Paul.

The group seems eager to enter the woods. Their only obstacle is Paul, who stands at the trailhead with a walking stick.

"We have come and gone," he says. "We have taken the riches of the land and left it barren, left it to rebuild and replenish." With his walking stick, he pokes the rotted stump of a fallen tree. "Today, I want you to keep your eyes wide and mind open for animal life, for the tracks and markings of the wild. Feel free to observe as usual, but be mindful of your animal friends." He steps aside and gestures toward the trail. "Proceed."

The group files onto the trail, narrowing into a line, two-by-two. I keep pace with the group, and when I reach the trailhead, Paul stops me by putting up a hand.

"Miss Hadley," he says, and steps close. He hands me a small notebook and a pencil. "Take this for now."

I lift the flap of the notebook and run my thumb over the paper. It's rough, almost veiny, not like the smooth paper I've seen at antique dealers. I suddenly think of Step and my heart momentarily sinks. I wonder where he is today.

Paul says, "Write down any ideas or observations you have along the way."

"Like what?" I ask, turning the pencil in my fingers. Like the notebook paper, the pencil is rough and unmanufactured, no branding. It's basically a stick inlayed with what seems to be charcoal.

"Anything you see that is new to you," he says.

I want to say, *Like this notebook?* But I know that he's talking about the surrounding forest. "I've never seen such a place as any of this," I say. I haven't. The clean, crisp air glazes everything with a sense of newness and purity. It seems almost untouched.

"Then," he says. "Start here." He places a finger on the notebook in my hand. "Start with one word. The first word that comes to mind."

I scan the wall of trees before us. A tunnel cuts through them so deep it's practically impossible to place a thought to it. I'm telling you, there are no words. It's like a small city street, except instead of buildings, trees tower over a narrow, overgrown path. And without lights, the path gets darker the deeper in it goes. But it's not haunting in the way the city can be with shadows lurking in alleyways. Instead, this forest is mysterious, dare I say mystical. The sounds alone will make you wonder. Instead of the murmur of traffic and blurts of passing portos, the trees hiss in the wind and the ground crackles underfoot.

I flip open the notebook and write, "Uncity." It's not a word, I know. But it's the first thing that comes to mind. My handwriting is terrible, unconfident, and scratchy. I can't remember the last time I wrote something with a pencil. Maybe I never have. I'm sort of embarrassed. When I look at Paul, he's smiling.

"Good," he says. "That is a good start."

I want to ask why I have to do this, but Paul leaves no room for questions. He starts down the trail, following the others already well ahead. I start to walk, taking in the way it gradually gets darker as I enter the woods. As I move, the trail curves away. And when I glance back, I see the van and the gravel parking area disappear behind the trees. The gray sky recedes behind a thick mesh of pine above. Far ahead, a line of porto screens float like slow, glowing insects. Sometimes there is a flash, somebody snapping a picture. It takes a moment for my eyes to adjust to the dimness of the forest. Daylight flickers between trees, and I wonder what it would look like at sunset, like that one time a year when the sun falls between the buildings in the city and shines down the streets in perfect strips of light. I open my notebook again and write, "Manhattanhenge."

We keep moving through the woods and I have yet to catch up with the group. I'm far enough back that I can't hear their voices, only rustling branches, the occasional snap of a twig and birds chirping in the distance. I'm not completely concerned, though, as long as I can still see their porto screens. I bend for a closer look at the forest floor, mostly brown pine needles, and wonder why we're even following this path. If Step was here, he would run howling like an animal as he wove through the thick of trees until he reached daylight at the forest's edge. He would make sure to trace every inch of the forest floor, climb over every log he found, peer into every cave, just like we did with each avenue and alley in the city, until there were no other places to go, until we knew it all and made it ours.

I step off the trail and onto the thin bed of needles that stretches throughout the forest. I take another step away from the trail and then another. With each step, I feel a great sense of opportunity and adventure. What I'm doing is not permitted or normal. At least it wouldn't if this were some overgrown city park. People don't stray from walking paths. Or maybe this is normal in the natural world. Maybe this is what we're meant to do. Only, nobody else in the group is brave enough to try. I might come upon a snake but I might also see something that nobody else has, something all my own.

I keep moving, climbing over fallen limbs, hopping over

large stones, each step coming with a swell of freedom. Far off, I can see the group dutifully moving along the trail. I laugh to myself, pull out the notebook and write, "Obedient." I keeping them in my sight as we move toward a ravine. Their trail slopes down toward a creek, and I keep pace by climbing a web of tree roots down my part of the ravine. I don't have the same primitive wooden bridge to get me across the creek but a few calculated steps get me across a series of stones. The group climbs the other side along a meandering trail that gradually switches back up the steep ascent, while I pull myself up an outcropping until I have nearly flanked them at the other side of the ravine. At the top, a few of them stop, the glow of their portos all pointed in the same direction, like they're taking a picture of the channel of water as it runs to a small lake on the edge of the woods.

In my notebook, I write, "They don't see me."

I tuck the notebook away and slowly back into the trees, taking light steps to not be heard. The group begins to move on, as I recede into the forest. Only, my heel catches a root and I lose my balance. I fall against the outcrop, and slide headfirst on back into the ravine. Roots and branches lash at me, jutting rocks slam my body, as I twist and tumble to the creek below with a hard *thud* that knocks the wind from my lungs.

I can't breathe. The water rushes through my jacket and my shirt and my jeans. It runs down my boots. An icy chill takes grip of me from the inside. My chest is seized. When I try to stand, my hand slips on a mossy rock and I end up back in the water.

I'm a fool for straying from the group. I don't know what I'm doing here in the woods and, for a moment, I have the sudden and fleeting urge to be back in the city where I know how to handle myself, what to expect around each corner, and where I don't have to worry about killing myself on some steep, slippery ravine.

I swat at the stream in frustration, trying again to get to my feet. My boot slips and I brace myself, ignoring the cold water as it rushes around me and pulls at my clothes. I take it slowly until I'm upright. Now I'm standing in the middle of the creek, each way out just as slippery and steep as the other. I might as well lie back down in the water, because that's where I'll be if I try to climb either side, especially now that my clothes are drenched and heavy with mud. I decide to work my way along the creek, leaning against the outcropping for stability, until I reach the small bridge of logs that the group crossed. Each step is heavy with water, and mud sucks at my boots from beneath. Once I reach the bridge, I climb up until I'm rested with my feet dangling above the water. There I lie, defeated. I'm not cut out for the woods. I wouldn't survive a night out here. Step talks about people roughing the wilderness, eating animals and berries, building fires. That's not me. I'm a city girl. That's for sure.

I stand up on the bridge and watch my clothes drip with creek water. There's a lump in my pocket and I realize it's the notebook Paul gave me. I pull it out to find a thick, soaked clump of paper. If I try to write on it now, the pencil tip will rip right through the page. I toss the notebook into the creek and watch it move with the current until it snags limply on a rock.

"Please retrieve that, Miss Hadley," a voice says from behind me.

I jump with surprise and turn to find Paul standing at the end of the bridge.

"We leave nothing," he says.

"I can't use it," I say.

"We leave nothing," he says again, a stern gaze accompanying his voice.

I want to tell him to shove off but I can't. He's my way out of the woods and back to civilization. I climb into the creek again and fish out the notebook. I slap the limp wad of paper onto the bridge at his feet. It's still open to the page I was writing on. He looks at the page curiously and then smiles.

"What's the sense in this?" I say. "Tell me what we're doing out here?"

Paul doesn't say anything. He just keeps that same contemplative look about him. I'm still standing in the creek, and he bends down on one knee.

"Do you want help?" he asks.

"No," I say. "I can get up."

I start to climb onto the bridge again and he puts a hand on my shoulder, holding me back.

"What the hell?" I say.

"Do you want help?" he asks.

"You're not helping," I say. I step back into the creek. I'm cold and wet, and I feel myself starting to shiver.

"Why did you come out here?" he asks.

"I don't know. To get away."

"Away from what?" he asks.

"From the city," I say.

He doesn't say anything, and I know he won't.

"I'm not the same there anymore," I say. "Is that what you want to hear?"

After a moment, he says, "Is that all?"

"I don't know."

"You do not remember," he says.

"What?" I ask. "No. I remember just fine." But I know this comes off as defensive, and even I wonder why.

"There are things you do not remember," he says.

"I do," I say. "I remember everything."

"No," he says. "You do not."

"What do you know?"

"I know what it is like," he says. "I know that you can and will survive. You will get through the day. You will feed yourself, clothe yourself. You will have a place to sleep. You will

134

hold a job. But you will not know the people around you, especially the ones most important to you."

"I was doing fine," I say, even though I know that's not true.

He points to the notebook.

"These are your thoughts," he says. "These are your observations. You will learn to think this way."

"What way?" I ask. I try to climb up and he shoves me back down.

"Through details. Not always concrete," he says. "Instead, you will find your way through the abstract details that make up the world around us."

I throw a leg up onto the bridge and see his hand come forward to stop me. I bring my leg back down and stay in the water.

"Have you ever loved?" he asks.

"Loved?" I say. "Have I ever loved somebody? I don't know."

"Sure you do," he says.

"Who?"

"You know who?" he says.

I do. And the thought of him knowing this terrifies me, not because Paul is a stranger but because I'm only realizing it myself. I know exactly who he's talking about—Step. I don't know how Paul knows this but he does.

"Do you remember when you first felt it?" Paul asks. "Do you remember being with this person and feeling that love, possibly in return?"

I don't remember. All I can think of are trivial times when we hung out. We're friends. Okay, we're family. Is this what it's like to love your family?

"Forget their face. Can you remember this person's company, maybe even their embrace?"

"I can't," I say.

"You can," he says.

I'm trying and yet I can't remember I single moment between Step and me that was any more significant than the others. Nothing that tells me why I feel this way now. And when I try to land on any specific moment, all I remember is the fight we had the other night, reminding me how he couldn't possibly understand me anymore and how, without him, there is no place for me in the city.

"You forget the most important things," he says.

I remember lashing out at him, at the way he made me feel for being different.

"I'm not the same person," I say. I've changed and have driven Step away. I've driven myself away.

"Nonsense," Paul says. "You're no different now than you were before."

I don't feel like the same person. Like the first time I looked in a mirror after the crash, I barely recognized my own face. I knew it was me but I had to tell myself it was. I had to say, "You are Hadley Hayden." I didn't feel like myself. I still don't. I'm not the same person. I'm not a Hayden. Not anymore. I'm nothing. And I want so badly to be something. For Step or for me. I want to be normal again. It's all my fault.

"I can help you," Paul says, as if he can read my mind. "Stay here with us and you will find yourself."

I want to believe him.

"Will you accept help?" he asks.

I want to think that I can feel like myself again.

"Please," he says. He holds out a hand to help me onto the bridge and I take it. Once I'm standing before him, he places a hand on each of my shoulders and looks me in the eyes.

"Repeat after me," he says. "I am who I am."

I don't say anything. It's stupid. In the distance, I can hear the group doubling back and calling for us. The trees rustle above. The creek babbles beneath our feet. I'm shivering and

Paul keeps his hands against my shoulders.

"Repeat after me," he says, again. "I am who I am." His eyes hold firm on mine, and I can't look away, as much as I want to.

I say, "I am who I am."

He says, "I am that I am."

"I am that I am."

He says, "I shall be that I shall be."

I repeat after him, barely able to speak. I don't want to be here but I can't imagine returning to the city either. I just want Step back. I want to remember us. I close my eyes and begin to weep. The group is closer now, almost to the ravine. Paul grips the shoulders of my jacket.

A breeze hisses through the trees, tall trunks creak and sway. I can feel my heart racing, my body warming beneath these wet clothes. My breath quivers. I think of Step and where he might be. I wonder if he'll be there if and when I get back.

"Tomorrow," Paul says. He rubs my shoulders, and I don't have the energy to pull away. "Tomorrow, my dear," he says. "You will still be."

***

It's one of those nights where I'm not sure if I'm dreaming or just awake the whole time and thinking. There I am in the suffocating darkness of my concrete tomb of a room and I'm thinking about Step and the other Haydens back at the Junction, and instead of missing them I start to pity them for not having a bed like mine or a cafeteria with plenty of okay food and trees and trees and trees all around. And then I think about Thomas, only he's a Hayden for some reason. Or he's just somebody like a Hayden, living on the streets and sad and lonely, and I still pity him, too, like the little boy I left in Madison Square Park. Only, I keep letting that little boy follow me to the park and I keep trying to make myself guide him to a safer place. And when we get there he's attacking me. And my mind goes back to getting off the train, letting the boy, my brother, follow me to danger. Over and over. Sometimes he's a little boy, sometimes the young adult who attacked me. Sometimes he's an OSU agent like Agent Stevenson, until he *is* Agent Stevenson. And then I'm waiting outside Ziggy's where Agent Stevenson appears with a throwback Volvo for me to drive to the middle of nowhere, to a bear in the woods among the rustling trees.

At some point in the night or in the morning—the concrete walls won't let me know—I'm as awake as I'll ever be and consumed with a ridiculous surge of energy that I don't know what to do with. I want to wrestle a bear or scale a mountain or, more likely, burst from this concrete bunker and find my way in this strange, new world.

CHAPTER FIFTEEN
LAVA ROCK

I'm going to have trouble here putting into words what the colony is like. I don't think you can understand it without actually being there and it's very unlikely you'll ever experience anything close to it. Recalling it now—and feel free to thumb through my cloud for pics—it is not very impressive. Rather, it's simple and very minimal. A plotted gathering of concrete blocks left in a wooded and wild field. Out of place. Unremarkable but memorable in its own way for being unnatural. Imagine a twenty-foot tree sprouting from a crack in the middle of 38th and Broadway.

Maybe that's a bad example. After all, that tree would be doing something, like getting in the way. The colony doesn't actually disturb the environment around it. It doesn't seem to do anything at all. Not when you look at it from a distance.

So, I guess it's best to start with what residents actually do there.

They play games.

I remember thinking this for the first week. All anyone here does is play.

I wake up. I eat. I play games. Paul says we're trying to draw out our deepest memories and restore the way we interact with the world around us. On the surface, it certainly doesn't seem that way, not even after days and nights of what he calls "retention challenges." After a week or so, I'm starting to wonder what good any of it is. But Paul assures me that I am making progress. By now, I have my porto back—good as new, in fact—and Paul pairs me with another resident at an iTable, where we test each other's ability to remember a random sequence of images. When it's my turn to quiz the other resident, I have to call up images of anything that comes to mind and in any order that I choose. If I didn't have my porto to keep track, I would probably be lost in the randomness of my own image sequence. In that way, it almost seems like I'm challenging myself to keep up.

Sometimes Paul watches and delights in how I might follow a picture of a giraffe with that famous shot of the Hindenburg disaster. Paul will add a layer to the challenge and ask the person observing the images to say the first thing that comes to mind when they see it, which isn't always the subject of the picture but some stupid thought that suddenly pops up.

One time Trevor and I are paired and for some reason I call up a picture of a shelf of candy like you might see in a drug store. For some even stranger reason, Trevor blurts, "lava rock," which sends us both into hysterics. Despite having to wrangle us back to the task at hand, Paul is pleased to witness our interaction.

Then there are the times throughout the day when Paul will simply walk up to you and say, "I'm thinking of a series of numbers and letters. Tell me what they are."

Sometimes I have to type them into my porto and sometimes he asks me to just say them out loud. I don't really think about it. I just say whatever comes to my lips, "7B7IR2320C."

He nods and smiles and walks away.

If you're more visually inclined, Paul encourages you to draw or paint. The concrete walls in some people's rooms are full of paintings and portraits. This one guy named Laars, who doesn't seem to like me all that much, creates amazing chalk art. I've seen his work on the sides of buildings. It reminds me of the graffiti you see around the city. Every few mornings a new one appears, sometimes over the remnants of an older rain-washed work. He draws these strange worlds of animated hand tools, like a chisel and a saw dancing hand-in-hand around a campfire. He does it in all sorts of colors. The one constant seems to be a hand drill, one of those old-timey things that you'd have to crank yourself, but his is all cartoony. And it's always flipping the middle finger toward you, like it hates that you're looking at it.

Most of Laars's work is done at night, pacing before the wall, chain-smoking tribal tobacco, which I wonder how he gets. Sometimes I can smell the smoke on my way to my room.

(I still smell that tobacco now, as I tell you this. Maybe that's why it makes sense to recall all of this as if it's happening now. Laars and the people like him whom I may never see again live on through whatever this is, this history that I'm telling you.)

Anyway, one night, I can't sleep and I find Laars drawing an image of a barn burning down, with all the hand tools standing in the foreground in mourning. This time the hand drill is holding its hands behind its back, middle finger extended my way.

I'm admiring Laars's work until he notices me standing there. He glances at me but only pauses for a second without saying anything.

"I really like what you do," I say. "It's tragic and cartoony at the same time."

Without looking at me, he takes a drag from his cigarette and keeps shading a part of his drawing. After a moment, he looks back and blows some smoke in my direction, seems to contemplate a thought, and goes back to work.

"Were you an artist back in the city?" I ask.

"Go away," he mutters without looking at me.

I take one last look at the mural and step away. Then I hear him mumble, "Hayden," under his breath. I don't entertain his jab. Instead, I make a note to steer clear of him from now on.

The days pass with more games and art and puzzles. Nobody seems to be bored or restless. We keep active and productive. When we're not retraining our minds, we have jobs to keep us occupied. The colony functions on the collected efforts of its residents. Each of us has a series of tasks from simple chores like sweeping floors and cooking meals to more taxing labor like tending to the garden and slaughtering chickens or whatever Weston brings back from a hunt. I've heard residents rave their newfound passion for this simpler life. Pete says he has tapped into his "inner farmer," and doesn't see how he could ever return to the city now that he's fallen in love with country living.

"I'm a man of the land," he keeps saying. He whistles as he tills the soil where we just harvested potatoes.

I'm not fond of gardening or cleaning up around the small chicken coop at the edge of the colony. I prefer to volunteer my time helping Renee in the kitchen. It's challenging enough, as we have a limited pantry. We do a lot with potatoes and eggs. Sometimes Weston will bring spices and sauces from the city. Other times, he comes back from hunting, and we have venison or rabbit or wild turkey for dinner.

If he's around, Paul turns our chores into memory games. He'll ask us to narrate what we're doing. Sometimes he'll tell us to name objects like they're our pets. I'll have some stalks of celery on a cutting board and he'll say, "What do you call that celery?"

"Earl," I'll say. Ever since he started asking, that's what I name all the produce I chop. If I'm dicing an onion, I'll say to Renee, "I'll dice up the Earl for our soup." It's sort of a joke. Renee does the same thing with eggs. She calls them little Joeys.

Paul thinks that I must have somebody named Earl in my

life but I don't recall anybody by that name. This doesn't keep him from asking from time to time like I might suddenly remember.

"Are you sure, Miss Hadley?"

"I'm positive," I say. The fact is, though, I'm not positive. I may actually know an Earl.

When we're not playing games or doing our chores, we take trips. Every few days, we drive out to a new place, usually another forest or gorge. We hike trails and gather around waterfalls. Paul asks us to take notes of what we think about along the way, and take pictures of anything we want. Because of this, we don't talk very much while we hike. Most people stay in their own little world, "tapping into their psyche," as Paul puts it. He wants us to keep visiting our minds, so that at the end of each day we can record our thoughts, typed or spoken into our portos, like I'm doing now.

In the morning, we record our dreams. This, Paul asserts, is meant to keep track of the sort of thoughts that we have most often. It allows us to hone in on what is most important to us, so that we can reacquaint ourselves with our desires. It's our desire, he claims, that drives everything about us. Not fear or need. Desire. It's the most revealing part of us.

Sometimes I listen through my notes but I can't quite make out what it is that I desire. And that scares me.

Not all of our trips are to the woods. Sometimes we venture into towns, which is usually more eye-opening than anywhere else. We learn about what it used to be like to live outside of the city.

Paul likes to bring us right down the main street, directly to the town center, where we can see shops and restaurants line either side of the street like one of those old model train sets. Have you ever seen one of those? It's like that. Always these small main streets with narrow brick storefronts. Very quaint but also sort of sad.

We stay in tight-knit groups when we get out of the vans, and Weston carries the rifle, not because of bears this time, but because of other lurking danger. In a nearby village, what used to be called Hometown, shop windows are broken away, signs ripped out of the ground, and there's evidence of looting and fires that happened long ago and now peek through ivy and overgrowth. Mostly, though, it feels like life is a distant memory. With weeds in the sidewalk reaching to the roofs of some buildings like trees, it seems like nobody has been through here since the First or Second Migrations. Wind and rain have washed whatever debris would have collected along the gutter. We walk down the center of the street, stepping around weeds the size of small shrubs. Paul says we should stay away from buildings in case anyone is inside.

In the village square, there's usually a tall marble monument to some great American war hero, and there's almost always the faint trace of weatherworn graffiti. I don't get close enough to read who or what the monument stands in memory of, but I take a picture of it with my porto.

As we walk, Paul tells us about the places he has seen outside of the city. He says that he traveled throughout the old states in search of a place to start his colony. He mingled with tribes, both welcoming and threatening, and he learned from them how to farm and hunt for small game. Along his journey, he met other lost souls, which is how he describes himself. "I am a lost soul," he says. "Only now, like you, I wander the corners of my mind, searching still for who it is I am."

He likes to talk that way, in strange parables and phrases. His stories often come with warnings.

"Throughout the countryside," he says, "there are many deserters from the last migration. These are people who left cities to be on their own. They are still part of the System, but they choose to carve their own lives into the forgotten land." He points to evidence of an encampment behind a building.

Remnants of a fire pit sits in the middle of what used to be a parking lot. Low-hanging cables stretch overhead, running from a rooftop to a line of trees at the edge of the lot. Paul explains how people would cook meat from those cables and hang tobacco to dry. When we come upon the athletic fields of an old high school, Paul shows us where the first generations buried their dead.

It was normal for people to resist moving to the cities. But anybody who stayed behind had to learn a new way of living, as their power was eventually cut off, their water untreated. It was toughest for those first generations. They were raised on modern convenience, only to have it all taken from them. Waves of wanderers, deserters, and tribal gatherers cleaned out these small towns and buried the remains of those who did not survive.

As we walk through town and listen to Paul's lectures, I can't help but think about what it must have been like. I heard about these things in history class, saw artifacts in the museum, but to see it firsthand makes it all the more unbelievable. Paul's matter-of-fact delivery highlights the impending fate of those he talks about. This destitution before us seems so real and inevitable, and it leaves me to wonder what might happen to the colony over time once we have all inevitably moved on. No small, unrealistic utopia can survive forever.

This one day, like so many others, we continue to walk along the main street through town, following Paul as he weaves a narrative of decay, until he turns a corner and takes us down a strip of similar buildings. Only, these structures are charred and demolished.

"War," Paul says bluntly. "Sometimes it came to this."

Crumbled brick walls stand jagged and blackened with piles of brick toppled into the street. Farther down the block, only foundations remain. Trees sprout from concrete slabs where buildings once stood. Even this seems so far in the past.

Somebody in the group asks if there are still battles over territory. We've all heard about tribal conflicts, but those seem so distance and abstract like something out of a history text. Nobody takes it seriously.

"Of course," Paul says. "We are not alone out here."

A few of us look around like there might be somebody watching from a window or a rooftop.

"What about the colony?" somebody else asks. "I mean, can they come after us?"

By *they* this person probably means tribes, but we all know it can mean anybody.

"Yeah," Pete says. "Are we even safe out here?"

Paul scans the war-torn landscape around us with a strange glint of excitement in his eyes. After a moment, he smirks through pursed lips. He looks at the person who asked the first question, then looks at Pete. We watch Paul study these ruins, his eyes growing wide with wonder. After a long spell of silence, he turns to the group again and says, "Safe?" A smirk creeps across his lips like the idea is so novel, so cute. But then Paul's eyes grow cold and serious, and he says, "Never."

CHAPTER SIXTEEN
CAKE

We are never safe. No one wants to admit it because once it's said, it's hard not to think otherwise. Before long, I begin to see scratches in the colony's utopian façade, signs that we are, in fact, vulnerable, maybe even more so than Paul suggests.

Some of that threat lies within. For the most part, people go about their days working and playing but it's clear that there are tiny factions among us, always ready to divide us. For instance, Renee and TJ like to do most memory exercises together and get snippy and impatient with other partners. Pete and Trevor are usually paired up, and sometimes they join a group that I like to call the Good ol' Boys Club, a troop of middle-aged to older men who like to sit around at night and drink and laugh. They hang out in the cafeteria or build a campfire outside. One of the older men, sort of a happy-go-lucky grandfather named Maurice, brings a jug of his moonshine to pass around these gatherings. Sometimes Weston can be found with them but he doesn't seem completely comfortable. Then there's Laars, who, like I told you, hates me for being a Hayden, even if that's a label I've left behind in the city. And yet, like me, Laars is sort of a loner. He doesn't mingle, except for during memory games when he's forced to pair up. Otherwise, he keeps to himself. Even on hikes or at meals, he minds his porto more than the people around him.

Yet, what concerns me the most aren't so much the holes

in the colony's veneer but the outside elements that might threaten it. I imagine they come from all directions, moving about the periphery just waiting for the right moment. I can't help but wonder what's out there in the shadows beyond the colony. At night, I find myself watching the hills that surround us, chasing what I used to think were figments of my imagination. But now, something tells me that there's more out there than trees and foxes. I can't shake the sense that we're being watched, and that maybe whoever is out there might soon try to come after us.

Each night before bed, I scan the jagged, pink horizon in search of movement, something that will confirm my fear. I stand not quite on the edge of the colony and I watch for anything out of the ordinary, which, you can imagine, to a city girl like me is just about anything having to do with nature. Out there, behind all the buildings, the only light comes from Laars's porto light or the Good ol' Boys' campfire, letting me know that I'm not alone.

More often, though, I am alone.

Then one night when I'm out there minding my own, that late autumn air creeps under my collar and I start to shiver. Even as I synch my jacket tight, my body keeps trembling like I know something in that darkness is watching me. But I stay out there because I want my eyes to get used to the dark. I want to make sure that we're actually safe. Or maybe I want to confirm that we're not.

I take a short walk along one side of the perimeter, away from Laars's light. That's when the Good ol' Boys start hollering.

"Kid! Hey, kid!" One of the Good ol' Boys calls to me. "Come here."

I wave them off because I don't want anything to do with them. They know why I'm out here. They've taken their shots at me. Trevor, especially, likes to say I'm just out here to burn energy. He'll say, "Isn't it past your bedtime, you twitchy little

drifter?" The rest laugh.

"Come on," Maurice says. "Get over here, why don't you. Them shadows'll stay put till you get back."

It's no use ignoring them. So, I make my way to the campfire, letting the light ruin any chance I'll have of seeing something in those hills.

"Have a seat," Maurice says. He raises his jug of moonshine and Pete stops him.

"Easy, Mo," Pete says. "She's just a kid."

I laugh like he's being stupid. Where I'm from, deep in the tunnels below System City, there is no drinking age.

"Mo's just a dirty old man," says another Good ol' Boy whose name I can never remember. He's a skinny guy, big nose, curly hair. He's funny, too. "Girl," he says. "Maurice doesn't mean anything by it. He just loves his moonshine almost as much as I love cake. And I love me some cake."

"That's for sure," Pete says, patting an open spot on a short stack of cinderblocks beside him. "Cake fiend."

I sit on the cinderblocks next to Pete and give a cordial, tepid smile.

"Cake," the man says, shaking his head like he can't take it. "Only reason why I've been married three times. All that wedding cake."

Everyone laughs but they each settle into a mutual silence, content to enjoy each other's quiet company.

"You won't find nothing out there," Maurice says, after a moment. He gestures to the dark hills around us. "Maybe a bear or some raccoon waiting for us to go in for the night. But you ain't gonna find what you're looking for."

"What about what Paul said?" I ask. Pete nods in agreement with me.

Maurice laughs, which prompts others in the group to chuckle. "What do you suppose is out there?" he says.

"People," I say. "Deserters, like Paul said. They might be

watching us."

"Do you actually think there are people watching us right now?" Maurice asks.

"Well—"

"Then why haven't they come down here or killed us like I'm sure you think they're going to?" he says. "Don't you think they'd have done that by now?"

"Yeah," Trevor says. "What do you think they're waiting for?"

I realize that it sounds ridiculous but I still feel that somebody's watching us. Call it an instinct I have from all the times I've had to watch out for cops while some other Haydens are selling tobacco in the city. Or how often I've had to look over my shoulder to spy any GCs in the area. Just thinking about them makes me want to turn and survey those shadowy hills. I know that I will see only darkness but I have to look.

"Let it go," Maurice says.

"Yeah, Hadley," Pete says. "Maybe you should stop thinking about it." But he doesn't sound convinced of what he's saying.

"I don't know," I say.

The fire crackles and spits some sparks at my feet. Trevor pokes at the embers with a stick. He moves a burning log, sending an upward burst of ash and sparks in the air, all of this perfectly visible to whoever is out there. It occurs to me then that if somebody is actually out there, they might need a fire to keep warm. And yet I haven't seen a distant fire. I can't see any smoke rising, other than the sulfuric fumes that the ground keeps spewing.

"You know," Maurice says. "Paul's just looking out for us."

"I know," I say.

"Has he told you about his accident?" Trevor asks.

I shake my head because I don't know much about Paul,

and I didn't think anybody did.

"He used to work for MIND," Trevor says. "You know, the agency that runs the System."

"He was one of them programmers or something technical like that," Maurice says.

"The guy is really smart," Trevor adds. "If you haven't noticed."

"And rich," Pete adds. "He made some serious money developing much of their software."

"Then one day he's crossing the street and...pow!" Maurice slaps his hands together. "Nailed by a truck. One of those big delivery vans."

"I hear it was a bakery truck," the nameless man says. "Run over by a van full of muffins and turnovers. Can you believe it?"

"Death by biscotti," Pete says through a giggle.

I try to imagine Paul being tossed through the air like a rag doll but I can only remember my own crash, hear the screech of tires, the sound of metal twisting and crunching. That memory ends in pain, an ache that I still feel sometimes in my hip and elbow. It's difficult to imagine calm-and-collected Paul feeling any pain at all.

"Got it in the noggin," Pete says, touching his own head.

"Grill smacked him right in the temple," Trevor says.

"Fried almost instantly," Maurice says.

"Just like us," says Pete.

A sudden and solemn mood settles over the group as we share a look around the fire. For a moment it seems like everyone gets lost in the roaring flames before us.

"Agency didn't want him anymore," Trevor finally says. "Like he was some kind of freak."

"We ain't freaks," Maurice says. "We are who we are." The rest nod in agreement. "But, you know, they don't like you when you're not on their System."

"That's the truth," Trevor says. "It sure explains what happened next."

"What's that?" I ask.

"Paul noticed that people were following him everywhere he went. You know what that's like, don't you?" Maurice says.

"Don't we all?" says Pete.

The others nod. I know exactly what they're talking about.

"So," Maurice says. "Rather than live like a freak and be tailed for the rest of his life, Paul took his severance and left town, where nobody could find him."

"I mean, seriously," Trevor says. "Who knows what they wanted with him."

"With any of us," Pete adds.

They all look at me like I might have something to add. I just shake my head like I don't know what they want. When I look into that fire, I can see Agent Stevenson's face. I can see that black sedan and some mystery man in a fedora. They're both burned into my brain like I'm still tapped into the System.

I casually look back toward the hills, because just the thought of Agent Stevenson makes me think again that there has to be somebody out there. Since my accident, it seems like there's always somebody watching.

The Good ol' Boys catch me looking.

"Are you serious?" Trevor says.

"Go ahead, girly," Maurice says, sharply. "Get on out there if that's what you intend to do. If you're waitin' for one of us to join you, there ain't no reason to dillydally."

"Look," I say. "Why am I considered the crazy one? It's not plausible that somebody might be out there?" I look to Pete because I'm sure he's still on the fence. "Why don't we ever just hike around here? I mean, we go out to all these places but we have plenty of nature around us. Right here."

"What are you saying?" Trevor asks.

"I'm saying that maybe Paul knows they're out there. Maybe he thinks that if we go out around here, we'll run into somebody in these hills. He doesn't want us to make any trouble."

"Well," Maurice says. "That seems like sound reasoning to me. I for one am fond of staying out of trouble."

"So, how come he doesn't think we'll run into somebody on one of our day trips out there in the beyond?" I ask.

"She's got a point," Pete finally says.

"Y'all are just talking this way for fun, right? Y'all are just speculating." Maurice looks us over, searching for the joke. When we don't laugh, he gets really serious. "Shoot," he says. "Girly, you ought to just go." He's shed his normal jolly demeanor, in favor of cutting me loose. He points past me toward the dark hills, and says, "Go on, now. Get out there. Go find out for yourself." He takes a long drink from his moonshine, winces, and spits. "If you think there's somebody watching us right now, go."

"I'm just saying—"

"Go!" he barks. He looks to Pete. "You too. If you actually think there's something to this kid's rambling. Get going."

"I'm not going anywhere," Pete says. I swear I hear his voice crack. He pans the group with anxious eyes. "I got nothing to prove. Really. I'm good right here."

I don't expect Pete to come with me but his cowardice is so revolting that I stand up and say, "Fine. I'll go." I zip up my jacket. "But don't blame me when they come kick in your door." I look Maurice in the eyes, and say, "*You* let them do it."

His eyes lock on mine. He's drunk and serious. Then he smiles and erupts into a hissing laugh. The others are still frozen spectators. Maurice waves me off and looks back to the fire, disregarding me as a fool. Maybe I am but I won't know until I've seen beyond those hills behind us. I turn on my heel and storm toward the edge of the colony.

Pete says, "Hadley, you don't have to do this. Stay. We're all safe here."

"Yeah, come on, Hadley," Trevor says.

I don't respond. I'm not doing this for them. And if Pete or any of these people meant anything to me, they would know that my name is Haddy.

CHAPTER SEVENTEEN
QUESTION MARK

There's no fence or wall, nothing to scale or climb under. There's only a faint line where the gravel lot gives way to weeds and dirt, and yet I hesitate. It seems too easy. Behind me I can hear Maurice trying to explain his behavior to the Good ol' Boys. Pete halfheartedly calls for me again. When I still don't respond, I hear Maurice say, "Look at her. She ain't goin' nowhere."

That's all I need to compel me forward. I step into the weeds and keep going. I don't look back. I just keep walking, cutting through a field of thick brush toward those hills. My sleeves snag on prickly branches, so I lift my arms high like I'm wading into the ocean, leap over a crack in the ground and crash through a column of thin, stinky smoke. My eyes sting and start to water but I keep marching.

When I reach the woods just before the first steep climb, I stop to listen. Trees bristle and creak in the breeze. I look up to see the moon through a web of thin, bare branches. Dry leaves faintly rustle in the distance, and I think maybe something is moving out there, hopefully only a deer. I keep walking until, when I look back, I cannot see their fire. I've crested the first hill and I'm now on the other side, alone. I wonder for a moment if I should go back, but that's what Maurice expects.

Guys like him are all too common. So many GCs act that

way around Haydens, like they know more than us. Even among the few male Hayden's, there are plenty of cocksure morons. There used to be this Hayden—of course, I can't remember his name—who just *had to* explain everything to you, make these declarative statements about anything and everything like he was a genius. He practically vomited *truths* at you. That's how he would put it—"Let me lay another truth on you gals." A bunch of us might be having a nice conversation about whatever, and he'd come up and interject himself, lay his truths, and practically expect a round of applause for it. In an odd twist of irony—a notion I'm sure he was unable to grasp—he had drawn a big question mark on the Junction wall. That's the mark he left. Yet, I don't think I heard him pose a single inquiry to anyone ever.

The woods get thicker with trees as I march down the hill and into a deep valley. This descent is far deeper than the valley where the colony rests. My eyes are wide and I keep close to the trees, sure to stop every so often and listen. I expect to come upon a small campsite or signs of somebody having been out here. But there's nothing. The constant rustle of dead leaves still clinging to branches overhead makes it difficult to place any other noises. I try to steady my breath and hold myself against a tree to keep still. That's when I hear footsteps. I'm sure of it.

I jerk around to find nothing but trees and darkness. I think that maybe there's something back there but when I squint, I can't see any movement. This is when I realize that my porto is back in my room. I have no way to call for help or shine a light.

I zigzag through the trees until I come to a stream, where I take a quicker pace as I follow the water in search of rocks where I may cross. Once on the other side, I crouch down and watch for whatever or whoever might be out there. Still nothing.

So many nights are like this in the city, especially for a Hayden. You're alone among the shadows. You never know who's around the corner or nearly on top of you. But you know that somebody has to be, or you tell yourself that to be ready, to survive.

When I don't see anything coming, I follow the stream farther down the slope toward the valley. After a while, I break away from the meandering stream and come upon an old white house in a clearing just up ahead. I keep it in my sight as I step through the woods, moving around the clearing to see if anybody is there. The house, with its broken windows and peeling and rotted roof, sits beneath several bare oaks. The property is covered in a thick layer of dead leaves and a brittle webbing of leafless vines. The rusted shell of a truck peeks from a heap of leaves and brush near a collapsed metal shed. Shiny eyes peer from inside the truck. It's probably a raccoon and it stays put as I walk past.

For some reason, instead of being followed, after a while I feel like I'm stalking something in these woods. Suddenly, I am the hunter but I'm not certain what or who I'm after. Around the abandoned house's property, I search the trees and fallen leaves for signs of life, all the while wondering just how long I will keep going or whether I even really care to find anyone out here. What if I don't go back to the colony? Will Paul come looking for me or send a search team? Will I eventually find another colony, another group of outcasts, and join them? If not, can I survive on my own?

Maybe in the city but not out here. The forest is alive. It moves and changes. I'm an expert in urban navigation but I wonder if I'd ever be able to really know these woods. I use to think it would be cool for the System to include a map of the city, so everyone simply new how to get around. It seems like an easy enough idea to implement. But that's because the layout of the city doesn't change much. It only grows upward. The forest, on the other hand, keeps morphing. Canopies of green disappear in the fall, return in the spring. The forest sways and growls in the wind. Trees collapse under their enormous weight. Floods ravage river basins. Streams carve new paths with time. Fires clear whole fields and new vegetation takes over.

Eventually, even manmade structures like this house will succumb to nature, be swallowed whole by ivy and rot. I'm surprised it hasn't already.

From the edge of the woods, I see nothing in the dark of the house. But that doesn't mean somebody isn't watching me from the shadows inside. Compelled by equal parts fear and curiosity, I follow the remnants of an overgrown gravel driveway to the road. Based on the moon's position, I decide to move west along the road. It feels good to walk so sure-footed on the hard blacktop after stumbling through weeds and brush. The road is cracked and fissured from the mines burning beneath, gnarly little weeds somehow bravely clinging to jagged scars in the pavement, but I feel confident walking such an open path, tunneling through the trees that loom overhead. If somebody wants to attack me now, they'll have to reveal themselves first. And if anyone is following me in the woods, they don't have it as easy as I do on this pavement. As exposed as I am, I can run farther and much faster.

I walk slowly and steadily for a short distance, listening to the murmuring forest on either side, when up ahead a glow sweeps across the road and back. The light moves swiftly along the trees, up and down and back again, tracing nothing in particular. It's not a car or a zipbike. There's no engine sound at all. I stop to listen. Voices. At least two. The lights are erratic like flashlights or portos searching the edge of the woods. Whoever they are, they are walking my way along the road. For a second I think I should confront them, let them know that I'm no threat. I stick to the edge of the trees and crouch a bit, wait for them to get closer.

Then something rustles among the trees, coming toward me. Before I can react, an arm wraps around my torso. My scream is quickly muffled from a hand over my mouth. It's a man's hand, rough, dry. When I draw a breath, I can feel powder or dust cling to my throat and I begin to cough. He makes no sound as he pulls me deep into the woods. I kick and fight and try to bite his hand or pry his grip from my torso. But I can't get my feet planted on the ground. Whoever it is has me lifted off the ground enough that I can't reach. He's big. My voice is lost in the tight seal of his fingers. He grunts, his breath heavy against my ear. That's all I hear, his strained breathing and some whispered words repeated under his breath. *Don't don't don't don't. Shushshushshush.* Once we're far into the woods, he lays me down and gets on top of me, putting his weight on me. I can't believe this happening. My chest is tight with panic, I can barely breath. His hand loosens from my mouth enough for me to let out a muffled scream before he clamps it shut again. My arms are practically useless against his weight. I'm crying and screaming into his palm and trying to throw any part of my body—knees, elbows, hands, feet—at him to make him stop. All the while, *Shushshushshushshush.*

When I finally submit in exhaustion, I realize that he hasn't been fighting back. He's just holding me down, shushing me, whispering almost inaudibly for me to not move. I want to cry out but I can't. He's not doing anything, just breathing. The heft of his warm and sweaty body settles against me. I can tell he's trying to calm himself. My face is pushed into the dirt and leaves, and I can't see more than his forearm. I feel his breath on my neck.

"Don't move," he whispers, more breath than voice. "They don't see us."

I try to calm myself, keep from breathing too heavily, just save my strength for when I can break his grip. Above us, a light sweeps across the trees, comes back, and lingers. He lifts his hand away from my back, his thick fingers still lingering like he might grab hold of me again.

"They're gone," he whispers. But he still doesn't release his hand from my mouth. He looks up again. "Be good. Will you be good?"

I shake my head yes. I just want to run. He rolls me over and I drive a knee into his groin. He lets out a groan and collapses to his side. When I try to get up, he throws his arm out to grab me. I kick at him, hitting him however I can before I'm on my feet and running.

"No. Wait," he says in a hushed cry. "Hayden."

For some reason, I stop. I don't know why. It doesn't even occur to me that he ought to know that I'm a Hayden if he's on the System. I just stop because his tone doesn't sound angry. It's cautioning. It's curt. I know this voice. I look back and he's on his knees, coughing and grunting. He looks at me and I recognize the ponytail, the sideburns, the hulking mass. It's Laars.

A light from the road sweeps by again. Whoever is out there must have heard us. They're doubling back.

"Go," Laars says. He gets to his feet and comes toward me. I keep my distance. "We need to run. Now."

"Who are they?" I ask.

"I don't know."

The light gets closer, just on the edge of the woods. He gestures for me to go, so I start moving through the trees. He follows close behind, straining to keep his breath. We stop, trying to use the trees to hide when the lights shine near us. When the lights sweep away, we move again. We're not quite running as much as we are stalking through the forest, keeping our feet light against the rooted forest floor. I clumsily step on a branch and it snaps, and one of the people in the road shouts, "Over there!" Both lights aim at us. We can hear the figures burst into the woods.

"Run!" Laars shoves me and we scramble deeper into the forest. The lights are frantic around us.

"We should split up," I say.

"No," Laars says. He's short on breath but keeping up with me.

"We can lose 'em," I say. I take a sharp turn away from the house that I know is just off to our right. Laars follows me and I have to stop.

"Go that way," I whisper. "There's a house. Hide there or keep going. But stay off the road."

"No," he says, trying to catch his breath. "We stay together."

We're crouched low and the lights scan the trees near us. Our hunters are gaining ground.

"What the hell, Laars?" I say. "We can shake them."

"No." Laars looks angry. He lets out a big sigh and says, "I'm lost out here."

"You can't get back on your own?" I say. This seems so strange to me. He's a grown man. Any Hayden worth their salt can retrace their path without hesitation. Then I remember that he isn't a Hayden. He's just Fried.

"I followed you out here," he says. "You had me going every which—" He stops talking when a light traces over us. We freeze. Then the light fixes on him and he shouts, "Go, go, go!"

We run. I take us back toward the abandoned house. The two lights are practically on top of us. When we reach the house, I look back and see two figures, men dressed alike, patches, maybe military but ragged. They come out of the woods and slow their pursuit, perhaps realizing that we're somewhere on this property. We get to a busted-out window and Laars hoists me inside the house. I help him climb in after me. The room is pitch black but for a beam of moonlight coming in the window. The floor feels rotted and shaky beneath me. I can just make out the partially torn away walls. Built-in book shelves are ripped down. There's debris and what looks like dried mud everywhere. Laars catches his breath, his face lit with panic.

I can hear the two men outside approaching the window.

"Back off!" I shout to our hunters.

Laars tries to shush me with a finger to his mouth.

I hear one of the men say, "Was that a girl? Oh, damn. I got this."

"You don't want what we got," I say. Laars and I crouch into the shadows. The men shine their portos into the window, but their angle doesn't allow them to find us. The light keeps passing overhead.

"Give it up," I say.

Laars pulls out his porto and whispers into it, "Flashlight," calling up the flashlight app.

"Put that away," I whisper.

"Might as well see what these guys look like," he says.

"And give them a target?" I say. "Put that away."

Laars thinks for a second and finally tucks his porto back in his pocket.

"You got us all wrong, little lady," one man says. "Just wanderers trying to keep on. You got anything to barter." He snickers something to the other man.

"Yeah," the other man says. "What do you got in there?" His slimy voice crawls like a snake through the window. Makes me shiver.

"Nothing you want," I say.

"Move on," Laars says, his voice unexpectedly booming within the confines of this rickety house. "You come in here and you'll regret it."

"Well, damn," one of the men whispers.

"We got all night," says the other man. "Come on out when you're ready." They whisper something to each other and then one walks away from the window.

I slowly move along the wall toward a doorway, keeping my feet light against the floor, trying to avoid creaky spots. In the hallway, more debris is piled along the walls, collected in corners. It's too dark to tell exactly what I'm looking at. I pass a doorway to what looks to be a living room with a fire place. Dead leaves are collected in the moonlit corners, that blue light spilling through three big windows. I think about going upstairs but that would do me no good, only trap me even worse.

Outside, I can see the top of one man's head pass the window. They must be scouting the perimeter of the house.

Suddenly, the floor creaks behind me. It's Laars in the doorway between the living room and the kitchen. He's holding a wooden breadbox with a broken lid.

"I'm going to smash this over that fella's head," he says.

Behind him, a man passes by the kitchen window, and I see a plume of smoke trail behind. Sure enough, a moment later, I can smell tobacco. That's how I get my idea.

"No," I whisper to Laars. "Give me your lighter."

"I don't have one," he says.

"Sure you do," I say. "You smoke like a chimney."

He reaches into his pocket and pulls out two familiar bars, a flint and steel, dangling from a short chain. I knew he had something.

"Do you have rolling papers?"

"Not on me," he says.

"Give me that box," I say. I take the bread box and the flint. I creep over to a pile of leaves and place the breadbox on them. The wood is nice and brittle, dried over decades. I strike the steel against the flint a few times, until a good spark catches the leaves.

"What are you doing?" Laars asks.

"We have to get out of here," I say. "I'm creating a distraction."

The dried dead leaves take a minute to fully ignite and soon a corner of the room is filled with smoke as they slowly burn. The smoke builds without much of a flame, but I know that the leaves are on fire. For a moment, I think about Step and how much this would excite him. That thought alone gives me courage. I take off my jacket and start fanning the fire. A faint orange glow swells within the smoke. Before long, the wall and the breadbox catch fire.

I can hear the two men outside come together to figure out what's going on. "It's your funeral, little lady," says one of the men. Then to his partner, he says, "Can you believe how stupid they are?"

I wave Laars over to me in the hallway, away from the smoke. The window frame and the wall around it are eventually engulfed in flames and the fire spreads among the leaves across the floor.

I point to some broken shelves and say, "Grab a couple of those. We need to spread this quickly."

We get a few boards on fire and carry them to a window. I throw my two boards into the leaves outside. No sooner do leaves around the boards start smoking. We move to a window in another room and peek out. One of the men is standing back and watching the house. I can see his face in the fire light. His beard is long and scraggily. Those patches on his clothes aren't military. They're homemade. His clothes are tattered rags. The flicker of light illuminates his astonished gaze. He clearly doesn't know what to make of the scene before him.

"Do it," I say to Laars.

He heaves his boards toward the man, just missing him. The burning boards land in the leaves around him and soon those leaves catch fire.

"What the hell are you doing?" the other man says.

"They're trying to kill us all," says the bearded one.

We grab some more boards. The living room has erupted

in flames and it's quickly spreading down the hallway. Smoke crawls along the ceiling, looking for an escape. The heat is intense. We light a few more boards and throw them out other windows. Outside, the men keep backing away from the smoke and flames that spread across the yard. I take off my jacket and hold it to my mouth and nose. My eyes water but I push through.

"We need to get out of here now," I say.

"How?" Laars asks, coughing. Outside, smoke rises around the house. The heat inside the house is growing unbearable. Smoke makes it nearly impossible to see.

"Follow me," I say. Laars is still coughing. I gesture for him to take off his sweater and hold it to his face. Out one window, I see the figures of the two men backing away. We decide to escape through the window we entered. I climb out and onto the charred remnants of leaves and sticks just around the house. Just like Step showed me, the flames have spread away from the house, creating a ring of fire and smoke that surrounds the property and keeps moving outward, driving the men away but leaving behind harmless smoldering embers.

I step into the charred leaves but Laars hesitates. "It's okay," I say, and wave for him to follow.

We creep along just behind the spreading ring of burning leaves. It moves toward the forest edge in a great big wall of smoke, enough to separate us from whatever is on the other side. In the opposite direction, the two men scamper to the road, coughing and wiping tears from their eyes. The smoke has driven them away. They're busy watching the fire take over the house, while we make our escape toward the woods. When the spreading fire reaches the metal tool shed, a gap forms in the flames where Laars and I make a run for it. We keep going as long as we can, putting distance between us and those two men.

When we reach the stream, Laars stops to rest. He's

gasping for breath, coughing into his sweater. We're far enough from the smoke and he pulls his sweater away from his face so he can breathe more easily. He nods with gratitude. I put my jacket back on. Laars washes his hands in the stream. He looks back toward the house in the distance, now a massive bonfire glowing just beyond the trees. He looks at me and smiles. I've impressed him.

"Why did you follow me out here?" I ask.

"You don't know what you're getting into," he says.

"And you do?"

He sits beside the stream. "I don't know who those guys are," he says. "Whether they're drifters or tribesman, I don't know. But there are people out here." He shakes his hands dry and wipes them on his pants. "I know why you come out every night. You're right. They're out here and they're watching."

"You think those guys will follow us to the colony?"

He shakes his head that he doesn't know. "Maybe. They looked like scavengers. But those aren't the ones who keep an eye on us."

"But you've seen somebody watching?"

"I have."

"Does Paul know?"

"Sure," he says. "Paul has to know about them." Laars puts his sweater back on and fixes his ponytail. "I've been out here maybe a year. If I know about them, he's sure to know about them."

"Why are we here?" I ask. "I mean the colony. Does it work? Do all these memory games do anything?"

"I don't know," he says, and lets out a small chortle. "It might not do a whole lot for us. Maybe it does. But none of us really want to go back. You know what I mean? There's no place for us in that city."

He might be right. There might not be a place for us. But I think I do want to go back. Too much of me is in that city.

There's a hollowness to these woods that makes me feel empty inside, and I suddenly feel more like that raging fire just beyond the trees.

We start hiking back up the hill toward the colony and neither says much for a while. We just walk. Laars glances back every so often to see if we're being followed but something tells me that nobody will mess with us now that we're closing in on the colony.

"So, really," I ask. "Why did you come after me?"

"You're a stupid Hayden," he says. Showing a bit of remorse for that curt response, he sighs and says, "Look, I just don't want you to start anything with whoever it is out here. They don't fuss with us. We don't fuss with them."

"You act like it's a mutual agreement," I say. "Nobody back at the colony seems to think that these people exist. What makes you so certain?"

He smiles to himself. "Folks may not act like it," he says. "But they all know somebody's watching. As long as we have this." He pulls out his porto and taps it with his finger. "They've been on us since we went off the System."

When we reach the top of the hill and see the colony below in the opposite valley, I stop and scan the surrounding landscape again for anyone coming. It's a perfect vantage point with the whole area in view and the rest of the hills rolling off into the distance. Laars seems to disregard the view.

"Don't bother," he says, starting down toward the colony. "You know what they say about ignorance."

I do. As I follow him back toward the glow of buildings below, I can think of nothing blissful about this.

CHAPTER EIGHTEEN
EYEGLASSES

So little happens at night. You may not think it, what with all that seems to go on in the city. But out here it gets quiet, too quiet, especially when you know that something is just beyond your reach, watching and waiting. Which is probably why I can't sleep. Holed up in my tiny room, my mind reels with worry from one thought to the next—about those men, whoever is watching us, the fact that we're all Fried. We're so vulnerable out here.

All the while, I'm fighting the urge to ping Step. I want so badly to see him right now. But I can't. And reaching out to him will do nothing if I can't get back to the city.

Instead, I do what I'm supposed to do. I write it all down. Everything that happened tonight. Paul keeps saying that a key to mindfulness is to be present and aware.

(And now you too know this, I guess. Maybe that makes you present. You're aware.)

Alone in my private cell with nothing but my porto, I describe what it's like at the colony, how I've been pacing the grounds each night. I talk about the Good ol' Boys Club and going off into the woods. I explain what happened with the drifters and the house and that wonderful fire burning so bright out there in the middle of nowhere. I even talk about Laars. Only, I do this as if I'm explaining it to Step, like I want him to know every last detail of what I've been through, how it feels to be away in this strange place, and how, for all its comforts, I just can't seem to settle in. I plead for Step to understand why I left in the first place and why it seems like nothing is going right for me. I just want to be normal again. I want to be a Hayden and be able to know people's names. I just want to remember who I am. But first I tell him that I want to come home.

***

I must nod off because when I come to, it's morning and there's a knock at my door. I don't answer it. Instead, I listen to Pete and Trevor standing outside.

"You think she came back?" Pete asks. "I really should have gone after her."

"She's fine," Trevor says. "I'm sure she didn't go that far."

"But what if they found her? I mean, you know. What would they do?"

"She's a tough girl," Trevor says.

They knock again.

"Should we just peek in?" Pete says.

"Do you think she's in the east wing?" Trevor asks. "Maybe out on the lanai, tanning beside the pool? It's an eight-by-five prison cell. I'm pretty sure she'd hear us knocking if she was in there."

"I just feel like we led her into danger," Pete says.

"We didn't do anything. That was all Maurice."

"I'm going to check," Pete says.

The knob turns and the door is about to open. Then it quickly shuts.

"Stop that," Trevor says. "If she's in there, we look like a couple of creeps. Cut it out and let's grab some grub. She'll be around."

They walk away and I hear the hall door open and close. There are some other voices at the other end of the hall, the normal morning banter.

I wait for the hall to go silent and then wash up for breakfast. The cafeteria has the normal crowd. Not everyone goes to breakfast and those that do usually gather at a single table, sometimes with Paul and Weston, if he's not running errands to the city.

I grab a tray and serve myself some eggs and grits. Renee sees me from across the kitchen and shoots me a baleful glance that seems subdued beneath her funky green eyeglasses. I don't think I've seen her twice in the same pair, and these are probably the most over-the-top eyeglasses yet.

"You're supposed to be back here," she says.

"I'm sorry," I say. "Can I grab a bite and help clean up?"

She walks over to the serving counter and looks me over. "You get any sleep last night?"

"I'm fine," I say.

"Pete was asking about you," she says. "Something happen between you two?"

"The Good ol' Boys got a little rowdy last night," I say. "We had some words."

"Ooh." Renee hisses. "You got some sass." She smiles and says, "Take your time. I'll be back here."

I sit down alone at another table and immediately catch Paul looking my way. He gets up and walks over.

"May I?" he asks.

"Sure," I say.

"Is everything okay?" he asks, and sits down.

"Fine," I say, not ready to talk about what happened last night. I take a bite of eggs and a scoop of grits onto my fork.

"You know, Miss Hadley," he says. "You have really become part of the community here. It is not an easy entry into the boy's club. Just ask Miss Renee." He smiles like this is supposed to be a joke.

I don't want to entertain his comment. I'd rather ask him how long people have been watching us and how much we should trust him with our safety. I want to know what other secrets he's been keeping. Instead, I regard the forkful of food before me and Paul's coy smirk just beyond it.

"Miss Hadley," he says, prying.

I drop my fork to the plate and say, "I want out."

"Come again?" Paul says.

"Take me home," I say. "I don't want to be here anymore."

The others must hear this because they look our way. Paul resists the urge to look over his shoulder at them. Instead, his eyebrows lift and he says, "May we talk about this elsewhere? Outside?"

"You're not going to change my mind," I say, and I stand up.

I follow him out the door. I think that maybe he wants to pull me aside and yell at me but he calmly gestures for us to take a stroll across the grounds. We walk slowly side by side, and I purposefully steer us toward the edge of the colony.

"Miss Hadley," Paul says.

"It's Haddy," I say.

"Haddy," he says, and it sounds forced. "Forgive me, Haddy." I don't like him saying my name this way and I immediately regret letting him do so. "You will understand why I do not talk about this upfront." He hesitates and then casually walks with his hands folded behind his back, clearly thinking about his words. "Everything you have heard about these...well, the others, let us call them. Everything you have been told about them is true."

"There are people watching us," I say, more as a statement than a question. I don't care how he knows that I found out.

"Always," he says. "Yes."

Hearing it from him only makes me angrier.

"Why don't you actually come out and say this from the beginning?"

"Each finds out at their own pace," he says. "We all know already."

"I just don't know why we allow this to happen?"

"What would you do differently?" he asks. To that I have no answer. He knows this and continues. "The government had American Indians under surveillance for decades. Look what happened to them. Did they rise up?"

"They barely have anything," I say.

"They have everything they ever wanted because they had patience," he says. "They have their land, their traditions. Most of all, they have sovereignty."

"What good is sovereignty when it's rundown and desolate," I say. "When it's under surveillance. What good is that? At least when we were on the System—"

He stops and takes my arm. I try to jerk away but he has a firm grip.

"You cannot be part of their System ever again," he says. "It is impossible. Do you understand that?" When I don't respond, he continues. "The only alternative is freedom. That is the price of freedom." He releases his grip and gestures to the colony around us. "We have it here. And, yes, they watch. So what? Let them watch everything we do. Let them see the world we have created for ourselves. They watch us. But they watch us live free."

When I turn back around to see the colony of sterile, primitive cinderblock bunkers, the roughly laid gravel paths, with the only splash of modernity in Weston's black sedan, I'm convinced that I want none of it.

"I want to go back," I say.

When I think of freedom, I think of city streets, the

smells of too many people living on top of each other, the possibilities for good or bad. I think of having it all in my reach, even if I have to take it when it won't be given to me. Freedom isn't living on an island.

"Freedom isn't isolation," I say. I start to walk toward the cafeteria. "Have Weston take me back today."

"They will kill you," he says, a tinge of desperation in his voice as he calls this to me. Maybe that's why I stop, because he might actually be telling the truth. "If you go back, they will find you," he says. "It will not be long."

I'm not sure I want to hear what he has to say, especially since Agent Stevenson already told me that I should be dead. But I listen anyway.

"You are not the first to go back," he says. Paul takes a deep breath and flashes a sympathetic grin. I try not to think that this is a conversation he's had a dozen times already. I'm bracing for one of his philosophical lessons. Instead, he says, "Tell me about the night of your crash."

"Why?"

"Humor me," he says.

"I don't know," I say. "I got in a car. A tire blew on the skyway. I went over the guard rail. Woke up in a hospital."

"Where did you get the car?"

"Somebody gave it to me," I say.

"A man in a nice suit, I suppose," Paul says. "A well-kept gentleman who would otherwise have nothing to do with you?"

"Sure," I say. "A gray suit. How do you know that?"

"Was there anything else out of the ordinary that night?"

It seems so long ago, even if it has only been a few months. My life since then has been so different. It's like I started over and now I have to think back to the night I was apparently reborn. It begins to reel through like a choppy film—the man in the gray suit, the old throwback car, zipping around

173

town, taking it up to speed on the skyway. Then I remember. "The onboard porto let me drive," I say. "And my porto still worked in the car."

Paul nods like he knew that already, like this is expected. "Did you use the onboard GPS?"

"Yes," I say. "Why?"

"Did you get a message on your porto at any point?"

"Yes," I say. "But I don't remember it."

"And did you respond?"

"I guess. Yes, I did."

Paul nods again. He takes a deep breath through his nose. He has my attention.

"The man you met that night, the one in the suit—he intended to kill you." Paul puts his hand on my back and we start to walk. "That man works for MIND," Paul says. "You, no doubt, have heard about MIND."

"You worked for them," I say, trying to assert some of my own knowledge.

"Yes," he says, smirking. "I did but not like this gentleman. You see, his job is to make sure you are able to receive their message."

"The one I got in the car," I say.

"Likely," Paul says. "Yes. You were supposed to read it and reply. Doing so opened a portal in the System, so that MIND could update their data."

I don't understand and my grimace must show this.

He explains, "It used to be that the System updated every six hours when somebody at MIND manually entered a password. Before long, they realized that no single person should wield such power, so they enhanced their security efforts. They began to preprogram people's chips with codes, and those people would be randomly selected to enter a code, which opened the System for its update. It was a rather ingenious move, if I do say so myself. We called it *human*

174

encryption, a form of crowd sourcing security."

"We?" I say.

"We," he says and nods his head. "The moment your preprogrammed chip is prompted, you automatically respond with your password like a mental reflex" He stops walking and says, "Are you following?"

"Yes."

"Not long ago," he says, flashing a coy, knowing smile, "let us just say that MIND became wise to certain threats and they ramped up their human encryption. They were still sending people messages by their porto and still unique to that person. Unique to people like you."

He points a finger in my face and smiles because he knows that this is more than I expected. It's true. Everything he says is unreal. I can't imagine being part of something so big and intricate. But we all are.

"The only secure password is an expired password," he says. "You see, the software is written to push updates through a tiny window of time, only a millisecond, long enough for data to pass through."

"That's good, right?" I say.

"If the password is gone," Paul says, pointing to my head. "It is not gone. You still have the code in your head. Therefore, to MIND you are a liability."

"MIND tried to kill me," I say. I have to say it because I can't fathom anyone wanting me dead, let alone some enormous agency like MIND.

"I am sorry," he says. "It was never meant to be that way."

It's too much. It's not real. "I'm Fried," I say, almost pleading. "I can't remember some code."

"You do not live with such a mental trigger for so long without it influencing your thoughts," he says. "You might remember your password, and then what? Like everything else you have ever learned or experienced, it is still up here." He touches a finger to my temple. I don't flinch.

"So, they want me dead," I say.

"Either they kill you or they watch what you will do," he says. "That is why you are here."

I can't help but believe what Paul is saying. It doesn't make sense but then I think about everything that has happened since I left the hospital, about the man following me, about Agent Stevenson.

"He told me I was supposed to die," I say. "He said that they were going after Haydens." I don't know if I mean to say this out loud but it's the last thing Agent Stevenson said to me, and it suddenly feels important.

"He," Paul says. "Who?"

"The man who was following me, he said that more Haydens would be killed."

Paul's mouth parts into a lustful smile. "Yes," he says. "It used to be so random." He rubs his hands together thoughtfully. "But you are expendable. Yes, nobody would care."

"Do you know Agent Stevenson?" I ask. "The OSU agent?"

"I know him by many names," Paul says. "And I know that he is not OSU."

"He told me—"

"OSU is a social service. They are glorified guidance counselors. Does that sound like your Agent Stevenson?" Before I can answer that it certainly does not, Paul says. "No, he is not going to help you. Your Agent Stevenson has a very different motive, and I have reason to believe he and the man in the gray suit share an employer. They might as well be the same person."

I don't know who to believe. Between the two of them, Paul has been much more forthright with information. And when I think of how mysterious Agent Stevenson has been, I can't help but question him. It would make sense that Agent Stevenson works for MIND. But so did Paul, at some point.

"Maybe you should go back," Paul says. "I think you should go and warn your friends, the other Haydens."

"I don't know if they'd believe me," I say. "Let alone care, for that matter."

"Yes, yes, yes." Paul starts pacing, working his hands together, scheming. "I think you should go back and find out if anyone has come across your friend, the man in the gray suit. You can bring them back here."

"Wouldn't they be dead?"

"Not necessarily," he says. "Tell me, are all Haydens so trusting to take a strange man's offer like that?"

I suddenly feel foolish for being where I am. Had I been less trusting, none of this would have happened.

"Just ask around," he says. "You might be surprised by what you learn."

"Am I still in danger there?" I ask.

"Yes," Paul says. "I will not lie. Nothing has changed for you. From what I know of MIND, you will be of great interest. But I think you can save your friends."

Here I thought I was escaping danger by returning to the city, and suddenly I'm entering into a suicide mission. It feels imperative that I go back and yet all the more foolish.

"Will you help your friends, your fellow Haydens?" Paul asks. "They are in danger in the city. You of all people should know that. They will be safer here. Will you help them get to safety?"

"I want to go back," I say, suddenly trying to convince myself. "Send me back."

"You are doing a good thing, Miss Hadley," he says. "I mean, Haddy." He squeezes my shoulder, and I cringe at both his touch and the sound of my name on his lips. We start toward the cafeteria, and he says, "Weston will take you today. If all

177

goes well, you will be back here in a week or two."

I wonder why I would ever come back to the colony after being so certain of the dangers here. But I'm also scared to find out what I'm walking back into when I return to the city.

Paul stops short of the cafeteria entrance and says, "Agent Stevenson."

"What about him?"

"He has been watching you."

"Yeah," I say. "He was following me."

"Be careful of him," Paul says. "Please."

"I will," I say, almost dutifully. I try to remember what Agent Stevenson was like, whether or not he truly seemed like a threat. "I'll be okay," I say, like I'm trying to reassure Paul that my return to the city is safe.

"You are supposed to be dead," Paul says, frankly. "When the time is right, Agent Stevenson will finish the job."

CHAPTER NINETEEN
SNAKE AND PIANO

Weston doesn't speak. His classical music plays from the onboard porto, providing a soundtrack to the rolling hills outside my window, the same landscape that I once regarded as beautiful but can only look at now with suspicion. In the distance, the occasional column of smoke rises into the early evening sky, more mine fire smoke, or maybe an encampment of outcasts or a remote tribal enclave. Those hills and trees are hiding so much danger. Of course, I have plenty of time to imagine what threats I will face in the city. Every time I think about the lights, the smells, the noise—my breath gets weak and I can't tell if it's in anticipation or fear.

On one hand, I just want to see my friends, especially Step. It pains me to think about how we left things. And so much has happened since then. I need him to understand what I have been through. But I also have to warn him and the others. If what Paul says is true—and if I'm to believe Agent Stevenson—any one of them is in danger. Of course, I can't even imagine how I will explain this. It barely makes sense to me. All that about the System and MIND, or the codes and passwords and people being killed—it feels straight out of a porto series. This isn't life. This sort of thing doesn't happen to people like me. It simply doesn't happen. I reach for my forehead and feel the scar just along the hairline and think that maybe it already has.

"You must have done something really bad to be sent home," Weston says.

"Don't act like you haven't already been briefed," I say.

As Paul's right-hand man, Weston must know everything that goes on. And given how shameless people are in guarding these secrets, I can't exactly trust Weston to be honest with me, even with what I already know. He plays the meathead crony on cue and the obedient chauffer when duty calls. But for now he sheds both. His grimace fades into a cunning smile as he watches the road.

"Do you think Paul would have let me go otherwise?" I ask.

"Honestly," he says. He glances at me from the corner of his eye "I don't know."

Before long, we're among the factories and warehouses of old north Jersey, a ring of industry that feeds and guards System City. The city itself appears like a nostalgic graveyard, both beautiful and morbid, just on the other side of that dark river. Weston takes us into the Lincoln Tunnel along with all the trucks that run supplies and food into the city. We are a single sedan among big rigs and vans. Very few people venture out of the city, so few that we're a rare sight to these truck drivers. Nevertheless, they're too tired or apathetic to bother with us. After inching along for some time, we reach the other side of the tunnel where a customs officer scans onboard portos for cargo reports. The officer looks down from his window with a curious squint. A toll charge appears on our onboard porto and the officer waves us on.

"Where to?" Weston asks.

"Where did Paul tell you to leave me?" I ask, taking a jab at his obedience.

He smirks again and sighs. "Where I found you."

We pull up to the curb by Madison Square Park. Weston cranes his neck to survey the street around the car. People shuffle along the sidewalk. Dogs bark on the end of leashes. Kids carelessly run around in the dead grass. Some people are headed home late from work. Couples stroll to dinner. I recognize none of them but I feel at home among the bustle and noise.

"Take it easy," Weston says. "And be careful."

"You really worried about me?" I ask him, somewhat playful.

"Just watch yourself," he says.

Before I close the door, I say, "Paul got you picking anything up while you're in town? I can point you in the direction."

Weston shoots me a snide look and says, "Shut the door."

I do and the car jerks into traffic. When Weston is gone, I take a deep breath, try to pull all the exhaust and food smells into my lungs. It's pungent and disgusting and all so beautifully familiar, a bittersweet respite to the colony's sulfuric odor. I think of Renee's commentary about the colony smelling like farts all the time. I might miss her but for now I'm overcome with relief to be back.

I pull out my porto to check the time, when I see that I have a message. I didn't hear it chime. The porto screen awakens to the notification—a message from Paul. It reads, "I have transferred credit to you. Stay safe. There is always a place here for you."

Sure enough, when I check my cred, I have 500, which I can certainly use. And yet I suddenly want to hurl my porto into the fountain to get away from Paul. If it's that easy for him to reach me, I don't want this stupid thing. I don't want to be found.

I step into the park and try to forget the colony for a while but the contrast from where I was and where I am is too harsh to ignore. The trees around the park seem so hardened and gnarly, probably from having to endure a city that chokes out the light. The sound of their rustling leaves has been replaced with horns, construction noise, and people arguing somewhere nearby. Being here feels new again, almost unfamiliar now that I'm an outsider. But I recognize it all. I want to say to the city, *You haven't aged a day. Let's catch up sometime.*

(You must know what I'm talking about here, the city being an old friend, albeit a mooch and a thief. If you've spent your life in System City, you understand how it has its own way of thinking and acting. Sometimes the city has a carefree swagger, not really concerned about whether you sleep, whether you eat or starve or live or die. It'll casually kill you. It'll take your cred and hit you up for more tomorrow. Sometimes it treats you to a beautiful sunset across the Hudson or offers a clean breeze over the deadened grass in Central Park. You learn to obey its forces and take everything you can when it lets you. System City is everyone's mother. I'm not sure what I'm trying to say here but that I think you have to have a relationship with the city to really understand it, to see its beauty, and to forgive it for being so damn hard on you sometimes. You don't get that outside the city.

I remember once at the junk market I saw an advertisement in a magazine—which is something people used to read back in the day. Sort of a throwaway book but shorter. Lots of crap, really. Anyway, this ad was for one of those national parks. You know, how the government apparently used to maintain natural areas like they had all the cred in the world. It's hard to believe, I know. But there was this advertisement for Yosemite National Park, which I hear was all the way in the western territories. Nowhere you or I will ever see.

Anyway, this ad said something like, "Be one with the wild," which I jokingly took to mean that you go there and get lost until you die and become fertilizer for the trees. But I sort of get it now. Only, I don't think that you actually can be one with the wild, not like you can with the city. I've tasted what it's like to be in the wilderness. Everything is alive and moving. It doesn't want you there and you're sure as heck never going to get to know it, let alone be one with it. Not like how you can buddy up to the city. Buildings, bridges, power lines, trains. These things are all dead, and they need you and I to bring them life.

Maybe that's what it is. It's not the city so much as it's the people. No people in the woods. Just trees, dirt, and hungry animals. In the city, you know each other, and more than in the way that the System provides. That shoeshine kid on East 93rd. He plays mandolin sometimes in old Times Square. Or look at the lady downtown who wants to hug everybody, keeps stopping people by name. "Want you a hug, Oliver? Come on over here for a hug, Kelly. You too, Laurel." She's apparently a beekeeper. You wouldn't know it. Just another crazy. But she has one of those rooftop hives somewhere in Chelsea. Hugs and honey is her thing, I guess. But you wouldn't know all that unless you lived here. I don't know if it's the people or the place but I think it's both. I guess I didn't know it until I left. And then it was like leaving part of me behind.

Anyway, I just have to hope you know what I mean. Because I sometimes think I can make it on my own. But other times I'm so desperate for somebody else that I don't know what else to do. That's how I feel when Weston drops me off at the curb.)

I've been back all but a minute and here I am saying, "Porto. New message. Stephon Hayden." His face appears on the screen and I barely recognize him. But not because I'm off the System.

You know how the System wants you to update your photo every three months. Most people ignore those messages, right? You might go six or nine months without updating it. Not

Step. He's funny that way. Kind of a rule follower about the most random things. He must have changed his picture while I was away because his hair is trimmed really short and his sideburns are gone. He looks completely different, not at all like himself. But I mean, it's him, for sure.

(I'm not talking about how it is now when you look at people. Before all that. But I'm getting to that part. Don't worry. That's why I'm telling you all this stuff, so you know what happened, so you know why you are who you are, or why people expect you to be somebody you're not.)

Anyway, you won't remember Step's face. I'm surprised that I do. He had scraggily curls, patchy facial hair, those dark sideburns that crept down his jaw. I remember it vividly, his face, the way I saw it just before I left. I never realized how clear a memory can be.

I tell him that I want to meet up.

He pings back, "Sure. Got stuff going on now. Meet up at Ziggy's tonight?"

I write back, "Ok." It's like I never left.

**

The bouncer at Ziggy's—an older Hayden whose name I don't remember, of course—says, "Haddy, where've you been?"

"Nowhere," I say, a little distracted. I'm staring at the curb where I stood when a strange man asked me to drive his car to Brooklyn. I suppose this is where it really began.

The bouncer opens the door to Ziggy's and a throng of noise rushes at me. I pull out my porto to pay but he waves me along for free. Inside, the place is packed. People squish toward the stage, where a death metal band called Fleshy Giftwrap shredding on their instruments like children having tantrums. My ears need to adjust. Lights flicker and a haze of tribal smoke

184

lingers above the crowd. I weave and push my way toward the left of the stage to find Step in his usual spot in front of a tower of speakers. Just like in his picture, his hair is cut short and he's styled it with a neat part to one side. Beside him is another member of his band who has a very similar style of haircut. They're both dressed in the same fashion, tight vests over cotton button-up shirts. It must be a new look for their band, a cleaner image. They seem more mature, or maybe I've been gone so long I just feel unknowing and inferior.

As I approach them, I can feel the music sway my hair with the beat of the bass drum. A fuzz of noise burrows into my ears like a drill. Step doesn't see me until I'm right next to him. I lay a hand on his shoulder. He looks at my hand before he sees that it's mine. I'm about to comment on his attire because he looks good, unexpectedly so. Maybe because I haven't seen him in so long or because I hurt so badly when we last saw each other, or because I'm just so tired of having to adapt and I need to be held, instead of saying anything stupid or snarky, I just hug him. We pull each other into an embrace, and I push my face into his shoulder. It feels so good to be held that I almost start to cry. Even through the scent of new hair oil that I don't know, I can smell him. I don't want to let go. I'm home.

We listen through this band and then his band goes on. At some point in their set, Cammy finds me in the crowd. I can barely hear what's she saying but she seems angry. She gestures for us to step outside and practically pushes me out.

We get to the sidewalk and Cammy's already shouting, "Where the hell have you been?"

"That's what I asked," says the bouncer.

"Shut up, Randall," Cammy says. "Haddy, seriously. I heard you were dead. Like for real this time."

In the streetlamp light, I can see Cammy's outfit, a charcoal gray pant suit with an orange top peeking out. She obviously didn't have time after work to change before coming here. Her hair is up in a way that hides the bleached strands. Shiny, ornate earrings dangle above a starched, clean collar. She carries herself stiffly when dressed this way.

"It's a real long story," I say, not sure if I want to talk about it now.

"Have you been back to Hayden House?" she asks.

"No," I say. "I've just been sort of lying low."

"Dammit, Haddy," she says, and punches me in the arm. "I thought you went down with Inman."

"Shame," says Randall, still listening. Cammy shoots him a look.

"Inman?" I say, because I can't remember him.

"Are you serious?" she says. "I guess you didn't roll with him. He has that snake tattoo up his leg."

"You know," says the bouncer. "The snake looks like it ate a piano or something."

I actually do remember the snake and the piano, and I'm sort of proud of myself. I remember the kid, too. Not how he looks but that he drew a piano on the wall in the Junction. He's the piano kid. That's what I called him, anyway. I once asked him if he could play, and he said something like, "What do I look like, Beethoven?" But the way he said it, *Beeth* rhymed with *teeth*, and *oven* was like the appliance. I remember laughing at him.

"What happened?" I ask Cammy.

"He got mauled by some dogs," she says. "Apparently he got lost in this house he'd been sent to break into and ended up in a room with these fighting dogs."

"What do you mean he was sent to break into a house?" Inman was just a kid.

"You know what I mean," she says. "Somebody paid him to bust into some house. Probably had something specific in mind like jewelry or whatever. You know how it goes."

"Is he alright?"

Cammy's eyes narrow with annoyance. "No. Of course not. You know that."

I suppose I would if I was on the System.

"Look," I say. I pull Cammy away from the bouncer to talk more intimately. "Remember how I got in that accident?"

"Yeah," she says. "Why do you think I'm so worried. Haydens are dropping like flies lately."

I tap my temple and say, "I'm not—"

She doesn't get it at first, but then her face sags a little. She steps away almost like I have something contagious and she doesn't want it.

"Oh, man. Damn," she says. "Oh no. Seriously? I'm so sorry, kid." She reaches for me but then pulls away, like she can't think of how to act. "So, like, you're totally Fried?"

When I don't respond, it's probably because I feel like I might start sobbing if I have to explain it. She sees this and takes me in her arms.

"Dammit, Haddy," she says.

It feels good that another Hayden knows, and I wonder why I've been so embarrassed to tell them. "I don't know anyone," I say.

Cammy takes my hands in hers. Her nails are polished and manicured. She looks me over like there must be some physical sign that I'm Fried.

"It's weird," I say, trying not to blow it out of proportion for her. She can't possibly understand and I don't feel like trying.

"Dammit," she says again, and smooths a hand over my cheek.

"It's okay," I say. "I'm okay."

"Yeah," she says, still in awe. "You're okay now."

"I am," I say. "But Inman. Have there been others?"

"A few," she says. "Too many, actually. Last night some Brooklyn Hayden ended up in the river. Word is he was just messing around and fell in. Kid couldn't swim. But who knows what really happened."

I think about what Agent Stevenson said, that we're all in danger. I don't want to get into where I've been or what I know. Something tells me that Cammy knows enough about MIND and the System to suspect something. She's smart. She's been around. So, I simply say, "I think we're in danger."

Cammy snickers and says. "No foolin'." The worry on her face has already faded and now she's back to her normal cynical self.

"Cammy," I say. "Has anyone been hurt recently? Is anyone else Fried like me?"

"Probably," she says. "But it's not like people make that known." She gestures to me as an example and then straightens the cuffs of her suit jacket. It kills me that even with her fairly normal life—which is a success by Hayden standards—she's still preoccupied with our plight. "We got kids getting banged up all the time," she says. "Nothing new. GCs coming down on us. Police don't exactly handle us with kid gloves, either. Sure, a Hayden will take a blow or two to the head. Some end up in the hospital, if they're lucky enough to get any care at all. You know all this though, Haddy. Why are you asking?"

I have nothing to say to this. It was a stupid question, and I realize that it shouldn't take Paul or some OSU agent to tell me that Haydens are in danger. Cammy's right. The reality for Haydens isn't that there's suddenly a threat. There has always been a million threats. Danger has existed for far longer than I've been around. Nobody seems to know this more than Cammy.

"Look," Cammy says. "I just got freaked out. I'm glad you're back. Don't worry about anything. It's just been a little nutty lately."

The resignation in her voice saddens me. Here's a woman who came from nothing, left for dead just like any other

Hayden. She came up on the streets, got out of the Junction, and made a new life. She's self-sufficient, makes a decent income, and hasn't had to hustle in years. And, yet, that doesn't make her any safer, as long as every GC can look at her and know exactly what she is. The threat on Haydens is as permanent as our names. We can all wear suits and drive fancy cars but as long as our last name is Hayden, we're nothing but moving targets. Nothing I can do will change this. I just have to stop thinking about it. Forget about Paul and the other Fried people at the colony, and forget about the fact that every few hours another Hayden will be dead as long as the System updates.

"You ladies alright?" Randall asks. "Had yourselves a little pow-wow over there."

We're not alright. I want to tell him that but he already knows. He's not alright. I'm not alright. Not even a woman like Cammy is safe, not with her one-room apartment in Queens or her job or her other, completely non-Hayden life.

"Come on," Cammy says, and reaches for my hand to lead me back into Ziggy's. She ignores Randall as she opens the door for herself. "I'm sorry I scared you like that, Haddy," she says. "We're fine. Come on."

She sounds no more convinced than I am.

CHAPTER TWENTY
MARBLES

There's a parking garage in Hell's Kitchen that, for longer than anyone can remember, has doubled as a junk market. On the weekends, dealers from all over the city appear with knickknacks and primitives from decades past. Along the walls of these chilly concrete parking decks, dealers set up booths that might resemble somebody's basement with shelves billowing with salt-and-pepper shakers, New Year's noise makers, old advertisements cut from magazines, things you wouldn't believe existed at one time or another. They have actual paper books and tattered pamphlets of every subject from crazy religious doomsday scripture to what types of fertilizers are best for what crops (this from a time when the average person grew things on their own property, when they *had* their own property). There are parts to old combustion engines, when cars actually ran on gasoline, and you can still smell the oil and grease. If you're missing a serving dish (if that's the sort of thing you have the luxury to worry about) you might just find it among the various incomplete patterns in Yari's booth. If you want interesting and cheap costume jewelry (like one Hayden often wears but as ironic mismatched earrings) there's a booth dripping with gaudy necklaces and hoop earrings and rings adorned with knobby stones. Eli the Electronic Guy has old cellular phones and laptop computers, these gargantuan machines that people would drape over their laps. He sells them as collector's items and gag gifts to enthusiasts of fossil technology. Another booth on the lowest level, in the darkest corner, has nothing but Christmas and Halloween items. One side of the booth is orange and black, while the other is green and red. A creepy plastic Santa Claus—its paint chipping and faux-hair beard gnarled with dust and grit—stares back at a rusty die-cut tin of a snarling black cat that hangs on the opposite shelf.

In full swing, the market is alive with sounds of bartering and haggling. Patrons like Step and I mill about, ogling more than buying. I like to hold things and imagine how people in the past used them, like this plastic toy in Eli's booth. He calls it a mouse, maybe because it has a cord running from it like a tail. He says it used to be part of a computer, for pointing at things on the screen. I hold the mouse thingy up to an old computer monitor, drag it across the lifeless screen, and he shakes his head and laughs. I ask if I'm using it correctly, and he says he has no idea.

The market is where Step and I can peer through a window into the past, images that stay with me for hours and days. My eyes close at night and I suddenly see a blur of colors—the pastels of Easter decorations, the faded primary colors of old wooden children's toys, the earthy tones of rust and soot on primitive hand tools—like a mosaic plastered across my mind. I'm able to see each item, especially the ones I've held, so clearly. Traces of history stay with me until the next time Step and I visit, and I'm introduced to more wonderful treasures.

This is how I spend my days, rediscovering the city with Step, observing everything I've always known but through a new lens. We walk the same streets we have so many times before, but it feels like I'm in somebody else's body, living their life.

(I guess you can say I haven't been myself for a long time. It isn't all that bad. You get used to it.)

I start to see the city differently, maybe because I've experienced the world outside and now I know why I love it here so much. I'm thankful for the honking car horns, people cussing, and stray cats hissing as we pass.

My first morning back, Step and I sit in the park and watch people hurry past to get somewhere faster than they probably need. We listen to birds chirping, children playing in a nearby playground, dogs barking at pigeons. In the afternoon, we watch the sun gather off high-rise windows and shine over a courtyard downtown, so much that people can be found sunbathing on steps under refracted light. In the evening, a Hayden who works as a custodian at an upscale fitness club lets us into the pool. I sit by the shallow end with the Jacuzzi jets blowing against me while Step playfully follows a serious swimmer as he does laps. Every time the swimmer kicks off the wall to turn around, Step darts beneath him against the bottom of the pool and waves up at him, until the swimmer finally quits, clearing the pool for Step and me to splash around like idiots.

And, of course, we have to survive. So we go back to hustling. We try squeegeeing car windows at traffic lights. We wash windows on houses again. Sometimes we go our separate ways for the day. Step gets on a tree-trimming crew up in Morningside. I get back on Imp's radar for deliveries, and he hooks me up with another guy named Morris in Queens, who I remember for his obsession with marbles. He sucks on one in his mouth like it's a hard candy. Morris's delivery region is more difficult to navigate without a car, so he gives me half a dozen packages along the rail line, and I only have to hump the parcels two or three blocks off the line. I use a backpack I made with straps sewn onto a tarp. It's big and awkward but it keeps the rain from getting at the packages.

Step and I don't make much but we cobble together an income. It's not enough to dream of having an apartment, not even on Staten Island, but we're still really young. Step has the idea that we might start our own food cart, serve up something simple like hot dogs or sausage. Only, he sees it as a front to sell tribal tobacco. I'm not opposed to the idea but I know that if we can even get it started, it won't last long unless we wear masks. Nobody's going to buy a hot dog from a Hayden. Other Haydens have tried similar operations with fleeting success. People expect the worst from us. They'll buy our tobacco, let us clean their toilets, and do odd labor. But, according to them, we need to know our place at the bottom. Nevertheless, we keep trying to make it, keep hustling. We have to. Only, now Step and I are doing it together.

I guess you can say that when I left, we each realized that, separately, we couldn't cope the way we do together. We just need each other to lean on. Isn't that how family's work? It sounds stupid but it seems to make sense to us. And before you go thinking there's more to it, stop right there. We've never hooked up. Friends are convinced we have. But I don't think it's really crossed our minds. He's my brother.

Anyway, before long, Step and I make a place of our own down the east tunnel from the Junction. While I was gone, Step foraged a bundle of scrap wood that was used on scaffolding at a construction site uptown. He bummed nails and a hammer from a friend and built a small lean-to with enough room for sleeping pads, a make-shift stove, and a storage nook. I can't help but think that it's not much smaller than Cammy's apartment, and her rent is at least two thousand cred a month, which she splits with a florist who runs a shop in Harlem. We have this space to ourselves and it's relatively safe. Mostly, I like that I have a home to come back to. I don't feel like I have to search for a place to lay my head at night.

For weeks we bust ourselves with work. Step gets more tree trimming jobs. He runs tobacco at night sometimes. Imp starts sending me into Queens more often because Morris needs help with deliveries. I don't mind. Morris pays about as much as Imp, if the packages are big enough. I aggravate passengers on the train with my sack of parcels but I guess they're already aggravated to see a Hayden. I let it roll off my back. It's amusing, actually.

Probably the only problem with this delivery job is that I'm Fried. So when I'm greeted at somebody's door, I don't know if I'm talking to the recipient of the package or just some person who happens to live in the same apartment. Most of the time, I just assume that it's them and say, "Mr. Lafferty, sign here," and have him sign my porto, which has a dummy signature pad, because Morris won't give me a company porto. Morris later forges the signatures on his porto for company records.

Morris also puts up with me cutting corners. And I have to if I'm going to make time. Trains don't always run so consistent out there. Sometimes I leave a package on a doorstep instead of waiting for somebody to answer the door. We're not supposed to leave a package in the open or even in a hallway, in case somebody steals it, which happens a lot if no cameras are around. I can't just toss the package back in a truck, so I leave them to lighten my load. If somebody complains, Morris can dock my pay.

Then one day I have some packages for a crummy area just south of Jackson Heights before you get to where the old stadiums used to be. If you've never been out there, a lot of the houses throughout the area are old and dilapidated but somehow survived much of the development that occurred north of the tracks. Many of these homes have two or more families in them, especially if they have a basement. I have three packages to deliver and I'd like to get back to the Junction before dark. One of the packages is a heavy plastic tube that's easy enough to carry in one hand. It takes me to a narrow house with cracked and faded vinyl siding, and surrounded by a short chain-link fence. The name on the tube is "Arthur Lowell."

There's a sign on the front porch railing that warns of a guard dog that probably doesn't exist. I knock on the outside storm door and it creeks open off its latch. I'm about to leave the tube when a man opens the door. He's in a beat-up robe and a t-shirt. His hair is thin and scraggily.

He doesn't say anything but reaches for the tube. I guess I don't care whether this guy is Arthur Lowell but he looks at the label and calls to the dark room behind him, "Pa!" He shares a brief glance like his *Pa* must be slow, and then sizes up the tube, puts it to his ear and shakes it.

A heavy smell of rice comes from inside the house. Somebody in there says, "Is that my goddamn tripod?" He's an old man. This must be Pa. He glances over the younger man's shoulder and says, "Who let the goddam Hayden on our stoop?"

The younger man looks at me and shrugs. He looks over his shoulder and says, "You have to sign for it, Pa."

Then the older man, says, "This dirty Hayden has to get off my property." He looks at me. "You hear that, Hadley. Get lost."

They both shoot me the same narrow glare while Pa signs my porto. On my way out of the gate, I check my porto to see that the next closest delivery is six blocks away. Only, I don't make it as far as the street before the younger man in the robe stops me.

"Hadley," he says.

"What?"

"Hadley Hayden?"

"Yes," I say, not in the mood for a confrontation. "What do you want?"

He doesn't say anything at first, just stares at me like I might know what he's thinking.

"You dumb or something?" I say.

"You've been to the colony," he says.

I'm not sure if I'm rattled more by a mention of the

colony or by the sudden crazed and tired look in his eyes. "I don't know what you're talking about," I say, and try to move on.

"Yes, you do," he says. "Trevor told me about you."

"Trevor who?" I play dumb.

He sighs. "Listen," he says. "Because of you, I got bumped."

I shake my head like I don't know but I'm sure he's the one who left the night I arrived.

"I'm Owen," he says. "Mr. Owen. Surely you heard people talking."

I put up my hands to show I'm not a threat. "I didn't know, man," I say, backing away. "That's all in the past."

"I wanted out," he says. "You understand?"

"Great," I say, sarcastically, and I keep backing down the sidewalk.

"I just didn't know it then," he calls to me.

"Sounds good," I say, turning to leave.

"Who bumped you?" he says. "Why you back so soon?"

I don't know why I stop. Paul sent me back with a purpose. But maybe it's the idea that somebody did replace me, another unfortunate person gone Fried. I turn to see that Mr. Owen has stepped out of his gate. "Maybe I wanted out, too," I say.

"You learned quick," he says, and flashes a sad smile. "Anyway, I should say thanks."

He turns to go back inside and I stop him. "Wait," I say. "Are we in danger?"

Mr. Owen looks up at the sky for second. He adjusts his robe and turns to me.

"I mean, you know," I say. "Since you've been back—"

"That," he says, and points to the porto in my hand.

I hold up my porto. "Yeah."

"Hope you wiped that clean," he says.

I look at my porto and back to him. He's already to his front steps. "Wait," I say.

"You don't want them to come after you and finish the job," he calls back, now opening his door.

"Wait," I say. "What do you mean, 'wiped clean'?" I rush back to the gate. "Please, wait."

He stops and looks back. "If you haven't done it, then he's probably tracking you right now."

"Who? Paul?"

"Who else?" he says. He scouts the street each way as if suspicious of his neighbors. "You might want to talk to some of the others. There's a Fried support group, you know. A few of them have been to the colony. Some real dark stories there."

I come to the bottom of his stoop, ready to listen.

"I was real angry when I first came back," he says. "Had it out for Paul and for anyone tied to him, especially that Weston. Figured I'd find him back here one time. Almost plotted some stupid rendezvous to ambush him." Mr. Owen chuckles to himself. "Anyway, I just had to let it go." He scratches his chest and his robe parts a little to reveal a deep scar burrowed through his chest hair. "You know, for a second there, I thought they sent you after me. Thought that was the end."

"You mean MIND?" I ask.

"I mean Paul," he says. "I mean, whoever's going to do it." I can see that he has just realized something. He steps closer. "I gotta know," he says in a more hushed voice. "How'd they get a hold of your porto? Did they confiscate it like they did Renee's? Said she was making contact with folks back in the city. Or did they steal it one night like they did Pete's, just snuck in your bunker and nabbed it?" He emits a creepy, low chuckle. "Or maybe they did to yours what they did to mine and a few others, and *accidentally* smashed the damned thing."

"I don't know," I say, because I can't believe him. He's crazy.

"You do," he says, backing up the stoop. "Get that porto wiped." He ties his robe again and opens his door. He looks back at me and lets out a raspy chortle.

I'm far too stunned to speak. I'm already replaying that night in my head—Thomas and his friends, my smashed porto.

When I look up again, Mr. Owen is already inside and the storm door is hissing closed. "Get it wiped, kid," he says, and then he slams the door between us.

CHAPTER TWENTY-ONE
MANTEL CLOCK

Dimitri's is about as fancy as we get. The restaurant is small and posh, but not too uppity, and it has a reputation for having survived the South Street Seaport floods, even though some people contend that it wasn't even around when the water rose. Step and I came here once a long time ago when a Hayden was a hostess and let us in. We didn't get past the water and free bread before we were driven out by angry patrons that demanded we leave. This time we come prepared after splurging on new outfits, hoping that we can play the role of normal people. Step has his vest and a fresh white button-up shirt tucked into brown trousers, and he had some kid shine his shoes. I got a new dress—well, new to me—from the thrift store and sweater for over my shoulders. Another Hayden named Summer cut my hair. She wanted to give me bangs but I refused. (Which reminds me—I should update my System pic, if we're still going to bother with that anymore.)

We have a reservation, which Step put under the name Harrison Gibb, a coworker of his on the tree-trimming crew. He even had to use Gibb's porto to make the reservation, or else they would have known it was Step. Of course, this doesn't make our dinner a sure thing.

"You're not Harrison Gibb," the host says.

"Yes," Step says. "I know this. He couldn't make it." Step subtly places his porto on the host's station and slides it toward the host. The screen reads, "Send credit to Edwin Baumgartner: 20."

The host's lips tighten and he glances across the dining room, presumably scouting the tolerance level of the other diners who will, no doubt, recognize us as Haydens. "50," he says. "But I can't guarantee that service will be...optimal."

The host places his own porto onto the counter and bumps it against Step's to receive the credit. He grabs two menus and says, "Right this way."

To my surprise, we aren't seated at the worst table in the place. We get a table not far from a window, but still in the middle of a few other parties. There's a well-to-do family of four with two grown children to my right and a middle-aged couple to my left. Step pushes in my chair and we settle for a moment in our seats, waiting for the sideways glances to begin once people see our faces. My hope is that our new outfits will allow the immediate neighbors to tolerate our presence for a meal. Our waiter, a boy probably not much older than us, provides the first reaction.

"Evening," he mutters, nervously. His hand is shaky as he pours our waters. Then he tells us tonight's specials through a hushed, unconfident voice. He tries to be charming through his unsettled nerves.

"It's okay, man," Step says. "We're not going to dine and dash, if that's what you're worried about."

"Of course." The waiter blurts a sad chuckle and says, "I'll leave you to your menus," which appear on our portos. As he walks away, his eyes scan the other tables to make sure nobody is uncomfortable with our presence.

Step and I know it isn't a crime for us to be here but the social order dictates otherwise. Looking around the room, I expect to see faces of scorn but instead everybody's faces are illuminated by their portos. If they're not looking at the menu, they're busy messaging with somebody or playing games or doing whatever they're doing while their food gets cold on the table before them.

At the table next to us, each member of the family of four has his or her porto in hand. The parents, probably in their sixties or seventies chuckle and show their portos to each other before busying themselves again. The son and daughter, probably in their twenties or thirties, are engulfed in their own devices. The son looks like he might be watching a series show or a movie. He's so entranced.

Step has finished looking at the menu and starts swiping around on his porto like everyone else. I can tell he's getting into whatever he's typing with this thumbs.

"Let's not do that," I say.

"Sure," Step says. "Sorry. It's lame." He puts his porto down but it buzzes. He knows so many people, it's always buzzing. He peers at the screen. "Romeo, the idiot," he says and smiles. He's about to reply when he sees my scowl. "You're right."

He pulls it back under the table, about to slide it in his pocket, when I say, "No, let's leave them out on the table. We can police each other. You know, so we're not tempted to sneak a look."

"I don't do that," he says with a coy smirk.

"The hell you don't," I say. "I do it, too, all the time."

"Maybe I do," he says. His porto buzzes again. He looks at it. "Stupid Romeo."

"Then put it on the table," I say. "But no touching."

"Is this a challenge?"

"Yeah," I say. "Leave it right here." I sweep aside the fake candle and place a finger on the table cloth. I pull out my own porto and place it facedown.

"Accepted," he says, and he places his facedown beside mine.

We sit for a moment, staring at each other like the other

might snatch their porto and start diddling with it. After a moment, the nervous waiter returns for our orders. Step asks for a plate of grilled vegetables and a cheese plate with fruit. He doesn't judge me when I order a seafood bowl.

The waiter leaves and Step smiles from across the table. "Look at us all fancy," he says.

"I really like this," I say, even if I don't feel completely comfortable getting all gussied up.

"Yeah," he says, with a stifled laugh. "But it's a little weird, right?"

"Completely," I say.

And we both laugh.

It seemed like a good idea when we came up with it. A way to celebrate life and our new beginning. We've been working a lot and doing okay. So, why not treat ourselves?

"I feel like we're on a date," I say.

"We probably screwed that up a little," he says. "Sorry." He nods to the family next to us. "Should have shot a little more for the family outing," and then he nods to the couple to the other side, "rather than the romantic evening."

We both look to the couple beside us as we laugh. They hear us and glance our way. They're immediately horrified by us and look away in discomfort, which only makes us laugh harder.

Our food arrives and it smells perfect.

"Look at that," Step says, commenting on my seafood bowl. "Lots of goodness in there."

"Oh," I say, calling his bluff. I spear a scallop and bring it close to his face. "You wanna try some?"

His eyes widen with alarm and he pushes my hand away. Despite the small portion, he seems delighted by his meal. He grabs his fork and knife and is about to dig in, when he sees me drape my napkin over my lap. He does the same with a sheepish smirk. Without hesitation, he cuts a stalk of asparagus and devours both halves in two quick bites.

"Don't choke," I say.

His porto buzzes and he almost reaches for it, when I go to swat his hand away.

"Fine," he says, and takes another massive bite of food. Through a mouthful of zucchini, he says, "Probably Romeo again," but I can hardly understand him.

We quietly eat for a moment, occasionally smiling to each other across the table.

"Yours any—?" he says, and coughs. He clears his throat and says, "Is it good?"

"It's great," I say.

He coughs, grunts again to clear his throat, and takes a deep breath. Annoyed by something in his throat, he gulps down most of his water.

"Did they debone your squash?" I say.

His smile quickly turns to concern as he massages his throat with his hand. He puts up a finger to a passing waitress and mutters, "Restroom?"

The waitress grimaces and points.

"Should probably eat slower," I say.

Step flashes a strained smile before he gets up and scurries to the restroom. His eager strut to the bathroom has gotten the attention of the family beside us, and the daughter scolds me with her eyes.

I slink in my seat, break some of my baguette, and dip it the broth to busy myself. The daughter says something to her father, and now they're all staring at me. I try not to look at them, and instead glance out the window when I swear I see a black car drive away. But now I'm just nervous and uncomfortable, so I don't make a big deal of it.

I keep picking at my food and glancing to the restroom but Step doesn't come back. Suddenly, a commotion starts over by the host's station. A man points back toward the restroom, and soon people are whispering throughout the restaurant. I hear a few say, "Hayden," under their breath, and I immediately think that maybe Step got into a fight with somebody in the bathroom. Soon the manager is at my table.

"Your friend is having an episode in our restroom," he says, almost accusingly.

"What do you mean?" I ask.

The man who started this commotion says, "He's drunk. Your boyfriend's in the restroom all hopped up on something. I heard him gagging." The man still has a crab claw cracker in his hand like he's not willing to let some Hayden's problems ruin his dinner.

I look at Step's plate of grilled vegetables and wonder what could possibly give Step an allergic reaction.

"Is he okay?" I ask.

"We've already notified the authorities," says the manager.

"An ambulance," I say, more as an assertion.

The grimaces as if to say he wouldn't bother.

"The Hayden's drunk," says the crab claw cracker man.

"He's not," I say, and I get to my feet. "Let me see him."

I move toward the bathroom but the manager leans in my way. "I can't let you go in the men's room, ma'am. Maybe you and your friend better pay and leave," he says. "Otherwise, the authorities will be here to see that you will."

I try to move again but the manager puts up a hand. Behind him, a diner, probably a GC stands up in case the manager needs assistance.

The manager picks up our portos and hands them to me. "Just leave," he says.

I glance at our portos. Step's screen is lit and says, *New message*, the one he received a moment ago. But there's no specific sender.

The manager takes my arm and I pull away from his grip.

He escorts me to the door but I'm still looking at Step's porto. I know his password, so I enter it and swipe to the ping app.

The manager says, "Ma'am. Leave now."

I look up and past his stupid face to the restroom. There's a busboy in the doorway, looking concerned.

"Hadley," the manager says.

"Shut up," I say, and open the new message. It reads, "What does the Mantel Clock say?"

It's nonsense. And for some reason I recall the black car that recently pulled away from the curb and I rush to the sidewalk. The manager says something behind me.

A police car comes around the corner, and I head back into the restaurant. "Call an ambulance," I demand. "He's having an allergic reaction!"

I try to fight my way past the manager to the restroom but now a GC has entered the mix. I quickly ping for an ambulance on my porto. More sirens draw near and soon there's a dazzle of lights outside. The rest of the diners brace themselves for what's unfolding before them.

"Miss," says a cop, as he puts a hand on my arm.

I jerk around and first see his chest. He's a big man. A really big man. "Where's the ambulance?" I say, "Get an ambulance!"

"Miss," the cop says again. "You'll need to pay and leave now." He goes to put a hand on my arm again and I swat it away.

There's a gasp among the other diners. I try again to push my way to the restroom, where other officers have already gone. The big cop steps in my path with his hands out.

"Let me see my friend," I say.

"Pay your check," the cop says. The manager offers me his porto with the check on the screen. "Let's make this quiet," the cop says.

I take another step toward the restroom, but the cop

leans in my way. For a second, I consider what will happen if the ambulance that I pinged doesn't arrive in time. I can't lose Step. I won't let that happen. Another cop comes from the restroom and says, "This kid needs a wagon. He's not responding."

The big cop gives me a baleful glance, and then he talks into his watch. "Need a wagon down at Dimitri's off South Street." He listens to the squawk from his watch, then says, "Copy that." Looking at me, he says into his watch, "The kid's a Hayden."

His watch squawks back.

"Not responding," I say. "What's that mean?"

"An ambulance is on its way," he says. "Now, the check."

I look at the manager's porto with the check and then at the manager. Over the cop's shoulder, I see the other two officers near the restroom. Their expressions look grim and I think I hear one say that they're wasting their time. And then I glance back over to the restaurant entrance and I see Agent Stevenson coming in. My heart nearly stops. This is the end.

But there are too many people around for him to do anything to me or Step. Of course, I can't trust the cops to protect us. And I can't let him near Step. So I have to lead him away from here.

Diners demand their checks and begin to clear out. There's a moment of commotion as so many people try to leave at once, while waiters rush to appease their tables in hopes of rescuing their dwindling tips. Even the cooks are out from the kitchen. There has to be a backdoor off the kitchen, I think. I make sure to catch Agent Stevenson's attention, and then I take off before he gets any closer. He wrestles through the crowd after me.

"Hey!" the manager yells.

Cooks leap aside as I dart through the door and run into a large metal shelf, making stacks of dishes crash to the floor. I skirt around the shelves and a prep table and slam through the back door and into an alley. When I look back I can see Agent Stevenson burst into the kitchen. He sees me outside. The alley door closes between us.

I run toward South Street where cobblestone peeks from beneath the encroaching river. My dress shoes are immediately logged with flood water. I dash for a boarded-up shop across the way where Haydens have been known to bunk when the heats on them. There's a passageway on the second floor to the adjacent theater catwalks. The first boarded-up window is too tight. I can barely get my hand in. I try another to no avail. When I look back, Agent Stevenson is already coming out of the alley. The third window board moves and I struggle to squeeze my way in. There's no way he will fit. I'm almost through when I feel his hands get a hold of my leg. I scream. His hand slips along my bare leg and I keep kicking and shrieking. I can only hope that a Hayden is somewhere inside the shop or theater to hear me. But nobody appears.

"Hadley," Agent Stevenson growls. "You're not going to get away."

I must land a kick against his chest because I hear him grunt and cough and his grip loosens. A nail snags my dress and gouges my skin but I get through.

Once on my feet, I rush through the dark shop showroom, feeling my way around mattresses and heaps of blankets and old pizza boxes all wet and stinky with mold. I get to the back room where I find the stairs to the second floor. Agent Stevenson has the window board mostly pried away and is about to get through.

Up the stairs, I find more mattresses and rats. Rats and cockroaches everywhere. They scatter from my porto flashlight as I search the wall for the opening to the theater. I can now hear Agent Stevenson downstairs, so I shut off my porto light and feel along the damp brick wall for two small wooden doors. The first one is open to the patched brick wall behind it. The second is closed, and when I open it, a rat leaps at my feet and I gasp.

Agent Stevenson calls out, "You're wasting your time, Hadley,"

He comes stalking up the steps. So I quickly climb through the small door and into the theater catwalk. There's a hole in the roof, allowing moonlight to spill over my only escape route, a rusty walkway suspended over a flooded theater and a stage that has caved in. I try to close the wooden door behind me but it latches on the other side. I make my way down one end of the catwalk, only to find it ends abruptly where it has collapsed into twisted, rusty metal. I rush back along the catwalk, and Agent Stevenson peeks his head through the small doorway as I approach. He swipes for me as I pass but I dodge his reach.

I get to a dropdown staircase that has also partially collapsed above the stage. There's no other way out but to climb down the mangled staircase and wade through the watery graveyard of theater seats. The staircase becomes more like a mangled ladder as I slowly work my way down.

"Just stop running," Agent Stevenson says. He's at the top of the staircase now. I'm a few feet below him. I'm tired and cold. I don't know where my next footing will be, and he will likely get to me before I find it.

"What do you want with me?" I say, still feeling around the rusty metal.

"You're going to hurt yourself," he says. "Come back up."

Below me, the rotted boards of the stage floor disappear into a dark, watery pit. Who knows what else is down there.

"I know about you," I say. "Don't come any closer."

It feels like the rest of the staircase is gone, leaving a long drop to the collapsed stage below.

"Listen, Hadley," he says. "Let me help you back up."

If only there were Haydens here now. If only Step were around. I can't believe what's happening. I hope an ambulance has gotten to him in time. He needs to make it through this, even if I don't.

I try to reach my porto to ping the nearest Haydens but I can't keep my grip on the staircase at the same time.

"Hadley," he calls. "Come on."

"Who sent you?" I say.

"Nobody," he says. "I'm here for you." He crouches down on the catwalk and extends an arm toward me. "Come on."

"Go away," I say.

We stay like this for a moment. I secure a better grip on the staircase but my arms are getting tired.

"Suit yourself." Agent Stevenson pulls his hand back up and rolls onto his side like he's relaxing. He picks at a rusty part of the railing and lets flecks of paint flutter to the murky pool below. "Where's Reuben Mayfield?" he asks, casually.

It takes me a second to register the name as the GC that Nona and Cammy were talking about, the one who used to prey on Haydens back in the day.

"How am I supposed to know?" I say.

"You do," he says.

"I don't know him," I say. I adjust my grip. "Never did."

"You know him," Agent Stevenson says. "He sent you back here."

He must be kidding if he's talking about Paul.

"I've been looking for Mr. Mayfield for some time now," Agent Stevenson says. "He used to work for MIND. But you know that already, don't you?"

When my foot slips, I climb up a little to get better footing and give my arms a rest. "I really don't know him," I say.

"You know about him," he says. "You know why I want him." He sits up and rests against the railing directly above me.

"Of course, MIND has an eye on him too for their own reasons. And they won't let me know where he is."

"Paul warned me—" I say.

"Paul," Agent Stevenson says. "You mean Mayfield."

"He warned me about you," I say.

Agent Stevenson laughs to himself and leans over the railing to look at me. He's just above me and could easily spit in my eye. When I look up at him, he stops smiling. "I'm going to kill you, right?" he says. "Or maybe that man out there, the one who just poisoned your friend, the one who works for MIND...maybe *he's* going to kill you. Sounds like a lot of bad people want a crack at you. I know where I'd put my money."

I need to save Step but I'm worried I won't get out of here. I look down again at the stage and the mangled seats. The first two rows are fully submerged in water. I'll never survive the fall.

"Self-importance aside," he says. "You can't hang there all day."

"You said it yourself," I say. "I should be dead."

Agent Stevenson lets out an annoyed sigh. "They've moved on and so should you," he says. "Mayfield is plotting something, probably against his former employer. Otherwise they wouldn't have such an interest in him. I'd like to stop him before that happens."

"I don't know about any of that," I say.

"Why would you? You're just a Hayden." He reaches a hand down toward me. "But you can help me get him."

"How?" I say. "Why?"

"You know where he is," Agent Stevenson says. "You know what he's done."

"He saved my life," I say.

"And for what? What has he gained from you? What does he want from you now?" Agent Stevenson urges me to take his hand. If he wanted to kill me, he would have done so already.

That's what I have to tell myself, anyway.

I grab for his wrist and he slowly pulls me up. The rickety catwalk creaks against our collected weight. I grab the railing with my other hand and help myself as he pulls. Once I'm up, I quickly back away from him and step toward the small doorway to the shop next door.

"You still need him to save your friend, don't you?" Agent Stevenson says.

I don't answer and he doesn't need me to. I put one leg through the doorway to get away, when he says, "They're not going to save a Hayden. Not unless Mayfield pulls some strings like he did with you."

He knows as well as I do that Step is as good as dead, even if he gets to the hospital. Haydens have no priority in an emergency room. And as far as I'm concerned, if Step doesn't make it, I don't want to either.

"I know what Mayfield can do if he sees value in it." Agent Stevenson gets to his feet and brushes himself off but doesn't come any closer. "I also know what he's done to people that he doesn't value."

For a moment, neither of us speaks. Water drips somewhere in the hollow of the theater. A board squeaks against a broken door frame toward the lobby. I feel cool air rushing from the shop into the theater through the small doorway.

"I think you're wrong about Paul being Mayfield," I say.

"Either way, you're going to contact him," Agent Stevenson says. "And I'm going to be there the next time you meet him."

"Step's first," I say. "He's all I care about. Do whatever you want to Paul or Mayfield or whoever he is, but only after I get him to save Step."

"Fine," he says.

"I have no other choice but to trust you," I say.

211

"That's correct," he says. His face is almost sympathetic. "You have Step's porto, don't you?"

"I do," I say, and pull it from my sweater pocket.

"Good," he says. "Then I think I have a way for all of us to get what we want."

CHAPTER TWENTY-TWO
HAND DRILL

Agent Stevenson wants to follow me out to the colony but he suspects that Paul is monitoring my porto. So, instead of putting a tracker on my porto, he puts a tracker on Step's porto, which will also make its way to the colony with me. Paul will want to see it, even if MIND has already wiped Step's porto clean from the backend like they did with mine.

My plan is to save Step. Plain and simple. Whatever Agent Stevenson is looking for is secondary to my goal. Once I get to the colony, and assuming he follows me, we agree that whatever has to be done to ensure Step's safety will be complete before Agent Stevenson makes a move. After that, I don't care. I was already done with Paul and his colony. As far as I'm concerned, the man can rot for whatever he's done.

In exchange for giving him access to Step's porto, Agent Stevenson agrees to track down where authorities took him.

On my way to the hospital, I ping Paul and tell him that I have somebody for the colony. It makes me sick to think that Paul might be Mayfield, but I'm having trouble processing any of that right now.

He write's back, "Are you sure?"

I tell him to look up Stephon Hayden in the System. There he'll see an updated file on Step that lists him as deceased as of earlier tonight. For once I'm glad I'm not on the System to see that. Once I send Paul a photo of Step in the hospital, he'll see that MIND has jumped the gun like they did with me. He'll want Step alive and see that it happens, however he does it. In the meantime, he agrees to send Weston.

At the hospital, a security guard stops me before I can get into the emergency triage area. I know better than to say why I'm here, so I fake an emergency and act like I've swallowed poison and need immediate care.

"Stomach pump. Ammonia," I grunt, and I stumble past him like I might vomit. The guard gives no resistance.

Once in the triage area, I try the same charade with a nurse. She has her porto ready for in-take information. We get halfway through the questions, when I get my own story crossed. I still need to find out where they have Step, then figure out a way to get to him. I'm too stressed to lie correctly.

"You told the guard that you swallowed ammonia," the nurse says.

"Sure," I say, not realizing what this means. Step is somewhere beyond those double doors and they don't want to touch him because he's a Hayden. To them, he's not worth even basic medical attention. He's, as Paul says, *expendable.*

"And now you're saying you swallowed bleach," the nurse says.

"What's that?" I say.

"Which is it?" she says.

"I don't know," I say. "I need help."

She lowers her porto and gives me a hard glance. Her eyes search my outfit. My nice dress is now torn and dirty from crawling through that abandoned theater.

"What do you want?" she asks, frankly.

"Are you gonna help me?" I ask.

"What do you *really* want?"

I decide to let down my guard. "I'm here to see Stephon Hayden," I say. I hate saying his full name.

She doesn't even say no or look him up in their records.

She just points to the exit.

Outside, I pull Step's porto from my bag and wonder if there's any way I can use it to get inside. I need to see him and know that he's going to be okay. The last thing I saw on his screen was the message he received: "What does the Mantel Clock say?" There was no contact name that I can recall. This must be what Paul meant about MIND sending an odd message to trigger a response in a person's chip. Maybe Step was supposed to respond. But with what? I can't make sense of it but Paul might be able to do something with this information. Of course, whatever happens with Step, another Hayden is soon going to fall prey to the same type of message, and I doubt there's anything we can do about it.

From the hospital, I walk one block east, one north, then one east, then another north, then two blocks east, and so on. It doesn't matter where I end up because Weston will find me if Paul is tracking my porto.

I pull out my porto and ping Agent Stevenson, asking him to check on Step for me. After a few minutes without a reply, I tuck the porto back in my sweater pocket. I really need to get my mind right. If Paul has stuck to his word, the hospital should be tending to Step right now but I can't be sure. I don't know who to trust.

My random hike through Manhattan takes me to Grand Central. It's late but folks still flow from the terminal, making it a safe place for lonely Haydens like me. It also makes for good people watching, even if I can't place a single name to any of them. As I watch the confluence of so many solitary lives bunched together without mingling, I wonder what sense it makes to even be able to know who each other is if we won't actually interact. It makes me sad just thinking about it.

Above the crowd, a clean-shaven scalp fishes its way like a stray buoy through the other bobbing heads. As it gets closer, I see that it belongs to Weston. Below that shiny dome are bemused eyes. Weston's crooked mouth stays shut and he stops ten feet from me, as if he refuses to take one more step. With a sharp sweep of the arm, he gestures for me to follow him back to his car.

"I'm not very happy to see you either," I say.

"Yeah," he says, a curt edge to his voice. "I had to double back for you."

When we get into his car, the onboard porto chimes and the screen lights up. It reads, "New Links: Hadley Hayden, Stephon Hayden," detecting the portos in my pockets.

Weston's eyes widen and he shoots me a look

"What's that?" he says. "Do you have his porto?"

"Yeah," I say.

He shakes his head and grips the steering wheel in frustration. Through clenched teeth, he says, "Why?"

"It's okay," I say. "Paul wants me to bring it." Weston doesn't seem convinced, so I say, "They wouldn't let me see him in the hospital. I wasn't going to leave it at the front desk."

Weston licks his lips.

"Look," I say, and pull the portos from my pocket. "I got nothing to hide," as if this would prove anything.

Weston starts the car and gives a big huff before moving into traffic. A moment later, I catch him glancing over toward Step's porto like he wants to throw it out the window, and I wonder if he suspects that it's being tracked. I think about the first time Weston picked me up. Thomas had broken my porto. Did Paul somehow arrange that, as Mr. Owen suggests? It seems like an awfully strange coincidence. Maybe Mr. Owen had a right to be paranoid.

The drive back to the colony is quiet. Weston's classical music does little to settle the heavy breathing through his nose. While the landscape outside my window grows dark and barren the farther we get from the city, I can think only of Step lying alone in a hospital bed. Even with nurses and doctors and all the little lights and monitors, it's just about the loneliest place on earth.

We pull into the colony at about the same time as when I first came here. When I open the door, the sulfur stench grips me by the nostrils like it wants to shove me back into the car. A faint scent of campfire lingers nearby, and I wonder if the Good ol' Boys are still outside. It's a bit too late for them though.

Weston takes my arm and leads me to the game building where he has me sit at an iTable. "Paul will meet you here," he says, and he starts toward the door.

"Do I have to wait until morning?" I say.

"It is morning," he says without looking back.

"Well, do you at least have a change of clothes for me? I'm freezing."

He doesn't respond and walks out the door. I place the two portos on the iTable and it comes to life, casting a glow around the otherwise dark room. The iTable chimes and reads, "New Link: Hadley Hayden, Stephon Hayden." Seeing his name again makes me weak. I look away and consider pinging Agent Stevenson to see if he's still in the city or if he has left already to follow Step's porto.

The door opens and startles me. It's Weston again with a bundle of my clothes from before. He drops them on the iTable, where he sees our names. I can see him clench his jaw.

"Where am I supposed to change?" I ask, pointing to a camera in the corner of the room.

"Right here," he says, and he leaves.

I get up and slowly open the door to see where Weston is headed. He gets into the black car and drives away. I go back in, kick off my shoes, and slide a pair of pants on. Cameras be damned, I step into a dark corner and change out of the dress and into a sweatshirt and jacket. I grab the portos, go outside, and follow the smell of smoke to the campfire, but all the Good ol' Boys have gone to bed already. I make my way to where

Laars usually works on his murals. I can't help but wonder about the watchers again. And suddenly I can feel them. When I look up at the hills where the darkness rises into the night sky, I swear they are there. I can't see them but I know they are watching. I almost want to run out there and confront them, but I know it will do no good.

Laars isn't at his usual post, but a new mural stretches the length of the building. The scene is of a playground with all the slides and jungle gyms and swings a kid would want. On the swing set, four cartoony hand tools happily swing, smiling as they flip their middle fingers out toward the hills. It's a great scene now that I realize what Laars has been doing all this time. I turn around to face those hills, exactly where I suspect the watchers are lurking, and I cast my own middle fingers in their direction.

"Miss Hadley," Paul says from behind me.

I quickly tuck my offending fingers into my jacket pockets and turn to face Paul. I can't imagine this little man being the disgusting Reuben Mayfield, and I wonder if Agent Stevenson is just mistaken. Besides, Paul thinks that Agent Stevenson is working for MIND. It feels like anyone can be lying.

"I cannot say the same for our friends in the hills," he says. "But I for one am glad for your return."

"My friend Step," I say, cutting to the chase. "Will he be okay?"

"Ah, yes," he says. "Of course. Stephon will be taken care of."

"Are you sure he will be fine?"

Paul places a hand on my arm. "I assure you," he says. "The hospital has my full credit backing. I promise."

I could cry with relief. It seems like such a simple thing for Paul to do and yet it means the world to me. I think that he and Mayfield cannot possibly be one in the same.

"You're welcome," he says, reading my gratitude.

We start back toward the game building and he asks me how I've been, like we're two old friends catching up. From everything he tells me, the others at the colony are making great progress. I tell him about Step and me, and about all the hustling we've had to do but how it's been good to be back in the city. Paul seems genuinely pleased to hear that, the way a father might feel about hearing from his daughter.

"This Stephon," he says. "He is very important to you. I hope to meet him soon."

"Yes," I say, and I suddenly feel eager to bring Step to the colony. Then I remember. "I have his porto."

"Here?" Paul says. He seems surprised, even delighted. "You brought Stephon's porto with you?"

I pull it out of my jacket pocket and reluctantly hand it to him.

He looks it over and then asks, "How did you get this?"

"I was there when it happened," I say, and I can feel my voice beginning to quiver, thinking about what Step must have been going through.

Paul wakes the porto and stares at the lock screen. I take it and enter the password. Paul nods, thanking me, and takes the porto back. He tries to navigate through Step's apps, but there's nothing visible.

"They wiped it clean," I say. "They did the same to mine."

Paul seems to think this over, his face flickering between disappointment and intrigue. "Did he get a message?"

"He did," I say.

"Did he respond to it?"

"No," I say. "I didn't let him because we—" I can't finish the sentence. It's so difficult to imagine how carefree we were just a little while ago. And now Step's in a hospital, clinging to life.

"It is okay," Paul says. He has a hand on my shoulder but

he's still looking at Step's porto. "May I hang onto this until your friend arrives?"

He sees that I'm crying and he leans close. "Your friend will make it," he says. I want to believe him. "Miss Hadley," he says, lifting my chin with his hand. "You made it."

I nod in agreement because this makes me feel better. I made it and Step is much stronger than me.

Paul looks me in the eyes, his face filled with hope and compassion. I want to believe that he cares. I'm so grateful that he's willing to take care of Step, and it's difficult to connect him to Reuben Mayfield and the stories that Cammy told me. I want to believe that he is kind, that he couldn't possibly be the same disgusting man.

"Please," Paul says. "You must be tired. Come with me."

We start walking the gravel path and he gently takes my arm in his, maybe for his own stability.

"We kept your room the way you left it," he says.

I try to show my appreciation with a smile but gently pull my arm free to close my jacket around me. "It's chilly," I say.

"Of course it is," he says, placing a hand on my back. We both look into the darkness beyond the lit gravel path. "It gets cold out here in the wild."

CHAPTER TWENTY-THREE
HOT AIR BALLOON

I barely slept and now I hear Pete and Trevor outside my door. Soon Renee arrives to shoo them away. The two guys are whispering about me and speculating why I came back. Renee is telling them that nobody gives a damn. "Just be glad she's back," Renee says, "Now get moving." When Pete and Trevor finally leave, the door creaks as Renee leans into it to listen for me.

"I'm here, Renee," I say.

"Oh, hey, Hadley," Renee says, through the door. "Sorry to wake you."

"It's okay," I say, and I wait for her to move along. But her shadow stays at the door.

"Kiddo," she says. "You okay?"

I get up and open the door. Renee's hair used to be in tiny knots but is now puffed up in a thick afro. Along with her bright smile and zebra-print eyeglasses, I actually feel a little at home.

"You left so suddenly," she says, pulling me in for a hug.

"I had to go," I say, playing off of our kitchen humor. "I had left a roast in the oven."

She laughs and says, "What's the roast's name?"

"Giles," I say, and we both breakout laughing.

At breakfast, I get a nice welcome from most of the crew. TJ gives me a hug. Pete, Trevor, and Maurice sass me a little bit like three drunk uncles.

"Thought it was something I said," says Maurice.

Pete says, "Had I known you'd be back, I'd have asked you to bring me a hot dog."

"A dirty-water hot dog," Renee says, nearly revolted.

"I love those hot dogs," he says.

"You love all that garbage," Trevor says. "Dogs, burgers, pork rinds."

"Sure do," says Pete. He looks to me and says, "You didn't get in trouble there in the city, did you? They kick you out?"

"Remember," Trevor says. "She's still a Hayden." He looks to Maurice.

"That doesn't mean a thing here," Maurice says.

"Oh, damn," says Trevor. "Look who's gotten soft."

"Anyway," Pete says. "Welcome back." He takes a bite of scrambled eggs. "We hear you got a friend who might be coming."

"Come on," Renee says, scolding him. "You know that's not right."

"Well, it's true," Trevor says. Then to me he says, "Isn't it, kid?"

"Yeah," I say, not interested in talking about it. I don't want to cry again.

"What's his name?" Maurice asks.

"Step," I say.

"Step," Maurice says, cocking his head back. "What the hell kind of name is that?"

"It's a fine name," TJ says.

"You'd say that, wouldn't you, Timoteo?" Maurice says.

"Well," TJ says, deflecting Maurice's comment. "I'm sorry your friend is Fried, Haddy."

I'm about to say that Step isn't Fried, or at least he probably isn't. And that makes me wonder why Paul would want him here. So, I keep that to myself.

"Is Paul taking care of him?" Pete asks.

"If Step's coming here," Trevor says, "then Paul must be doing something."

They all nod knowingly. I look around to see that Paul is nowhere in sight, which is strange for breakfast time. He likes this time to build morale before getting everybody into memory exercises.

"How does he do it?" I ask, trying to shift the focus away from Step. "How does Paul pay for all of us? For all this?"

"Credit," Trevor says.

"He has lots of it," Maurice says.

"How?" I ask.

They all look at each other, wondering who's going to tell me.

"The guy's a genius," Renee says. "You know, like a real deal smartypants."

"Master programmer," Pete says. "Coder, developer, whatever they call themselves."

"Hell," Maurice says, leaning in close. "He makes his own damned credit. You know, that cryptocurrency stuff. He writes his own cred like he writes programs."

"Counterfeit," I say.

They all laugh.

"Sure," Trevor says. "Counterfeit, if that's what you want to call it. Not even the real money's real money. That's why they call it credit."

Weston comes in to the cafeteria and everyone's giggling goes quiet. He walks by our table on his way to the kitchen and, without making much of a scene or bothering with dramatics, he snaps his fingers at me and says, "Paul wants you in the game building in five minutes."

Everyone jeers like this is primary school and I just got called to the principal's office. When I get up to leave, they provide a slow clap that turns to a roaring applause I can hear even after the door closes behind me. There's still quite a chill in the late morning and frost clings to brush beyond the colony perimeter. Nothing stirs in the hills but for a few strands of mine smoke teased by the breeze.

When I get to the game building, all the lights are on but Paul isn't there. None of the iTables are awake. None of the projectors are going. There is no music. I linger for a moment, thinking Paul might be back any minute, but then I hear, "Back here," from a door toward the back of the room. It's a maroon metal door that I assumed was a supply closet until now. I approach it and say, "Paul?"

"Enter," he says.

The door clicks and I try the handle. It opens. Inside, I find a room about a third the size of the main game room, only it's dimly lit and there are porto screens lining a curved, half-circle desk. Paul sits in the center of the curved desk. He has a set of small tools and a few boxes of tiny electrical parts scattered about his work station. There's a strange, grungy type of rock music playing quietly from the corner. It feels like a security station. Only, none of the porto screens show images from around the colony. Instead, the screens are full of programming language that I don't understand.

"Sit down," Paul says. He doesn't look up from whatever he's working on but he nods to a chair inside the curve of the desk.

When I'm close to him, I see that he has Step's porto in his hands, and the back of it is opened. He's delicately working some tweezers. His face is serious as he concentrates. He has bags under his eyes like he hasn't slept.

"You wanted to see me?" I say.

"I *want* to see you," he says, his voice a little sharp.

"Is it about Step?"

"It is," he says.

I suddenly imagine that Step didn't make it and my heart nearly explodes with hurt. I start to say, "Is he—"

"Your friend," Paul says, and stops tinkering. He puts the porto on the desk and turns his chair to face me. "Does your friend know Agent Stevenson?"

I don't know what to say. Of course Step didn't know Agent Stevenson. But what has Paul found on Step's porto to make him ask this? Does he somehow know that Agent Stevenson is tracking it?

"I don't think they know each other," I say, it's not a lie if I don't know for sure. Then I decide to play into Paul's favor. "I'd have to guess that if Step ever met Agent Stevenson, Step would be dead."

Paul nods and bites his lip. He says, "Yes," and sighs, looking at the opened porto. "You said he received a message the night of the incident."

"Yes."

"Walk me through that night," he says.

"Is this a memory game?"

"Sure," he says. "What makes you think he was targeted?"

"I saw the man in gray," I say. "Well, his car. I think he was the same man who approached me the night of my crash."

Paul nods, not surprised, just affirming. "Tell me what happened."

"We were eating dinner," I say. I can already feel my mouth getting dry. My stomach tightens. "He seemed uncomfortable but I didn't exactly realize it right away. You see, Step has these allergies. He can't eat a lot of different foods. It makes for a tough time, especially as a Hayden."

"What did he eat?"

"Vegetables," I say. "Always vegetables. They were grilled. Probably had no more than salt and pepper, maybe some oil."

225

"Oil," he says.

"Yeah. You know. Cooking oil."

Paul nods. "You were eating," he says, allowing me to continue.

"Yeah, so, we were eating and Step ends up coughing a bit. He turns real red, almost like he's choking. Only he's not. He's breathing but still kind of coughing. He had to loosen his shirt collar."

"Was this when he got the message?"

"No," I say, hesitating. "Yes. I don't remember. We had our portos out on the table in front of us." I want to cry but the thought of us making such a silly pact at the restaurant makes me smile, as well. "He ran to the restroom and I didn't see him again."

"So," Paul says. "When did he get the message?"

"I don't know," I say. "While we were eating. Before he got sick."

"He never responded," Paul says. "You told me you would not let him."

"Right," I say. "I didn't."

Paul doesn't seem to care why, and I don't care to explain. Instead, he says, "And then?"

"I took the porto with me when I ran."

"Why did you run?"

"They called the cops on us, and Agent Stevens—" I realize I shouldn't say anymore. I've already said too much and I can see that Paul is absorbing all of it.

"Agent Stevenson was there?"

"I think he's been following me," I say.

Paul nods again, a grimace painted on his face. "Go on."

"There's nothing else. I ran away and pinged you for help."

"You never checked his message?"

I'm not sure if I should admit that I had, but it seems like he already knows. "Yes," I say. "I did."

"Who was it from?"

"It didn't say."

"What was the message?"

"It said something weird. It was stupid."

"Nothing is stupid," Paul says. "What did it say?"

"Something like, 'What does the Mantel Clock say?'"

Paul's face tightens in bemusement. He sits back and drums his fingers against the desk. "That does sound like nonsense," he says.

I don't say anything because it is nonsense. Only, I have a feeling he really doesn't agree.

"You know Stephon quite well," he says.

"More than anyone."

"Would that make sense to him, the message?"

"No," I say. "I mean, maybe. I don't know."

"Is it an inside joke?"

"Not that I know of."

"And it said, what now? A mantel clock?"

"Yes," I say. "He's in a band called Grandpa and the Mantel Clocks but—"

"Wait," Paul interrupts. He leans forward in thought but shakes his head in confusion. "Stephon is in a band called Grandpa and the Mantel Clocks."

"It's a stupid name," I say, but I can tell that Paul isn't really listening to me now.

He turns away in his chair, rubbing his tired face. "This is really quite interesting," he says, looking at me. "I cannot wait to meet him. I think he and I will have much to offer each other. I would love to know what that message means."

"It's a weird thing," I say, feeling like I should give Paul more information. After all, he's just trying to help us. "I guess Step just thought of the band name one day. But mantel clock, I don't know. We all have our things, I guess, right?"

I'm already thinking about all the Haydens and their funny little mascots, the symbols we draw on the Junction walls like silly little children. It's foolish but it makes me smile just thinking about all those goofy people.

I can see that Paul doesn't understand or he isn't paying attention.

"There's a place underground," I say. "It's where we—the Haydens—hunker down. It's in an abandoned subway line." Cammy would be angry that I'm talking about this but it's not like we're even in the city, and I'm not being very specific. "The walls are filled with graffiti of all shapes, like hieroglyphs. We all sort of contribute to it, I guess. It's really amazing." And it is, when I think about it. No other place feels so rich with personality, with family. It's about the only place I can imagine ever calling home.

Paul's still distracted in thought, studying Step's porto and tapping his lip with his finger. He whispers to himself, "Mantel Clock," like he didn't hear a word I said beyond that. I watch him as he thinks, and I wonder what can possibly be going on in his head.

Once he realizes that I'm still here, he says, "Thank you, Miss Hadley. You may go now."

I get up and start toward the door, when he says, "Miss Hadley." I turn and see that he's looking my way. "I want your friend to pull through as much as you do. He will be alright. I will see to it."

I smile graciously and hope he's right.

***

At night the Good ol' Boys Club has a much bigger fire than normal and a few non-regulars make an appearance. Weston shows up with marshmallows and the boys let him stay. They have Maurice's moonshine and music is playing from somebody's porto. It's a nice chilly night, perfect for sitting around a fire. Everyone is in a good mood, except for maybe Weston. But he's always a little surly.

"He got you running ragged," Maurice says to Weston.

"Yeah," Pete says. "How many trips you make this week? Like five, six?"

Weston doesn't say anything, just emits a fake chuckle to appease them. And they keep going.

"Seriously, man," Trevor says. "Your butt must be sore from all that sitting."

"You might get trucker butt," Maurice says.

"Trucker tooshie," Pete says.

"It gets all numb and flat," Trevor says.

"Blood clots," Pete says. "You need to watch out for those. You know they say that if you—"

"I'm fine," Weston growls.

Pete goes silent for fear of riling up Weston even more. All eyes are on the fire now.

"Aw, come on, Weston," Maurice says. "We're all buddies here."

Only Weston's eyes look up, skeptical.

"Yeah, man," Trevor says. "Lighten up."

"You're a pal," TJ says.

Weston straightens his back. He looks at everyone. His grumpy scowl remains but the fact that he's still here suggests that he has warmed to these guys.

"I don't know what's riding you right now," Maurice says. "But we're here when you want to talk."

That's the last of it. Everyone goes back to watching the fire and roasting marshmallows. Weston simmers and, aside from not talking, seems to have an okay time. The others drink and tell the same stories about their lives before the colony, how TJ used to work construction for a living but also wrote poetry on his breaks. Renee managed a restaurant in Brooklyn and lived with her adult daughter who worked for her. Apparently her daughter now manages the restaurant. Pete talks about being an accountant. He and his wife took care of his parents who also lived with them. Once his parents pass, he wants his wife to come out here, so they can move farther into the country and start a farm. Trevor says he's still a professor of engineering, even though he has no intention of returning to the city. And Maurice operated a subway train for thirty-five years. He'll always say he loved every minute of it.

For as many times as these same conversations arise, nobody bothers to ask me about my life back in the city, probably because I'm a Hayden. I don't have a title like poet, professor, or restauranteur. I'm not a sister or a daughter. I'm just a Hayden, the only title I can be proud of.

At some point during the round of stories, I quietly get up and take a walk. As soon as I leave the fire, a chill engulfs my body. It's refreshing until the smell of burning wood is replaced with sulfur fumes.

I take a stroll through the colony, listening to gravel crunch beneath my feet while the group's laughter grows quieter. I follow the path to a glow in the distance, only to find that it's Laars. He has a giant chunk of white chalk and he's covering a drawing, perhaps to start over. He works the massive piece of chalk up and down the wall with two hands, extending upward as far as his arms will reach. Up and down, up and down, he wears the chalk into the cement. He stops to cough and wipe his brow. That's when he sees me. He hasn't come out since I returned and this is our first time seeing each other after that night in the woods. He looks at me and, without a greeting or a smile, says, "Hasn't rained in a while."

"Too bad," I say. "I liked this one."

The hand tools' feet dangle from their swings and are still visible at the bottom where Laars has yet to cover the wall.

"Do you take pictures of these?" I ask, wishing there was an archive somewhere in the cloud.

"I used to," he says, his voice lacking sentiment. "Not anymore."

He goes back to covering his mural and I watch for a moment, when suddenly there's a noise behind us. We both stop moving and I hear it again in the brush well beyond the colony's perimeter. But I don't see anything. Maybe it's crouching low. The noise is getting closer, and when Laars turns off his light, I think I see something moving in the shadows. Over the next minute or so, our eyes adjust, and we agree that something is coming toward us, slowly and deliberately. Shapes appear within a short distance.

"Are those—?" Laars says to me, urgency in his voice, and then calls out, "Ho there!"

There is no answer. My instinct as a Hayden is to run. Always run, even though there's nowhere to go. The shapes get closer, the crunch of the ground beneath their feet a steady march. Laars gestures for me to stand behind him for my protection.

"Friend or foe?" Laars calls. He stands his ground and raises his brick of chalk like a weapon.

There's still no answer. As they draw closer, it's clear that there are three individuals walking abreast. Just as they reach the perimeter, Laars says, "Identify yourselves," but they still don't speak. From the looks of it, the two outside men are leading the middle person by his bound arms. Closer still, I can see that the captive man is gagged. Laars snaps on his light and shines it on them. Only the captive man flinches, his bruised and bloodied face wincing. It's Agent Stevenson.

I feel a rush of adrenaline like I should do something, fearful that he'll say something to me that puts me in danger too. But he doesn't. The way he squints against the light, he might not even see who I am. The two other men are dressed in old, ragged attire, like the men Laars and I ran into in the woods. They have night goggles draped from their necks.

"Stop right there," Laars says. "Don't come any closer."

The men march past without acknowledging us. Agent Stevenson's legs step weakly between them. We follow close behind as they bring their prisoner into the colony. Agent Stevenson tries to glance back at me but he can't. The men walk as if they know exactly where they are going, which shouldn't surprise me if they've been watching us this whole time. I wonder how long Agent Stevenson was out there before they caught him. Probably not long.

They walk past the campfire and everyone leaps to their feet. Maurice wonders aloud who the hell these guys are and the rest just murmur among themselves. They abandon their fire and we all follow the three men at a safe distance deeper into the colony compound.

Everybody else is fast asleep in their windowless rooms, unaware.

Flood lights mounted on three of the buildings pop to life, drowning out the campfire's flicker. Then a door to the game building swings open and Paul emerges with a metal chair. He brings it to the lighted gravel parking area between two cabin buildings and sets it down. He is not surprised by our guests. Rather, he was expecting them.

"Bring him here, please," he says, gesturing to the chair.

The two men drag Agent Stevenson into the brilliant light, spin him around and shove him into the chair.

"Gently," Paul commands.

The two men adjust Agent Stevenson until he's sitting upright in the chair. His wrists are bound behind his back, so they drape his arms over the back of the chair and tie him down. They do the same with his ankles to the chair legs. Agent Stevenson remains calm, his eyes scan the group of us, never really settling on me but I know he sees me now. When Paul comes around to the front of him, Agent Stevenson's eyes fix onto him and they narrow slightly. Paul smiles in return. He leans in close to Agent Stevenson, who doesn't react. They both seem so calm like old friends who assumed this moment would come. Paul gives him a hard look and then straightens again without saying anything.

"What in the hell is going on here?" Maurice says.

Paul turns and shushes him with a long hiss like a snake.

"Thank you," he says to the two men who delivered Agent Stevenson.

These are the watchers, and it is clear that they are Paul's hired men. This seems to sink in among the group, and nobody knows how to process it.

"These two fellas," Maurice says. "They the ones in the hills?"

Paul smiles.

From Pete to Trevor, I can see in their faces a sense of betrayal laced with confirmation. It almost seems as though they were expecting something like this to happen, and now that it has, their pleasant but strange little world has been fractured.

"We ought to know who these men are," Maurice says. "If they're watching over us."

"Or just watching us," Laars adds.

"Not to worry," says Paul. "They are *with* us." He steps behind Agent Stevenson and looks at me. "Is this man your friend, Miss Hadley?"

I don't answer because it's not necessary. Paul might just be tormenting his prisoner or trying to rattle me, but whatever I say will not change his opinion. Agent Stevenson glances at me, and I expect him to act like we don't know each other. Instead, he seems only to be biding his time.

Paul steps toward me and says, "This place you spoke of, the one underground."

233

"Yes," I say, surprised he had been listening.

"The place with all the symbols," he says. "The graffiti."

"Yes," I say, curious as to why he's continuing our earlier conversation while ignoring the very present situation and its audience. I can hear whispering from among the Good ol' Boys Club.

"I had a thought," Paul says. He paces around Agent Stevenson. "And I would like to know something."

"Anyone want to shine a little light on this moment?" Maurice says, stepping forward. He comes up beside Weston, who has been almost sheepishly quiet. "Weston, my man. Any chance you want to—?"

"Shut your mouth," Weston says, in his usual growl.

"Shut my—what?" Maurice steps back, as if to square off with Weston. Pete reaches for Maurice's arm to stop him. Weston readies himself for a fight.

One of the watchers steps in and puts an arm between them.

"No need," Paul commands. Everyone freezes. Only then do I see that the watcher had is other hand on a holstered pistol. Weston straightens his jacket while Pete guides Maurice away from the rest.

"Miss Hadley," Paul says, trying to remain calm. "Did you contribute to that wall?"

I want to say something about Agent Stevenson, or the watcher and his gun. I want to address what's actually going on here, when Paul says, "What did you paint on that wall?"

"I really think we should be talking about what's happening—"

"What did you paint on the wall?" Each word punches through Paul's pursed lips. His patience has come to an end.

I'm too perplexed to answer or to even remember right away what I had drawn on the wall in the Junction. But when I do, I suddenly get it. I know what the message on Step's porto meant and I know what Paul is looking for from me. I have no idea how he can use it but I know what information he's after. And that scares me.

I look to Agent Stevenson. He gives a subtle shake of the head, telling me to keep my mouth shut. The others are clearly confused and scared.

"I don't know," I say, but it sounds like a lie even to me. "It was a long time ago and—"

"Stop," Paul says. "Just..." He snickers to himself. "Of course you will not tell me." He puts a finger to his lip in contemplation. Something is brewing behind those eyes. "I will need your porto," he says, and presents his open hand.

"What for?" I say, stalling.

"Where is it?" Paul says.

I can't keep him from getting it and I can't run away. I have no way out of the colony without him. "It's in my room," I say.

Paul looks to Weston and commands, "Get Miss Hadley's porto."

Weston, who has been staring at his feet nearly this whole time, looks up as if he missed what Paul said.

"Her porto!" Paul yells, only there's an edge of crazed anticipation in his voice.

Weston stalks away.

Paul straightens himself and grins at the rest of us. "This might turn out to be a very wonderful day," he says. "I have been wracking my brain—all of your brains, in fact—for so long. I began to give up hope. Your friend, Mr. Stephon, seemed so promising." Paul turns to Agent Stevenson. "And then this little gift." A smile stretches across his face. He turns back to me. "If I am correct, I may not need your friend after all."

Others begin to emerge from their barracks, groggy and confused.

Penny, the lady who loves bears, wraps a blanket around

herself and says, "What's going on out here? What are you all doing out so late." When she sees bloody and beaten Agent Stevenson tied to a chair, she gasps and backs into the others.

"My friends," Paul says. "I am talking about a new life for all of us. And you all, each and every one of you, will go from outcast to elite. The key?" He removes a porto from his jacket pocket. "It is right here."

Weston returns with my porto. Paul takes it but doesn't turn it on. Instead, he turns it over in his hands. His smile grows wider. I know what he's looking at, He scratches a sticker that covers part of my porto case, and licks his lips as he traces his thumb over what I have scratched into the back of my porto. I don't understand how it's important, only that it is. Just like Step's Mantel Clock or the hand tools that Laars draws, or, if I had to guess, my brother Thomas's candlestick. There's something to these quirks, these spirits that we cling to somehow. These aren't coincidental obsessions or eccentric tastes. These things have been placed in our minds on purpose, programmed along with our chips, and are far more important to MIND, and now to Paul, than they are to any of us. Paul starts to giggle and I know that whatever he has planned is much bigger than any of us can imagine.

He looks at me with crazed eyes and says, "Miss Hadley." I'm already looking at him. He has my attention, along with everyone else's, because there's no telling what he will do or say. He wipes his mouth and ever so gently asks, "Miss Hadley, what does the hot air balloon say?"

There is only one reply and it is right there in my head. I couldn't tell you it at random. I wouldn't know what I was supposed to say. My mind knows.

Paul repeats the question, this time with emphasis. It takes so much of my concentration to not answer. Everybody is watching, confused. My mouth doesn't want to say it. Paul seems to realize this and comes toward me. He awakens his porto, swipes the screen, and says, "Porto. Gateway. Hadley Hayden. What does the hot air balloon say?" He offers me my porto, which is vibrating with a new message in his hand.

I don't take it.

"Miss Hadley," he says. "Take your porto and come with me."

I take it and feel the etching of a hot air balloon that I left in the plastic casing, a similar image to the one I drew in the Junction. Paul starts to walk but I don't follow.

"Where are we going?" I say.

"You will see," he says.

"Let's just take it easy a second," says Laars. "I'm afraid I can't let you take her." He steps forward.

Paul looks at Laars with a pathetic smirk, and says, "Come along, Miss Hadley."

"Listen here," Laars says, stepping toward Paul, his finger pointed threateningly. "If you lay a hand on that girl, I'll—"

Paul snaps his fingers and, just as quickly, a pistol fires a bullet into Laars's knee. Laars cries out and crumbles to the ground, grabbing at his bloody leg. He lets out a single howl of pain and leaves it at that to silently writhe. Penny screams and the watcher swings his gun toward Maurice and Trevor, who have bravely decided to step in. I can't find my breath.

"Easy," the watcher says calmly, his gun trained between them.

Trevor and Maurice back away from the gun but stay together near the fire.

"Mr. Peter," Paul says, calmly. "Please go get Miss Laurel to tend to Mr. Laars."

Pete runs off toward the cafeteria to find Miss Laurel, formerly a nurse practitioner back in the city.

"Miss Hadley," Paul says. "Now, please come with me."

Behind Paul, Agent Stevenson shakes his head *no* in

defeat. Beside him, two watchers aim their guns at the rest of us. My only option is to comply. I follow Paul to the game building and into the back room with his work station. He sits down.

"What's happening?" I ask. I can feel my voice getting shaky. "Whatever you need with my porto or me, just please don't hurt anyone else."

"Please," he says, ignoring my plea. "Sit."

He has me sit behind the curved desk. Over my shoulder, he taps a screen to life and calls up some program code that I don't understand.

"I am not a monster," he says. "I am a programmer." He chuckles. "Or a reprogrammer, if you will."

"What's this?" I say, looking over the gibberish of code. "Let me guess, a virus?"

"No, no, no," Paul says, laughing. "Much better. I simply plan to jumble up a little bit of data."

"What kind of data," I ask. "Whose data?"

"Everybody's," Paul says, smiling. "Imagine reassigning everybody's identity. New names for everyone. Imagine it. Just think of what will happen when everyone becomes somebody else. Instantly! One second you are Joseph, and then—" He puts up his hands as if there's a giant, silent explosion. "You are Theodore or Charles or Mary." He giggles. "I never thought of that. A man might get a woman's name or a little boy's name or—" His eyes widen with ecstasy. "The possibilities are delicious."

"We'll all be affected," I say, but I'm unable to imagine what this all means.

"Everybody!" Paul cheers, like one of those old-timey circus ringmasters. "Even me. And, if I am correct, being Fried may have its advantages. But we shall see." He points to my porto. "The moment you answer one simple question."

I look at my porto. On the screen is the question: "What

does the hot air balloon say?" Below is a blank field where I can enter my reply.

"You have to take care of Step," I say. "I won't do it until I know he's safe."

Paul laughs to himself and then his face grows serious. "I do not wish to hurt anyone else," he says. And I take that for what it is—a very serious threat from a very sick monster.

He points again to my porto.

There is a sequence of ten characters—numbers, letters, and symbols—that swims in each of our heads. If asked, you could not simply tell somebody the sequence, as it is buried deep in the chambers of your subconscious. There is little-to-no chance that it would ever simply spill from your memory, as Paul has no doubt spent years trying with so many Fried people. If you're lucky, it will never surface. The sequence that has been assigned to me has only come up twice in my life—the night of my crash and now.

I start to type and Paul taps something on his screen. In a last effort to stall him, I say, "Are you Reuben Mayfield?" I hope maybe to startle him or get him to rethink his strategy.

He cranes his neck, maybe shocked or maybe impressed that I know this. His eyes dull with morose reflection but then he smiles and says, "Not for much longer."

I hesitate, thinking that maybe he'll change his mind or that there's something I've missed that can save us. But there isn't. Maybe there never was. And that's why I finish the sequence. When I hit *send*, the code on his screen scrolls quickly in a flicker.

Then it stops. No noise. No explosion. Nothing. And I wonder if his plan has worked, if anything has happened at all.

When I look at Paul, he's staring at his screen, tapping his lip, thinking or hoping. I can't tell. When he looks at me, his anxious glare melts into crazed delight. He lets a small giggle leak from his parted lips.

"Thank you," he says. He puts a hand on my shoulder and I nearly collapse under the weight of what I must have done. "I owe all of this to you...Ella."

CHAPTER TWENTY-FOUR
TYPEWRITER

My name is Ella Banks.

That's what Paul tells me, anyway. The coding he has uploaded to the System has rearranged everyone's name, including mine. Now, somebody else is Hadley Hayden. For now. Because it turns out that his plan doesn't end here. Paul wrote the code to scramble the database each time the gateway opens and for as long as MIND is unable to eradicate the errant code, which has replicated and planted itself in various parts of the System. This means that every six hours, four times a day, everybody's name will change. Again and again and again.

(You know this already. You live this. Or maybe it's over by the time you hear this.)

But when this first happens (as you know) none of it seems real. I don't feel any different. I almost don't believe it. And I'm shocked that Paul isn't actually fried. Maybe that's why he suddenly seems like an entirely different person—because he *is* an entirely different person to himself. He's so excited, he tries to hug me but I recoil in disgust. He gets up and scurries from the room. For a moment I have the idea that maybe if I destroy all this equipment that he's left me with, maybe I can stop his virus. But I know that's not true.

I follow Paul outside where I find that the watchers have gathered everyone around the campfire for warmth. Paul rushes over to them and starts pointing at each person, firing off new names. Renee is now Molly Prescott. Trevor is Harold Candler. Maurice is Susan Ratajkowski, which makes Pete, who is now Kyle Williams, laugh awkwardly. Miss Laurel is now Ingrid Sanchez wrapping the leg of Opal Marks, who used to be Laars.

Paul tells Agent Stevenson that his new name is Timothy Pendergast. Agent Stevenson doesn't seem amused. By the way his chest heaves, it's clear that he is angry. The two watchers seem befuddled, perhaps unable to grasp what just happened. Paul pulls Agent Stevenson's gag out of his mouth and says, "Tell me my name."

Agent Stevenson looks up with just his eyes.

"Come on," Paul says. "Be a sport."

"Reuben Mayfield," he hisses.

"Oh, no," Paul says, taunting. "You are wrong. You are so so wrong. Tell me. Who do you see?"

"I see a sick son of a bitch named Reuben Mayfield," Agent Stevenson says through his teeth. "A deranged, lowlife pedophile."

"Whip this one," Paul says to a watcher.

The watcher hits Agent Stevenson with the butt of his gun and the agent's head drops to one side. He spits and sits back up. He starts to say, "A cowardly little—"

"Again," Paul commands, and the same watcher hits Agent Stevenson across the cheek, cutting his face with the butt end of the gun.

Paul trots over to the car that Weston has been driving and kneels before the side mirror, craning his neck for a better look at himself. He begins to laugh. "Look at me," he chortles. He turns to the rest of us, his eyes wide. "My name is Lawrence Pinto. Lawrence!" He holds his arms out wide. He's taken on an entirely new persona. "Look at me. Hey, guys. It's me, Larry! How do you do?" He playfully offers his hand to Agent Stevenson. "Larry Pinto," he says, a sinister edge to his voice.

"Pleasure to meet your acquaintance?" He laughs and pulls his hand away.

"What now?" Maurice says, cutting into Paul's performance. "What do we do now?"

"We rejoice!" Paul says.

"What's going to happen from here?" Renee asks.

"Exactly," Maurice says. "If this is what you've been aiming to do, what's the point?"

"Let us just swim in this for a moment," Paul says.

"What does this mean for us though?" Pete says.

"None of you have to worry," Paul says, as if they're going to listen to somebody who has been lying to them all this time. "You all have the advantage now. Don't you see?"

Weston stands up from beside Pete and Trevor. He approaches Paul and says, "Tell me my name." Nobody but Paul, Agent Stevenson, and maybe the watchers know. Paul looks Weston's way and says, "Tobias Langhorne."

Weston doesn't react in any way but to look at his hands like they might be somebody else's. He keeps the same scowl when he closes his eyes, perhaps envisioning the faces of others he knows, trying to learn who they are now. He sits down again beside Pete.

Pete watches Weston, then looks at the rest of us, and says, "It all seems so..."

"Anticlimactic," Trevor finishes.

"But imagine," Paul says. "Come morning, everyone is going to wake and see themselves in the mirror and just...scream! They will not know the person looking back at them."

"It really doesn't feel like much," TJ says.

"Yeah," says Renee. "It just seems so trivial."

"Trivial?" Paul cries. "You must be joking. Imagine the mayhem. Maybe not here but think about what is going on in the city right now, as we speak! Imagine what it will be like tomorrow. Business will stop. All forms of life. Everything! Life as they know it will simply stop."

"You're fitting to make chaos," Maurice says. "That's what this is all about?"

"He's fitting to hide among the crowd," says Agent Stevenson. "He couldn't go back to the city if everyone knew who he was."

A watcher approaches Agent Stevenson to hit him but Paul puts up his hand to say that it's not necessary.

"Timothy," Paul says. "Dearest Timothy. The hunt is over."

"You have all this out here," Agent Stevenson says. "You've rebuilt your life. What you've done now... it wasn't necessary."

"Do you know what it's like to be labeled?" Paul says. He crouches close enough that Agent Stevenson can smell his breath. "Can you imagine what it's like when somebody looks at you and knows about the awful mistakes you've made? They judge you. They hate you. You're now only as good as those mistakes."

"You don't believe those were mistakes," Agent Stevenson says. "Neither did your victims."

"I couldn't live!" Paul says, leaping to his feet. "No matter who I met, I never had a fair chance."

"You pay for your crime," Agent Stevenson says.

"You pay for your ignorance!" Paul cries, and he spits on Agent Stevenson. "You all do. I am more than what the System tells you." He spins to address the rest of us. "We all are!"

Something in what Paul says feels familiar. I've always felt so alone, so detached and disconnected, long before I was Fried. I never had a chance to connect with other, regular people because to them I was just a Hayden. I'm what the System tells them. All the sideways glances and judging stares, the rejection and outright hate. The ignorance. So many times I wished I could just be somebody else in the System, something other than a Hayden.

And then it hits me. Paul needs to go back to the city to see what he has done, to feel what he has become. And I need to get him away from the colony for the others' safety.

"I was branded," Paul says, as if trying to convince the others of an injustice.

"You burned yourself," Agent Stevenson says, leaning back in the chair.

"Enough with you," Paul says, and he snaps his fingers. He points and a watcher raises a pistol to Agent Stevenson's head.

"No!" I shout. "Don't!"

Paul puts up his hand to stop the watcher, if for just a moment to entertain me.

"You don't need to kill anybody," I say. "You said you wouldn't." I slowly step toward Paul. "I get it. I understand completely what you mean. The System is unfair. I know exactly how that feels. Any Hayden would."

Paul seems to process this. He looks at me curiously, as if maybe he believes me.

"The System never gave you a chance," I say.

"No," he says.

"You haven't been able to simply be," I say.

"No," he says, sounding sorry for himself.

"I know *I* want to see what it's like to live," I say. "Don't you want to go back now? Don't you want to see what you have done? Don't you want to live?

A sinister grin smears across Paul's face.

"Ella," he says. "Little Ella Banks." He comes closer, takes my head in his hands, and brings his conniving face to mine like he might kiss me. "You are much smarter than they let you be. You are more than a Hayden." He pulls me close and wraps me in his arms. I want to pry away but resist. He whispers, "Let us

245

go back. Let us live."

"Let's go now," I say. "Before they wake. We can see it all unfold."

"Yes," he says, lustfully.

"Don't do it, Hadley," Laars grunts from the ground. "Don't play his game."

"Don't worry," I say. "Paul... I mean, Lawrence and I will be free. *We* will all be free."

Paul looks over the perplexed and scared group. "I never planned for this moment," he says.

"Let them sort it out," I say. "Nobody can hurt you now. You're a new man." As much as he repulses me, I touch his arm.

"Is the car ready, Tobias?" Paul says to Weston.

"I'm not going," Weston says. He remains seated with the others around the fire, shaking his head in doubt. I can understand. I am also worried about our fate among the chaos erupting back in the city.

"Very well," Paul says. "Nobody here knows the city better than Ella."

The thought of driving back alone with Paul—with Reuben Mayfield—worries me, too, but I have to separate him from the group. I have to make sure that nobody else gets hurt.

"Stephon," Paul says. "Your dear friend. Will I still get to meet him?"

"Certainly," I say. "We owe you that."

"Splendid," he says. Paul looks to the group again. "The rest of you, I have grown to adore many of you. I will keep you in my memory. Please enjoy the new you." He looks to his watchers. "After an hour, please let my friend Mr. Pendergast free."

Agent Stevenson looks at me, dejected and accusing. He shakes his head.

"Hold on," Maurice says. "You can't be serious. What do we do now?"

"Whatever you want," Paul says. "You are who you are. You shall be that you—"

"Don't give me that," Renee says. "Are you coming back or not?"

"Who's going to take care of the colony?" Pete asks.

"You will," Paul says. "All of you."

Confusion falls over the group and everyone starts to question what will happen next. The watchers are similarly confused but remain at the ready for any new confrontation. Paul and I get in the car. When Paul starts the ignition, the onboard porto awakens with, *New Links: Hadley Hayden, Stephon Hayden, Paul.*

"Why does it have our old names?" I ask. For a second I think he might have been lying about all this.

"Portos are independent of the System," he says. "Or they should be." He seems unsure. "They are assigned to you." He smiles. "I do not know how that will sort out, whether the System will reassign each time or how it could." Paul seems intrigued by the idea, another puzzle to solve. "Maybe the camera reads your face or grabs your fingerprint and then you have access to your new cloud account."

"So, I'll have somebody else's cloud?" I say. "I'll have their life? That's insane. That doesn't make sense."

"We are in highly uncharted territory now," Paul says. "The System as we know it may never be the same." His grimace is almost as curious as it is menacing.

He begins to drive, idling out of the parking area. I watch the others milling about the campfire circle, their futures so uncertain but maybe not as much as mine in the city. Paul places a foot on the accelerator. We lurch forward, spitting gravel and dirt, and I brace myself against the door and dashboard. Paul slams on the brakes before we get anywhere.

"I will admit," he says. "I am nervous. It has been some time since I drove a vehicle."

"I can drive," I say.

We get out and switch seats. The others watch, except for Agent Stevenson whose back is to us. I adjust the seat and we pull out of the colony, into the darkness beyond.

We finally get onto the open road but Paul doesn't speak. He runs his palms along his legs like an anxious boy, as he stares out the window. He does this nearly the whole way. At times he whispers something to himself, as if rehearsing a speech. Though, he also admits that he has no plan for his return, only to spectate and enjoy his doing.

Somewhere in the old New Jersey territory, I can hear his breathing quicken. I, too, have no plan. Each time we approach the columns of an overpass or a large tree along the roadside, I contemplate punching the gas and swerving us toward our deaths, maybe undoing Paul's safety belt just before impact.

Paul coughs and says, "What do you think we will find when we get there?"

"I have no idea," I say. "Do you think you will stay?"

"Of course," he says. "I have missed so many things. There is so much time to make up."

"I suppose you have prepared for this," I say.

"No," he says. "To be candid, I believe that the future is uncertain for all of us, so much so that none of us could have ever planned for this."

"What will happen to the colony?" I ask. "If you don't go back, will they be okay? And the watchers—"

"The watchers, as you call them," Paul says. "They are just former MIND agents that I was able to recruit as security."

"Are they Fried?"

"No," he says. "But they have nothing to lose anymore. Once they defected, they basically lost their lives."

I get the sense that his plans run much deeper than he lets on.

"And your friends will be okay for a little while," he says. "But I fear that without my leadership, they might not be so... productive."

"Do you mean in recovering their memories?" I ask.

He begins to laugh, first a small, stifled chuckle that soon grows into this enormous guffaw of hysterics. When he settles his laughter, he says, "You are sweet." He wipes tears from his eyes. "I am sorry but you should know that you will likely never be fixed. I needed access to your thoughts. I should not tell you this but I suppose there is no more harm in it than anything else I have done." He looks out the window, speaking to the passing town beyond the highway barrier. "I have been monitoring your portos, feeding everything you write and say into algorithms that formulate questions and answers, much like what we used to eventually gain access."

"It was all for this," I say. "To get us here."

"Yes. And it was desperate," he says. "I was chasing the shadows of your accidents. I was hoping, really." He takes a deep breath and exhales slowly. "I guess I never thought it would actually happen."

He's silent for a moment. The sky is brighter in the distance, and I know that the city will come into view very soon. Paul has pulled the sun visor down and he keeps looking at himself in the mirror, smiling proudly.

"So, this was all connected," I say. Suddenly, I'm forced to wonder about all that has happened, everyone I've met or encountered, since the accident. Which brings me to this: "Did you send my brother after me?" It comes out before I can even stifle it.

He looks at me, not so put off as I thought he would be. In fact, it seems like he expected me to ask. "I did," he says, shrugging casually. "I'm sorry. Truth be told, I did not know he existed until Agent Stevenson contacted the boy. I have had your agent friend tracked for years. I only knew you had made contact with him because of the photos in your cloud. I was surprised to find that you stalked him when you were younger."

Hearing that he's been prying into my life, that he has dug through my deepest secrets, fills me with helpless rage. He goes on to tell me how he paid Thomas and his friends, and how Thomas was reluctant at first to agree. Apparently, according to messages and notes in the cloud, Thomas aspires to be a MIND agent. So, Paul threatened to expose Thomas's most embarrassing secrets as a way of hindering his chances for admission into the MIND academy. And Thomas finally agreed.

All I can think is how much he has violated Thomas, me, and the rest of us. And now I want to slam on the brakes, drag Paul from the car, and beat the pathetic snot out of him. I look at the way he gazes longingly into the passing landscape like some innocent child, his doughy pathetic face lit by the dashboard porto. I want to claw that face, gouge out those eyes. This must be how Nona has felt for years, and I can only imagine now the bloodlust she's been harboring. This man is a monster. He needs to be stopped.

Paul takes a deep breath, runs his hands up and down his pant legs, and says, "Where do you want to go when we arrive?"

He doesn't even realize the hate seething beside him. I can send us off a bridge to his death, plunge us into a river, and watch his eyes freeze with fear as he drowns. A past version of me would consider doing that. After all, what good is a Hayden? What I know is that the worst Hayden, even a murderous one, is worth more than this pile of garbage.

My heart is racing with anger but Paul doesn't seem to notice, not even when I don't respond.

"I want to be there when people find out," he says. "When they realize that they are no longer themselves." He laughs to himself. "If only I could be there when they first see themselves in the mirror." He looks at me, clearly unaware that I want to see him suffer. "Wouldn't you like to see that?" he says. "Don't you just want to see the horror on their faces?"

"I do," I say, without looking at him. "I want to see the horror."

We go around a curve and the distant lights of the city come into view. Paul leans forward in his seat, his eyes wide, mouth agape. He seems like a giddy little school boy.

"It is gorgeous," he says. "Where do we begin?"

"I have the perfect place for us to go," I say.

"Fantastic," he says.

We reach the tunnel and find ourselves in line with overnight freight trucks. Paul seems just as spellbound in this dark corridor as he was seeing the city skyline just across the Hudson. When we reach the other end, the customs officer looks at his porto screen and leans down to see me. The toll charge appears on our onboard porto but our other portos must appear on the officer's scan, as well. When he looks at my face, he says, "You ain't no Hayden."

"No," I say. "I guess not." It feels sad and liberating at the same time to hear this.

"What are you doing with Hadley Hayden's porto?" he asks.

Paul leans across my lap and says, "Listen, Carl. You have been freed from the confines of your life."

"What?" the officer says. "I don't know no Carl."

"Yes, you do," Paul says. He points to the rounded mirror that extends from the officer's booth to view approaching vehicles. "Give yourself a glance."

"I don't have time for this, buddy," he says. "I don't see a Lawrence Pinto on here neither."

"Carl," Paul says. "Look at yourself."

Puzzled, the officer looks at me. I give him an affirming nod. "Man," he says, annoyed. He leans out the window and cranes to see the mirror, pulls it toward him, and almost immediately lurches back. "What the hell?" He looks again. "C-

Carl Haller—."

"Carl Halleran," Paul says. "You have some explaining to do. Your wife won't even know you."

The officer calls something over his radio. He's confused and angry but mostly scared. He looks at himself in the mirror again, mutters his new name to himself, and readjusts the mirror. Somebody calls back over the radio. The officer sees the line of vehicles behind us and, realizing we have paid, let's us move on. This is just one reaction. So simple and devastating. I can't imagine what will happen when the whole city wakes in a few hours.

(Of course, you know what happens. You're living it.)

When we emerge from the tunnel, we are both bathed in city light coming through the window. I almost expect Paul to weep. But that won't be enough for me. I need to hear him scream.

I drive us slowly through the city, letting Paul absorb the sights. I can't imagine all that has changed since he left. On the sidewalks, the few people out at this hour seem unaware, especially if they're alone. But then we see a group of guys, college-aged, spilling from a bar and into the street before us. A few of them shove a man until he tumbles to the concrete. He screams, "You got me wrong, guys. Lay off!" From the looks of his stylish, new clothing and expensive shoes, he's not a Hayden. But these GCs probably think he is now.

Paul raises his eyebrows with intrigue, no more moved by it than if it was on a porto series. He watches the brawl as we drive by, and once we turn a corner, he goes back to looking up toward the tall buildings like he's never seen them before.

As we drive, it seems that more people are coming out of buildings and looking around the street, as if to find an answer to their confusion.

I drive us toward the park and stop the car by the curb along 59th Street. We get out.

"Are we here?" Paul asks.

"Almost," I say. If he doesn't know where I'm taking him, then he will when we head underground. Though, I have to imagine he knows. He's only playing coy as I lead him to fulfill his fantasy. Why else would he want all this—to be somebody else—if not to prey undetected?

Paul looks up at the night sky, stars bleached away by city lights. He traces the height of a building back toward the ground and peers across to Central Park. He says, "They call that nature," and chuckles.

Paul doesn't question any of my directions as we make our way down to the Junction, using a doorway off the Columbus Circle station. It's a long way to go but an easier descent than crawling through a manhole. Paul has little to say, perhaps because he's still in awe. He sounds like he's getting tired as we take a short ladder to some abandoned tracks. It is so dark and remote down here, I could probably shove him from the ladder and break his neck. Nobody would find him. But that wouldn't be satisfying enough.

As we make our way down one more tunnel, Paul is entranced by his surroundings, the pipes and dripping water, the rats and debris, the graffiti. We pass a few lean-to structures that serve as homes for a number of Haydens. Paul studies them with great curiosity.

Then he asks, "Do you live down here?"

"I do," I say, and I'm not ashamed by it. In fact, I'm almost proud.

We straddle the tracks that lead to the Junction, and Paul follows me without question. As we draw near, I can hear a low rumble of voices. There is no music or laughter, just people talking over one another as if debating something very important. There seems to be confusion or unrest, which makes sense. We reach the Junction and find dozens of Haydens, maybe a hundred, gathered under the domed ceiling. The gathering could easily be confused as a party if it wasn't for a lack of music or beer. The fire in the center of the room is dwindling, because everybody is too preoccupied to tend to it.

People shout and gesture with their hands like they have to compete for attention. Somebody is crying, "Who am I?" Another person yells incoherent words, as if he's drunk. "Who are you? You're not even a Hayden."

"Neither are you!"

Paul stops short of the tunnel's opening. "Is it safe?" he asks.

"They're my friends," I say. "Looks like they've just found out."

He nods and starts walking again, cautious but curious. As we get closer, we see that people aren't fighting. It's as if they're trying to sort out some issue without having anyone to lead their discussion—everybody just shouting and crying and yelling. I move deeper into the mob and faces turn to me, some with fleeting recognition, some stifling their greeting, probably because they might recognize me but are still perplexed by the unfamiliar name attached. I know how they feel. You know a person by their looks, at least you think you do. But the System has made that part of our brains lazy.

When I look back, I see that I've lost Paul. He hasn't followed me into the crowd but instead somehow got separated. He staggers through the sea of Haydens, his eyes wide with wonder as he, I'm sure, takes in their names, probably no longer Haydens. After a moment, I can see that he's looking for me now. Instead of working back toward him, I recede to the edge of the crowd, making it harder for him to spot me. From there, I can see him standing among the group, his head dropped back to capture the magnitude of graffiti above us. He is frozen with awe. The fire's meager light flickers enough to see the mosaic of shapes and colors that span the dome. My eyes trace downward from the ceiling and toward a circuit box where I had left my mark—a hot air balloon. Only, I cannot see it through the crowd.

Paul steps backwards, haphazardly moving within the crowd, paying little attention to those around him, his eyes wide with disbelief. I watch as his gaze follows the ceiling from peak to the floor, and he begins to say something I can't hear. It's just too loud in here. I can't even tell who he's talking to.

Then somebody shouts something. It's not so much a bloodcurdling cry as it is direct, attacking. She keeps shouting it, but I can't tell what it is or who's saying it, only that it's angry and pointed. And as the crowd of Haydens goes quiet, these shouts grow clearer, until we all can follow the voice back to its source—Nona shoving her way through the crowd.

She's yelling, "Who's that?!" over and over. "Who is that? Who are you?" Everyone turns to see her, and the Junction goes silent but for her voice. "You can't be serious!" she cries. "Get over here!" She's fixed on Paul but he doesn't even realize that she's talking to him. Nona keeps charging toward him as people part to make way. Cammy isn't far behind her but even she doesn't know what has Nona so riled. When Paul finally realizes what is happening, Nona is already before him.

"You son of a bitch," she says, her voice quivering. I can see her eyes tearing and furious. She bares her teeth. "I can't believe it, you son of a bitch. Mayfield. Reuben goddamned Mayfield."

Whispers move around the crowd but they keep watching Nona. Paul seems perplexed that she would know his name. It looks like he might actually be saying, "Who me?" in some last ditch effort of denial. But I can't hear him. Nona is already shouting, "You've come to the wrong place. You don't know what you've done."

The confusion on each Hayden's face has contorted into blind understanding that if Nona is upset, then there must be

255

something wrong with this man. They begin to gather around Nona and Paul, hungry for what she will do.

Paul turns to find me, scanning the room. When he eventually spots me through the crowd, I can see his mouth form the words, "What have you done?" I say back, too quietly for anyone to here, "What have *you* done?"

Cammy puts her hand on Nona's shoulder, as if to protect her but it might as well not even be there. Nona is entranced, ravenous, suddenly an animal pacing around her prey. The crowd keeps circling closer and Paul doesn't seem to understand the gravity of the moment. His fear is still tempered by denial or curiosity.

Until Nona flicks open a box cutter, her eyes wild with rage, and says, "Welcome to the Junction."

The terror that registers on Paul's face as he sees the box cutter raised before him can only be described as everlasting. Before he can put up his hands in defense, Haydens seize his arms. He shrieks as they pull him to the ground, and I can no longer see him. Box cutter drawn, Nona kneels over him. More Haydens begin to shout as they emerge from tunnels to descend upon the scene. I quickly turn away, unable to witness the satisfying horror as it unfolds. I hear only a measure of his cries before even they are swallowed by howls of victory, and justice is served.

CHAPTER TWENTY-FIVE
LETTER OPENER

Most of this you already know.

Even before dawn, sirens fill the air like cries for help. People wander the sidewalks in bathrobes and pajamas, confronting each other, confronting me, asking, "Who am I? How can this be?" Nobody ever asked that before. Unfortunately, I can only answer one of those questions—how this can be.

That's why I'm telling you now—recording it all into my porto, in case one day you somehow find it in the cloud—so you know how the System fell. Maybe then you can make sense of this new world.

This all may have begun when they tried to kill me but I already plan to start over.

So, to me, it begins here. Lower Eastside Hospital. Immunology Ward. It takes close to an hour to find him here because, while he was admitted under the name Stephon Hayden, the current confusion around names has left everyone in the hospital's administration—and everywhere for that matter—in complete doubt.

I'm able to use that uncertainty to gain access to his room, claiming that I am his sister. Just that my name is, well, you know how insane it has been.

The morning sky is only starting to lighten and he's still asleep. He has no idea of the mayhem unfolding outside this hospital. In the calmer corners of town, where rioting hasn't begun, bus and train schedules are practically non-existent. By the time I get here, cops are trying to contain the sheer unrest on the streets, they themselves unsure of who they are. Schools haven't closed, they just haven't opened. The procedure to do either involves people to do their jobs. Only, those people are trying to make sense of the faces they see in the bathroom mirror this morning or on the person beside them in bed.

I don't want to turn on a light and wake Step, so I sit here in a chair across the room talking to you. His body moves calmly, a dark figure rising and falling as he breathes. A machine, probably some monitor, beeps a subtle cadence.

There's commotion outside the room and Step stirs. People are restless, nearly insane, especially now that six hours have passed and the name they've been coming to terms with has changed once again. I have no idea who I am.

Step rolls over toward my direction but I can't see his face in the dark. He might be looking right at me or searching the darkness.

"Hey," I say, quietly. "You awake?"

"Haddy," he says, his voice is hoarse. "Where have you been?"

"I'm here," I say.

"Come here," he says. He's frail as he tries to sit up.

I come to the side of his bed and lean over him, hold him. His embrace is weak but I need it. I'm already crying and I can only wrap my arms around him so much, pull him so tightly against me.

"Can you get the light?" he says, sitting back to look at me. "I need to see you."

I turn on a lamp near his bed and he squints against the light. When he finally looks at me, the flash of ease in his eyes blinks into bewilderment. I can see the shock, like his mind has betrayed him. Only, as he searches my face for an explanation, his eyes finally slacken with sadness. This all happens in a matter of a second, but I catch each stage like it's the length of a season.

"Why?" he says. "Who are you? I mean—"

"It's okay," I say, reaching to take his hand. He wants to accept my touch but I can see apprehension.

"How are you—?" he starts to say. "Your name."

"What is my name?" I say.

"You're Haddy," he says, struggling to form the words, his mind no doubt telling him otherwise.

"I am," I say, "But what is my name?"

"It's—," he says, an astonished quiver to his voice. "It's...Tara?" He offers a doubtful smirk. "It's Tara Steinweg." He emits a sad laugh to himself. "Or is it Stein-veg?" He shakes his head. "What is happening? That's not you. That's not your name."

"It's okay," I say.

"Are you in trouble?"

"No," I say. "No more than the rest of them."

I gesture to the window but he can't see outside or down to the street where more people are sure to gather in anger, frustration, fear. I turn on the porto screen across the room and call up the news. The screen blips to life. Footage appears. Fires. People running through the street. Looting. Some people just wander like zombies. Others seem to push through, already trying to make their day normal.

A reporter is talking from a train platform above all the mayhem somewhere in the city. A sparse gathering of commuters meanders in the background, their feeble attempt to normalize the situation. They all look sullen in fear and denial.

"This is Frank Hodges, formerly Max Neuland, reporting to you live as the chaos continues," he says, straining to keep his journalistic composure. "As of," he looks at his watch,

"Twenty-six minutes ago, at which time I was Winona Charles."

"What the hell?" Step says. He rubs his eyes and lets out a slight chuckle.

After a nervous laugh, the reporter goes on to speculate as to what has happened to MIND's System and begins to assure his audience that an explanation is surely to come very soon. He turns to a boy standing beside him. The boy's name is Minka Shropshire. The reporter asks for a reaction.

"I don't want a girl's name," the boy cries into the camera. "The kids at school are going to laugh at me."

The reporter pulls his microphone back and says, "Poor Minka is just trying to cope with what appears to be one of three things: an elaborate prank, a simple but tragic computer glitch, or an all-out act of terrorism."

He thrusts the microphone toward another person watching the chaos from the train platform.

"Mr. Manning," says the reporter. "Do you think that this confusion will lead to more crime, now that it will be more difficult to identify criminals?"

Mr. Manning looks anxious as he peers into the camera. "I hadn't thought about that," he says. "But I need to clear the air. My name is not Ivan Manning. My name is not Patrick O'Leary. My name is and always has been Julian Trudeau." He finds himself shaking a fist at the camera, as if threatening a bully. "My friends call me Jules. You got that? My name is Jules!"

"Sure it is," the reporter says. "Tell me, how are you handling it so far?"

"I'm headed downtown to find out just who Mr. Ivan Manning is and why it is that I have his name." He spits and says, "City Hall has to be held accountable."

The reporter laughs condescendingly. "I don't think that's the way this works," he says. "But good luck to you." He turns to the camera. "However this unfolds, good luck to all of you watching Wolf 93 in the morning. Back to Pam and—" He looks off camera, holding a hand to his ear, then looks back. "Or back to Erin and Sydney in the studio." He offers the camera a coy smile that barely masks the legitimate horror in his eyes.

Step shuts off the screen and asks, "Am I still—?"

"No," I say.

I go to the window and draw the blinds completely so that he can see his reflection in the dark glass. He stares for a moment and leans in close to make sure he isn't mistaken. I can hear a whispered cackle come from somewhere in his throat, as he looks down at his lap and shakes his head. He rubs his face.

"Are you okay?" I ask.

"I'm fine," he says. "It's just that..." He looks at me unsure. "I'm not a Hayden."

"I know," I say, forcing a smile. "It's weird."

I still can't grasp it myself. I may never be able to, even when I no longer have to hide or cower or feel shame for being neglected and abandoned, for being an outcast from society. It has been the only constant in my life, the only thing I could hold onto. And now I've lost that too.

"What does this even mean?" he asks. "Who am I?"

Without pause, I find myself saying, "You are who you are."

Step says, "Yeah," and nods more to himself. He looks off somewhere beyond the room, lost in thought, and then shakes his head in disbelief. I can't tell how he's taking the news, but he doesn't seem angry or scared. He must have so many questions, things that I'm not sure I want to tell him, because none of it matters. There's nothing we can do now.

After a moment, he looks at me, and I can see his body relax a little. I sit beside him and he takes my hand, gives it a squeeze. We sit like this for a moment, when a nurse comes into the room, clearly frazzled.

"Are you okay?" she asks Step. She stops when she sees

him sitting up. "Your monitor was racing."

"I'm sorry," he says. He gestures to me. "I was happy to see—"

"It's okay," she says. "Just...it's madness out there." She fiddles with some of his monitors and IV tubing. "We're trying to get our bearings. I'm running around like a loon. Gotta make sure my patients are okay." She rambles more to herself. "Can't stop healing just because the stupid System is on the fritz and now you go by some new name. Can you believe I was a Hayden for a while there?"

Step looks at me with a puzzled smile.

"And get this," she goes on, tapping something into the iTable. "In the middle of all this, I got the strangest ping on my porto."

"Yeah?" Step says, playing along, even though he doesn't know what she's talking about. Only, I do.

"It said something real stupid," she says. "Made no sense at all. Something like 'what does the letter opener say?'" She looks up briefly with a contorted face like it's the dumbest thing she's ever read.

I have the sudden fear that the man in gray might come through the door, and that whatever befalls this nurse will surely take us too.

"What did you do?" I ask, maybe a little too eager. "Did you respond? Did you answer the question?"

Step looks at me like why do I care. The nurse gives me the same funny look.

"Answer it?" she says, and goes back to reading Step's monitor report on the iTable. "Why? I don't have time for those silly games. I just shut the dang thing off."

It's that simple. She just shut off her porto. No worries. It's almost hard to believe.

I start to laugh and I can't stop myself.

"I mean, I got better things to do," the nurse says. She

straightens Step's sheet and says, "Are you okay, Stanley? You don't mind me calling you Stanley, do you? I mean, for now, that is. This whole mess is... well, a mess."

I'm still laughing. The nurse and Step give me a strange look, and I try to calm myself by squeezing Step's hand tighter. The nurse smiles and leaves.

Step looks at me and smiles, still confused but relaxed. He pulls me into him and I close my eyes, keep that smile imprinted in my mind so I will never forget it. This is where we stay, quietly holding each other like the city won't fall to pieces around us, like everything we know of ourselves isn't on the cusp of upheaval, soon to be lost among the turbulence of the very system meant to define us. None of that seems to matter because where we are right now, in each other's arms, is where we need to be.

And you. You are who you are. No matter what, tomorrow, you will still be.

Acknowledgments

Many thanks to Nate Ragolia and Shaunn Grulkowski for championing science fiction and giving this book a chance. Thanks also to Greg Hlavaty for encouraging me to step outside of familiar territory and just write something for fun.

About the Author

Greg Shemkovitz is the author of *Lot Boy* (Sunnyoutside Press).
His short fiction can be found in print and online journals. He
lives in Atlanta.

About the Publishing Team

Nate Ragolia was labeled as "weird" early in elementary school, and it stuck. He's a lifelong lover of science fiction, and a nerd/geek. In 2015 his first book, *There You Feel Free,* was published by 1888's Black Hill Press. He's also the author of *The Retroactivist*, published by Spaceboy Books. He founded and edits BONED, an online literary magazine, has created webcomics, and writes whenever he's not playing video games or petting dogs.

Shaunn Grulkowski has been compared to Warren Ellis and Phillip K. Dick and was once described as what a baby conceived by Kurt Vonnegut and Margaret Atwood would turn out to be. He's at least the fifth best Slavic-Latino-American sci-fi writer in the Baltimore metro area. He's the author of *Retcontinuum*, and the editor of *A Stalled Ox* and *The Goldfish,* all for 1888/Black Hill Press.